TIM PARKS

Born in Manchester, Tim Parks grew up in
London and studied at Cambridge and Harvard.
In 1981 he moved to Italy where he has lived ever
since. He is the author of novels, non-fiction and
essays, including *Europa*, *Cleaver*, *A Season with
Verona*, *Teach Us to Sit Still* and *Italian Ways*.
He has won the Somerset Maugham, Betty Trask
and Llewellyn Rhys awards, and been shortlisted
for the Booker Prize. He lectures on literary
translation in Milan, writes for publications such
as the *New Yorker* and the *New York Review of
Books*, and his many translations from the Italian
include works by Moravia, Calvino, Calasso,
Tabucchi and Machiavelli.

www.timparks.com

TIM PARKS

THOMAS & MARY

A Love Story

VINTAGE

1 3 5 7 9 10 8 6 4 2

Vintage,
20 Vauxhall Bridge Road,
London SW1V 2SA

Vintage is part of the Penguin Random House
group of companies whose addresses can be found at
global.penguinrandomhouse.com

Penguin
Random House
UK

Copyright © Tim Parks 2016

Tim Parks has asserted his right to be identified as the
author of this Work in accordance with the Copyright,
Designs and Patents Act 1988

First published by Vintage in 2017
(First published in Great Britain by Harvill Secker in 2016)

www.vintage-books.co.uk

A CIP catalogue record for this book
is available from the British Library

ISBN 9781784702007

CONTENTS

RINGS

This is how Thomas lost his ring. They were on Blackpool beach and wanted to go for a proper swim but they couldn't do this together because of the children, who couldn't swim and had anyway already been in the water and just wanted to play round the windbreak. So they decided to take turns. Him first. And because the cold water made his skin shrink a little and made it slippery, he pulled his ring off so that he shouldn't lose it. He didn't want to lose it. It was solid gold. He had a long swim, came back, got dressed and asked Mary for the ring but she frowned and said she hadn't got it. 'I gave it to you,' he said. 'No, you didn't.' She thought he must have put it in a pocket. 'But I'm sure!' 'Why are you looking in your pockets, then?' she smiled.

The ring wasn't among his clothes. He couldn't find it. So she thought maybe he had hidden it, somewhere. 'I would have some memory of having hidden it,' he said, 'wouldn't I?' Again she laughed. 'You forget all kinds of things!' 'Maybe *you* forgot I gave it to you,' he said. She shook her head. Unlike him, she did not forget things. She wasn't that kind of person. He was the forgetful one, the distracted one.

Thomas searched in the sand, first on the spot where he had changed, then round the poles of the windbreak. If he had hidden it, it would have been right next to something fixed. Mary said the kids had moved the windbreak. Hadn't he noticed the wind had shifted? Thomas began to feel panicky, because it seemed to him that a wedding ring was important, symbolic, quite apart from the money. 'I took it off to look after it,' he protested. 'Not to lose it.'

He grabbed one of the kids' spades and began to dig where he thought the windbreak had been. Not there, Mary thought. She wanted to go for her swim now and set off across the sand. 'Can we help, Daddy?' the kids asked. Mark crouched down and pushed sand back between his legs like a dog. 'Stop it!' Sally screamed. 'Don't you remember if I gave it to Mum, or if I hid it?' Thomas asked them. They didn't remember anything. By the time his wife came back they had dug up an area of five square yards. 'My towel is sandy,' she complained. 'Things can't just disappear,' Thomas protested. Drying herself, she shook her head. 'Somehow or other you've managed to lose it,' she said.

Later, half a mile down the beach, they saw a man with a metal detector scanning the base of the pier supports. Thomas offered him a reward if he found the ring and they walked back down the beach together. 'I thought I'd given it to my wife for safe-keeping,' he explained, 'but she says I must have hidden it in my clothes. So it's probably fallen in the sand, though I can't find it.' As they walked, the man told him how many rings he'd found with his detector, some of them lost decades ago. And coins. Pocket knives. Even a hand grenade.

When they reached the spot, Thomas wasn't sure it was the spot. The tide was coming in fast. Everyone else had gone. It all looked different. But almost at once the metal detector beeped. Thomas's heart twitched. The man unearthed a ring pull from a Coke can. In the end they found half a dozen ring pulls, a self-tapping screw and an old-fashioned tin opener.

Another week of sea and sunshine and all trace of the ring on his wedding finger was gone. The kids continued to dig in the sand, but nothing was found. The same year, towards Christmas, Thomas noticed that Mary was no longer wearing her ring. 'I thought,' she explained, 'that if you weren't wearing yours there was no point in me wearing mine.' 'But I've lost mine, I *can't* wear it.' 'You could have bought a new one,' she said. She was right, Thomas thought, but he wasn't sure that that would be the same thing. 'You didn't tell me to buy a new one,' he observed. She asked did he need to be told?

The more Thomas thought about this, the more distressed he felt. Yet at the same time he did not want to buy a new ring. Somehow it seemed to him the only thing that would really solve the problem would be to return to the sea and find the old ring with their names and the wedding date engraved inside, in 22-carat gold, and put it on again and then the world would magically return to what it had been before. Many years before.

This did not happen.

BEDTIMES

Monday evening, 10.30. Thomas is sitting on the sofa with his laptop reading for work. Mary has been talking to a friend on Skype.

If he is going to work all night, I may as well go to bed, Mary decides and goes upstairs without a word. Thomas joins her at midnight when she is sound asleep, face to the wall.

Tuesday evening, 10.45. Mary decides that their dog Ricky needs a late walk. Thomas, who has been watching a Champions League game in the old playroom, wanders back to the sitting room to find it empty. If she is out with the dog, I may as well go to bed, he decides. Mary joins him at midnight when he is sound asleep, face to the wall.

Wednesday evening, 11.00. Thomas is still out playing billiards with his friend Alan. Mary concludes she may as well turn in and leads her dog Ricky up the stairs to his basket on her side of the bed. 'Go to sleep now,' she tells him when he puts his cold nose between the sheets. 'Bed,

Ricky! Bed!' Thomas joins her at 1.30 when she is sound asleep, face to the wall.

Thursday evening, 9.30. Thomas and Mary are in their sitting room reading, he on the sofa, she at her place at the table. He is reading a novel by Haruki Murakami, she a book about training cocker spaniels. Unusually, their son Mark comes downstairs. It is warmer here, he says, and proceeds to open his computer to watch a film, with headphones. The boy is fourteen. Thomas looks up and says he'd like to watch the film too if that's okay. Mark tells him he won't like the film, but Thomas says he'll give it half an hour if that's all right. Mark says fine and unplugs the headphones. Thomas asks Mary if she would like to watch the film too. Mary says there's hardly room for three to watch a film on their son's laptop. Mark says they could go and watch the film on the TV in the playroom. Mary says it's too cold in the playroom to sit through a film and decides to take Ricky for a walk. Thomas finds the film dull, stupid and disturbingly violent. It's nice sitting beside his son but at 10.30 he bails out and goes to bed. Mary joins him at 11.30 when he is not asleep, but pretends he is, face to the wall.

Friday evening, 7.30. Mary has arranged an evening out with her friends from the dog park. She invites Thomas to come. He would enjoy meeting them, she says, and they are eager to meet him. Thomas is not convinced – he doesn't want to meet her friends from the dog park; it is not his scene he says; he will take Ricky out while she is at the pub. Mary repeats that their son can take the dog out, leaving Thomas free to come to the pub and meet her friends. He repeats that it really isn't his scene. He has some work to do. In the event he has a long conversation on Skype with an old friend. So as not to have to pretend to be asleep again, something he finds painful, he goes to bed early. Mary joins him at 11.30 and hardly cares whether he is asleep or not, since she has nothing to say to a man who she believes is having an affair.

Saturday evening. Mary says there is a good film on at the local cinema about ten minutes away in the car. She asks their daughter if she would like to go, but she wouldn't. So she asks Thomas if he would like to go. Thomas asks for some more details about the film, which she provides, and he decides yes he would like to go to see this film, so Thomas and Mary go to the cinema and watch the film which is called *We Need To Talk About Kevin* and both of them enjoy it up to a point and afterwards they go out to a bar and have a drink and talk for quite a long time about the film and about their children and their relationship with their children, since the film is largely about parents and the terrible mistakes you can make with your children, and both of them feel how pleasant it has been to chat together and what a good decision it was to come out together and see a film. Back home, Mary asks Mark if he took the dog out and Mark says he did, about two hours ago, and Mary says that since they are back much later than she expected she feels the dog should be taken out again for another quick walk and she keeps her coat on. She asks Thomas if he would like to come with her to walk the dog for a few minutes, perhaps just around the block and back, but he says he'd better check his email since there's an issue with one of his company's clients in the USA and this is prime time for people emailing from the USA before the end of their working day, and so she goes out alone. As it turns out there is no mail from the USA. Thomas sends a few private emails and text messages and waits, expecting Mary will be back, but after forty minutes she is still out. Thomas is feeling conflicted but now decides he may as well go to bed and is in fact fast asleep when his wife follows him half an hour later. 'Tom,' she asks, checking to see if he would perhaps like to talk, but he doesn't respond, face to the wall, snoring lightly.

Sunday evenings Thomas has always taken one or both his children out for a burger or even to a restaurant, depending on their choice, and since his daughter is home today he takes the two of them out to a burger bar. He asks his wife and the children ask their mother whether she would like to come, but she says no, she doesn't really want to come and have a burger, they are so fattening; the children then suggest that in that case she could have a salad, why not?, and she says there is no point in going out to pay for a salad that she could perfectly well have at home, so they say let's go to a restaurant then, maybe Indian or Japanese, but she says no you go, she doesn't want to go out to eat, and so Thomas takes his son and daughter out to the burger bar where they chat and joke very merrily eating burgers and drinking Coke, and afterwards Thomas persuades them to go to a pub as well so that he can have a beer and the children discuss music and boyfriends and girlfriends and how not to get fat despite eating burgers and drinking Coke, and Mark who is four years younger than his sister worries about school and Sally who has left home now worries about university and they all have a good time laughing at some of the other people in the pub, one of whom has an offensively loud voice, and in the end they return home around 10.30. Given the early hour, Thomas is surprised to find that Mary has already retired to bed. He sits at his computer to look at email while his children go to the playroom to sit in the cold with a sleeping bag on their laps and watch a horror film, and he smiles on hearing them giggling down there and decides to go to bed, where he finds that his wife is not sleeping with her face to the wall but reading a book.

Thomas is taken aback. 'Coinciding bedtimes,' she laughs, and there is something of a challenge in her voice. 'A miracle,' Thomas agrees and he takes off his clothes but for pants and T-shirt and lies down beside her. Propped up on a pillow, she continues to read with the light of the bedside lamp. Thomas lies on his side, face towards her, watching. The air between them is tense. Thomas feels his wife is a good-looking woman. She is aware of the pressure of his eyes on her. 'How can you go on reading so many books about dogs?' he finally asks. 'They're fascinating,' she replies at once. 'Absolutely fascinating. Aren't you, Ricky?' she addresses the dog, which is dozing in its basket and raises a silky ear. 'Speaking of which,' she suddenly says, 'he probably needs a last pee. Poor thing.' And she climbs out of bed and pulls on her jeans. Thomas watches. He feels he should protest, but doesn't. Perhaps she is waiting for him to protest, but if she is, she doesn't make it clear. 'Do you really think he needs to go out again?' Thomas eventually asks, but it's too late, the dog is now racing round and round the room in inane canine excitement and she is saying, 'Come on. Come on, darling!' And she disappears through the door and downstairs.

Thomas lies on his back. He has had a nice evening with his children but now he feels drained and lost. He wonders, should he wait up for his wife and confront her, but in the end it is only a passing thought. Surely it's she who should confront him. These thoughts are discouraging and eventually he rolls over towards the wall and falls asleep. Finding him in that position forty minutes later, Mary sheds a tear or two before falling asleep herself. Another week has gone by. In the playroom the two children are wondering whether there's anything they can do about their parents.

COMMON FRIEND

Thomas and Mary do not have friends in common, though they do sometimes have people to dinner. For example, they had their daughter's boyfriend's parents over recently and served them fish. Unfortunately, it turned out that the one thing the mother never ate, in fact absolutely couldn't eat, was fish. It was a shame because on the rare occasions when she does cook dinner for guests, Mary does it in style and here she had prepared a truly wonderful dish of salmon trout, as well as fish soup and some fishy hors d'oeuvres.

'You don't eat fish? Oh, for heaven's sake! If only I'd known!'

While the others sat down at the table and raised a glass or two, Mary rushed back into the kitchen to prepare an equally elaborate meal *without fish* for her daughter's boyfriend's mother. Thomas knew Mary wouldn't mind doing this because in the end Mary doesn't like to spend too much time sitting at table with other people. Often she eats alone. But she does like a chance to show off her cooking skills and generosity. So actually this was a rather successful evening for Mary. Thomas held the fort conversationally, Mary cooked, then cleaned. All well.

This wasn't always the case. If Thomas's mother came to stay, for example, particularly if she came at Easter or Christmas, the older woman would fuss around trying to help. 'For heaven's sake, Mum! Sit down,' Mary would say. 'Take it easy when you're on holiday.' And the younger woman set to work. Thomas would have liked to do some cooking himself, with Mary or with his mother or alone, but Mary's kitchen was Mary's kitchen. As the (elaborate) lunch was served, there would be a little tension around the table. Why? There just was. Almost the only thing that could be said was how good the food was. And again it was. Beyond that, an abyss. Mary served, running back and forth from kitchen to sitting room, because they ate at the big table in the sitting room when there were guests. Just occasionally she sat a moment or two before springing up again. The children wolfed the food down and hurried off to their computers. Often for hours on end each separate member of the family was in his or her separate room with his or her computer. Then there was peace.

But enough of dinner guests! We were talking about friends in common. Had Thomas and Mary *ever* had friends in common?

In the distant past, for example?

Well, acquaintances certainly. Joey, who had introduced them, was one. Thomas had been passing through the college bar when he spied Joey at a table with a group of girls. This was Durham twenty-five years ago. Joey lived across the corridor from Thomas in graduate accommodation. Afterwards, Thomas asked Joey for Mary's phone number but Joey objected that Mary was *his* girlfriend. Later the same evening Mary phoned Thomas and when he asked how she had got his number, she said from Joey. 'Your boyfriend,' Thomas observed. 'Not at all,' she insisted. 'What an idea!' After which, so far as he could recall, they had never really met Joey as a threesome, or even in a group, ever again. Though sometimes Mary met Joey on her own and sometimes Thomas met Joey on his own and on those occasions everybody got on fine. Joey never seemed to resent their having become a couple. Go figure.

Otherwise, at the time of their first meeting, Mary had two friends of her own, Patty and Liz, old school friends from Glasgow with whom she would let her hair down and giggle. But she and Thomas didn't go out together with them, or not more than once or twice. Or maybe three times. That is, at the beginning they did have a meal or two together but there was something that didn't gel. Perhaps Mary felt that Thomas was paying Patty a bit too much attention. Patty had quite a figure. Perhaps Thomas felt that the three of them made too much giggly fun of him. They pulled his leg non-stop. Thomas could be prickly.

Perhaps Patty and Liz felt it was time to find boyfriends of their own rather than having to watch Mary prancing round with hers. But when they did get boyfriends, going out in foursomes or sixsomes didn't really work, either. Liz's man was much older and seemed bored. He was pushing fifty. Patty's boyfriend was sensitive and felt criticised. He was an ambitious young engineer. Sure enough, later, in bed with Thomas, Mary did criticise him. She criticised both men. Her friends had chosen badly, she thought. Thomas joined in and criticised too. Not just the men but the women. He wanted to cut those giggly friends of hers down to size. They had a field day. In fact a lot of Mary and Thomas's being together seemed to have to do with criticising the acquaintances they had in common, which is maybe why those acquaintances never quite became friends in common. After they left Durham, Mary never found friends like Patty and Liz again, never again had the kind of friends you could really let your hair down with. That must count for something.

Others who never really became friends in common, or only very briefly, were his old pals from the church youth club in Bristol where they lived for a year or so in the early stages of their marriage. Nigel and Jenny and Timothy and Kate were both established couples before Mary met them. Thomas had been friends with Jenny in the one couple and with Timothy in the other. Not really close friends. Just friendly. So the common friends thing seemed possible because Mary need hardly fear that these were friends *against* her; they hadn't, as it were, lost Thomas to her, as perhaps Patty and Liz had lost Mary to Thomas, and at the same time Thomas didn't need to worry that Mary would gang up with them to make fun of him. They just weren't the kind to make fun. But perhaps because Mary and Thomas always criticised these people, indeed any people they met, something queered the air. Not that they criticised them to their faces. Only when they were alone. All the same, something must have come across. Nigel was pompous and Jenny such a ditherer and Timothy was also a ditherer, though in a different way, whereas Kate was ferociously bossy, and Nigel and Jenny's kitchen was such a mess and they always cooked too much in a sloppy kind of way, though never enough meat (one chicken for six!), and Kate's kitchen – because clearly Timothy had no say in it – was not exactly squalid, but mean somehow, and her cooking drearily austere in an army-rations, cold-bedroom kind of way, and Timothy would keep the wine bottle on the floor by his leg of the table, so you could never help yourself. What was odd about it was that Thomas and Mary really loved these friends and really, genuinely loved spending evenings with them, when they did. It just wasn't very often.

Another odd thing was that Thomas and Mary never imagined that the others might be criticising them. Or maybe they assumed that all couples criticise other couples and so hardly cared. Perhaps they were right. Once, years later, they managed a Cornish holiday together with Timothy and Kate at a time when both couples had two small kids, toddlers, perhaps because they hoped that company might relieve the growing tension between them – between Thomas and Mary, that is – but since it didn't, they never repeated the experiment. The problem with a foursome was agreeing on the shopping and cooking and eating out. Timothy never wanted to eat out despite having the biggest salary of all of them. And he baulked at buying good wine. Mary thought Kate too strict with her children. She wouldn't go to them if they cried in bed. It was madness. Also Thomas tried to confide in Timothy about his marriage problems and even about the girl in Accounts he was growing fond of but Timothy didn't want to go there. He really didn't. Perhaps in the end both these couples, Nigel and Jenny, Timothy and Kate, had started to steer a little clear of Thomas and Mary because they sensed their relationship was getting a bit rocky, they feared contamination. Yet in both cases, long after the foursomes ended, they were always happy to see Thomas on his own or Mary on her own. That was odd. And having made those now-solitary visits, Thomas and Mary, or rather Thomas *or* Mary, whichever it had been, would always bring back enough info on these old friends to go on with their previous criticisms, which now more than ever seemed the only glue that held Thomas and Mary together. Nigel was pomposity itself. Timothy let Kate walk all over him. Everybody but Thomas and Mary had got it wrong, it seemed.

All this was a very long time ago. Hard to believe it happened, really. Now, after the move to Manchester and his promotion to a seriously prestigious job, Thomas has had just one close friend for a decade and more, but Mary doesn't want to see him. Thomas knows that Mary thinks Alan is her enemy. Actually, this isn't true. If anything, Alan worries for her and is also a little frightened of her. But there you go, the idea of the three of them getting together for drinks or dinner or just a pleasant evening in front of the TV is unimaginable. Thomas would be thinking that Mary would be thinking that Alan knew all kinds of secrets that Thomas wasn't telling her. And he does. Thomas and Alan play tennis together, drink beers and talk women. Occasionally they offer alibis for each other. It's on this questionable 'relief' that Thomas and Mary's marriage seems largely to depend these days. Imagine if they spent an evening together and all that came out. Not that Mary doesn't know, because in a way perhaps she does, but it's important that nothing be said. A common friend could be fatal.

Meantime Mary has got into a habit of making friends with people who are younger than her or somewhat weaker character-wise or simply at a different level. Subaltern is the word that sometimes comes to Thomas's mind as he observes the development of this phenomenon. Who are these people? A cleaning lady, their younger child's swimming instructor, the wife of a client Mary does some freelancing for, a girl she has met at her Pilates course.

None are people you would ever invite to dinner or who would ever invite you to dinner. Mary sees them for coffee, or does aerobics with them or goes for walks with them. Often she helps them in some way. Almost as if they were children. They're grateful. Often she gives them gifts. She's a generous person. But Thomas has almost nothing to do with them, they don't interest him at all and he can now more or less predict the moment when Mary too will suddenly stop seeing them. That's how it is. For a while Mary will be extremely friendly and generous with these people, then lose interest, rather abruptly, perhaps even complaining that she has been exploited. Perhaps she has. Thomas has given up trying to understand. He has reached the point where he feels they both need help. They need to be saved from themselves, from whatever poison it is that makes their married life so hard. But looked at another way, everything chugs along much as it always has, he with his one close friend, she with her many shadowy, unobtrusive friends, one after the other.

Until she got the dog. And this, you might say – the dog, I mean – was really the first friend Thomas and Mary had ever had in common. Though it didn't start that way.

One day Mary announced she had decided to get a dog. Apparently Thomas didn't need to be consulted on this. In fact, he didn't object. Anything that kept Mary happy, he explained to Alan, was fine by him, left him with more time for tennis, or an amorous adventure perhaps, or simply the Champions League. The Champions League and a couple of bottles of Beck's was not a bad way to kill an evening. This was the sort of thing Thomas would say to Alan. But on another level he was furious. He didn't want the dog at all.

Mary wanted a dog because she had never had one. That was sufficient reason. She hadn't got a dog earlier because she didn't believe in having dogs around small children. Dogs carried diseases. But Mark was in his teens now. So it was time for a dog. After long navigation on the Web Mary identified a cocker spaniel breeder with a newborn litter. In Devon. A month later Thomas was asked to drive her and their son the two hundred and fifty miles down there to choose a pup. Thomas tended to be dutiful about these matters, to earn himself his freedoms elsewhere. Anyone seeing them together that evening at the restaurant of the small hotel where they stayed would have wondered what on earth could keep this couple together when their son left home. The answer would be Ricky.

Things might have gone differently if Mary had chosen the pup she wanted. Sitting in a farmhouse kitchen watching half a dozen animals fall over each other, she was immediately attracted to the most combative, the most lively, the one flouncing about and nipping its brothers and sisters at the heels and behind the ears, first to the food and water bowls, confrontational, loud, in command, looking for trouble. The breeder pointed instead to a fluffy creature half asleep in the pack. Brought out for examination, this puppy licked Mark's fingers with lazy affection. The other dog was too much of a handful for a first-time owner, the breeder thought. Mary asked for half an hour's time out to think it over, and in the farmyard expressed her opinion that the breeder was trying to cheat them of the best dog and sell them a lemon. Mark said, 'Mum, you're amazing.' Thomas thought the breeder lady was simply trying to be helpful. 'That other monster will tear up the carpets, and pull down the curtains and dig under the roses.' On the drive home the sleepy pup was christened: Ricky.

At the beginning Ricky seems more likely to end the foundering marriage than save it. With little left to do for the children, and having long since wound down her free-lance work, Mary gives the animal all her attention. She buys toys and treats and grooming products. She reads books. The dog must sleep outside. They buy a kennel. The dog must be allowed to stick his nose in the earth; they need a pen in the back garden. Thomas spends a whole weekend building a pen but as soon as Ricky is in it he yips and howls and scratches until he is let out, then sticks his nose in the earth of the flowerbeds. The flower-beds are Thomas's domain. He loves flowers and bushes and pruning clippers and compost. Ricky destroys the flowerbeds.

Another book now says that young dogs get lonely if obliged to sleep alone, so from this point on the dog must sleep indoors. However, there is the problem of the burglar alarm; the dog can't be left on the ground floor, where the alarm has its sensors. Consequently, the dog basket is placed on the landing outside the bathroom and a child-proof gate is dug out of storage to block the stairs so that Ricky can't go down and trip the alarm. To get to the bathroom two or three times a night Thomas has to step over the dog, which wakes up and licks his heels, or pads in to watch him peeing.

How tiring all this is, Thomas thinks. He hadn't wanted a dog at all. He is not in control of the expensive house a lifetime of work has bought. Both his wife and his adolescent son are entirely absorbed in an escalating competition for the affection of a mere animal. But at least Ricky is a handsome creature and happy as Larry. His waggy cheerfulness is infectious. Mary takes him out morning, afternoon and evening. She discovers new paths in the countryside around their house. She discovers new, ever-unobtrusive friends at the dog park on the nearby estate. In fact, she is soon queen of the dog park community. She regales Thomas with stories of other dog owners and the sacrifices they make for their pets. The stories are interesting. People who keep dogs are actually more humane than people who don't; of that Mary is convinced. Thomas appreciates that he falls into the category of people who don't. On cold days she takes flasks of tea to the park. She stays out for hours. On warm evenings a bottle of wine. She can't pick up Mark from school or take him to karate because she is out with the dog. She is taking Ricky to 'agility' lessons. In a town twenty miles away. She is taking him to the vet. She can't miss her appointment with the vet just to take Thomas to the airport. Thomas takes a taxi. It seems to him the dog is already agile enough, healthy enough. When they go to a café together on Sunday mornings Mary buys a bun, she who never eats buns, and feeds it to Ricky. Not to Mark or to Thomas, who is very partial to cakes. The dog licks the sweet crumbs off her fingers. She picks up his shit in the road outside. Mark rolls around with Ricky on the carpet. Mother and son argue over hygiene. Now the dog takes to whining on the landing at night with the result that Mark allows the creature into his room. Ricky sleeps on his bed; but then Mary decides that Ricky should sleep in their bedroom, her and Thomas's room, not Mark's – it's not good for a boy to have a dog on his bed. Thomas tries to put his foot down and object; the dog's nervous padding back and forth from basket to bed, or rather to Mary's fingers trailing invitingly over the edge of the bed, makes it hard for him to get to sleep, and just when he does he's woken by a warm tongue licking his nose. When he complains Mary laughs and it's the same laugh she used to laugh with Patty and Liz, a mocking laugh, Thomas thinks. So Thomas goes downstairs to sleep in what used to be his daughter's room. Mary doesn't seem to mind. It is the end of any pretence of married business as usual. Is it the beginning of the end?

From time to time Thomas takes the dog out. Either Mary has some other appointment she can't miss or she has to visit her sick mother up north. She is away for a few days. Ricky is intelligent and obeys Thomas more readily than he obeys Mary or Mark. It's true Mary has taught Ricky to do a few tricks, give you a paw to shake, touch his nose on your hand, roll over on his back and wave his legs in the air, that kind of clownish, exhibitionist thing. But when it comes to sitting still, or coming when his name is called, he actually responds better to Thomas. It's been a while since Thomas was able to command anyone. Even his girlfriends tend to run the show. It's a pleasure.

'Here Ricky!'

Since Thomas absolutely refuses to pick up dog shit – he's too squeamish – he walks the dog in the country, which after all begins about a hundred yards from their house on the outskirts of Pendlebury. Doing so, he realises how much he likes to walk in the country. It's been a while. He's reminded of his childhood when there was always a dog around. He likes weather, landscape, any weather, the smell of the soil, the drizzle on the leaves, sunshine on stone. He likes life. Ricky hares off but eventually returns when he's called. Thomas watches him. The dog lives through his nose. He is entirely connected with the soil and the breeze. He is part of life, of everything. Now he's pushing into a thicket after a hedgehog. Thomas stands and watches. In a tangle of branches the dog is yelping at the balled-up hedgehog. Both animals are absolutely in the here and now, one excited, one terrified. Both happier, Thomas shakes his head, than a man who feels trapped and can't make up his mind. A coward.

On a summer evening he lies down in a field and closes his eyes. Ricky comes to lick his face. The dog seems contemplative, a little troubled. His master has never lain down on the grass before. Eventually the animal settles beside Thomas and puts his head over Thomas's ankle. The fur under his throat is luxuriously silky. It has to be said, Mary keeps her pet clean. The dog pants a little and whines. 'What do you think of Mary, in the end?' Thomas asks Ricky. His eyes are still closed. The dog wriggles, probably scanning the horizon for movement, scenting the air. 'She has so many good qualities, don't you think? We have done so much together.' The dog is still, but very present. Thomas can feel a hum of life through the warm fur. 'I don't love her any more,' he announces. The dog listens. 'We drive each other crazy.'

Suddenly, Rickly leaps up to dash at something in the distance. His claws scratch Thomas's ankle. Thomas sits up abruptly to inspect the damage. The dog is streaking along a hedge; there's a wonderful golden brown purpose about him darting through dusty green. Thomas shakes his head. When Ricky comes back he grabs the dog by the ears and looks him in the eyes. The animal's panting is like laughter. His breath is friendly and foul. The eyes are quizzical, optimistic. 'What am I going to do?' Thomas demands. 'Tell me what to do, Ricky.' The dog lets out a bark and shakes his head free, shakes his fur as if coming out of water, but then comes back to put his wet nose on his master's neck.

'You're a trophy dog,' Thomas accuses him. 'My wife's trophy dog. To replace me. To tell me she prefers a younger dog these days.'

Ricky smiles. He knows.

'What's she thinking, Ricky? Come on now, she's your friend. I bet she talks to you. Does she want me to leave? What does Mary really want?'

The dog sits and pants. Thomas gets up to walk home.

'It's childish sleeping elsewhere just because of the dog,' Mary says some days later. 'In the end you like him as much as we do. It's just an excuse.'

Thomas doesn't answer. He stays in what was once his daughter's room. But he feels the pull of going back to his old bed, their bed. To be precise, he feels the pull of pretending all is well. Now when he doesn't go up the final flight of stairs to their room the dog comes back down and scratches at his door. Thomas won't open. In their separate rooms he can hear both Mary and Mark laughing. It's *that* laughter.

Or perhaps it's my problem, he thinks.

Sometimes Mary stays out at the dog park till eleven and even later with her young dog and unobtrusive friends. Ricky looks exhausted when he gets home. He crashes. Sometimes Mark goes with his mother, but mostly the boy is busy at his computer.

'Mum does seem to overdo it with the dog,' Thomas remarks.

'Ricky's a faithful companion,' Mark says drily. Thomas watches him. How much does the boy know? Why has the dog become so important in their lives?

Eighteen months after they brought the pup home, Thomas is half asleep when Mary shouts. 'He's poisoned. He's dying!'

She had taken the dog out late on a stretch of land at the bottom of the hill. Ricky ate something there; now back home he has started to vomit. He is in convulsions. Mark rushes from his room. It's Sunday after midnight. Thomas drags himself out of bed and climbs the flight of stairs to the marital bedroom. Ricky has his four legs splayed wide, shaking violently. With no plan Thomas grabs the dog and starts downstairs. 'Check on the Net for an emergency vet!' he shouts to his son. As he passes the boy's room, Mark sees the dog twisting and turning violently in his father's arms.

'He's going to die,' the boy starts to yell wildly. 'Ricky's going to die!'

The dog is fully grown now and flings himself back and forth in Thomas's arms. He arches his head back with surprising power.

'Find where there's a vet,' Thomas tells Mark. 'Doing night duty.'

Downstairs, he's forgotten the alarm and it goes off. Woo woo woo woo.

He leaves his wife to fix it and struggles out through the back door to get the animal some air but the dog wrenches

26

himself free and is on the ground, yelping, pawing. Thomas gets down on the grass and puts his hands in the animal's mouth, to see if there's anything in there, or maybe to make the creature vomit, if he can. The dog writhes and bites. He's taken some skin off Thomas's hand. It's impossible to see anything, with all the saliva and fur in the half dark. Thomas becomes aware of sobs behind him. His son is standing at the back door in blue pyjamas shaking his head furiously: 'He's going to die, he's going to die. It's horrible!'

'I told you to get on the Net!'

Woo woo woo, goes the alarm.

Mark is beside himself. Who would have thought the dog was so important to him? Thomas leaves the animal and grabs his son's shoulders, shakes him hard.

Inside the house, his wife turns the alarm off, which makes Mark's voice even louder.

'Ricky's dead, Dad, he's dead, he's dead!'

Thomas slaps the boy across the face. 'Check the fucking Net! Now. Emergency veterinary services. Postcode. Go!'

Mary arrives on the scene. Thomas is on his knees trying to calm the dog which is retching and tossing its head from side to side. They are on the back lawn with the light from the kitchen window coming through the branches of the apple tree. The dog rolls its eyes. They are yellow. It spasms and is rigidly still, fiercely still. His wife is weeping. 'He was so good, he didn't deserve this, he was so good. Such a good doggie. He really didn't. He didn't.'

'Get the car out of the garage. Get a blanket.'

'He was so good, he didn't deserve this.'

On the lawn, Thomas looks at the dog lying still and rigid. Is it dead? He crouches beside it, turns it on its back and puts his ear to its chest. The heart is beating fast. There's such a doggie smell. Not entirely unhappy with the situation, Thomas hurries into the house and finds his son at the screen. He has an address.

The boy is calmer now. He looks at his father differently. 'Is he going to die?' His voice trembles.

'I've no idea,' Thomas says and hurries to his room to get some shoes. The address is the other side of Salford.

Thomas drives fast and efficiently. The dog is convulsing on the back seat, wrapped in a blanket now. His wife is beside it, crying, endlessly repeating what a good dog he was. 'Don't die, Ricky. Don't die. Please don't die.' This is mad, Thomas is thinking. As if the animal were a child. He's on the point of bursting out laughing. Am I acting to save the dog, he wonders, or to show my wife and son who counts in this family when there's an emergency? There is no traffic and the car races through the streets entirely ignoring warnings of electronic speed controls. The address corresponds to a door in a block of flats between two shops. They have to ring the bell twice before a window lights up, then the door buzzes open.

The vet is a tired young Indian in his thirties. He pulls on a white coat, injects the dog with a tranquilliser, lays him on a table and starts to set up a drip. As he works, shaving away fur, tying an elastic cord round a leg, Mary talks on and on about what a remarkable dog Ricky is, how playful, how good tempered. If only he hadn't picked up whatever was left on the path. Who would do such a thing, leaving poisoned food where there were dogs!

Thomas is struck by the intensity of his wife's emotional investment in the creature. How much love she has to give! But not to Thomas. 'He always greets me so warmly when I come home,' she is explaining, as if the vet could be remotely interested. 'Always happy to see me.' She is crying. She brushes tears from her eyes and blows her nose. 'He's such a beautiful person.' The vet is ignoring her completely as he pushes a needle into the dog's leg and sets the speed of the drip. Thomas understands that what she is saying is that he, Thomas, never greets her in this way, that he and she are never really happy to see each other. Talking to the vet, she is addressing him. Suddenly he is overcome by a deep sympathetic sadness for her. For himself too. He will never be allowed to experience the love she gives the dog. Or her unobtrusive friends, for that matter. He will never be able to show her the affection he gives to his girlfriends. He wishes he could. He really does. But he can't. For some reason it's impossible. On the table their common friend Ricky twitches. He's still alive. Bubbles rise in the drip bag. The vet frowns and pulls off his gloves.

'That's it. We'll know tomorrow. Call around midday.'

Mary begins to press him. 'Will he survive? Do you have any idea what he ate?'

29

The vet shakes his head. 'If he's alive in the morning, he'll probably live,' he says.

Approaching home, towards three, Mary puts a hand on Thomas's wrist and says quickly, 'Thanks, Tom. You were fantastic.' 'It's nothing,' he says. After reassuring Mark that Ricky is still in with a chance, Thomas hesitates on the landing, then climbs the stairs to the marital bedroom. It's a mistake but one he feels he has to make. In the night, getting up to pee, he wonders if it wouldn't have been better if the animal had died. Better for their relationship, for the end of their relationship. When Thomas brings the dog home two days later, Mary throws a party and invites her friends from the dog park. She serves them assiduously. She has cooked all kinds of treats. No one seems to notice Thomas. Mark rolls around with Ricky on the lawn. The dog appears to have forgotten everything. Soon his son and his wife too will have forgotten how it was that night, Thomas thinks, how hysterical they were and how efficient he was, when it counted. Going upstairs to the marital bedroom, he finds his wife is letting Ricky lick her eyes. 'Oh, come and give him a hug,' she beckons her husband. 'He wants you to admit you love him, don't you, Ricky?'

FOUR-STAR BREAKFAST

'You'll gobble up that boy for breakfast and spit him out before lunch.'

This was the burden of what Mary's mother told her daughter the day she was introduced to Thomas. Mrs Keir, from Glasgow, was famous for her way with words.

There were other unhappy omens: the man who stopped them on the street in Durham a couple of months after they met and said: 'You're in love now, but in ten years you will hate each other'; the love-match astrology encyclopaedia in a bookshop in Leeds that presented every possible combination of birth dates and declared theirs a catastrophe in the making.

Was it an omen, too, that at Patty's Christmas party Mary had poured the dirty dishwater over Thomas's head when he flirted with the big Russian girl who promised, 'I will drink you under the table'? If it was, they didn't recognise it at the time. They felt very sure of themselves and in bed they laughed at dumb astrologers and creeps who pestered young couples on the street. Out of envy. Because they were in love.

But let's go back to that instructive first meeting with Mary's parents. Mr Keir was in Newcastle on business with his wife in tow. They arrived mid-afternoon; Mr Keir had appointments, then there was a dinner with old friends. The following day they had to be in Edinburgh for lunch. So the only moment to catch up with their daughter was at the Grey Street Hotel near the station for breakfast. Since she had told them this new boyfriend was serious, they were eager to meet him.

At the time Thomas had never been in a four-star hotel, let alone eaten there. His parents never got beyond boarding houses and bed and breakfasts. Mary's family, he sensed, moved in a different world. No sooner were they through the gleaming doors than a blonde woman let out a little shriek and enveloped Mary in a fierce embrace. She wore a broad-brimmed red hat above, of all things, a Mexican poncho. Mary cried out too and hugged her mother hard. Looking on, Thomas found himself sharing his disorientation with a small squat man in a grey overcoat and trilby. The man put out his hand. 'You must be Tom.' 'Good to meet you, Mr Keir,' Thomas said. Mary's father stood back and sized him up. 'How old are you?' he asked.

All Mary's friends were saying the same thing. Thomas looked so young. Actually, he was six months older than her. But he was so fresh-faced. The beard fooled no one.

If anything, it underlined his anxiety to appear adult. No sooner had they drunk their orange juice than Mrs Keir more or less lifted Mary from her seat and took her off to the Ladies. 'What are you doing with such a baby?' she demanded as they both looked in the mirror. 'Whatever's got into you, girl?'

Thomas was thrown by the sudden disappearance of the two women.

'Girls' talk,' chuckled Mr Keir in his soft Scottish accent.

He began to ask Thomas what he was studying, what his plans were, when he expected to be looking for a job. Thomas answered as best he could. He couldn't see the sense, he said, in worrying too much about employment when he still had another full year's scholarship to run. The university was a prestigious one. Mr Keir shook his head. The world wasn't like that any more, he said. One had to be constantly establishing contacts and building on them. There was no other way. In his briefcase, which he kept beside him on the floor, he found a wallet stacked with business cards. He pulled them out, and began to tap the edges on the tabletop as if he were aligning a pack of cards before shuffling them. Very soon Thomas was being invited to consider a bewildering array of career choices, mainly in the construction and manufacturing industries, each one represented by a card laid out on the table as if in a game of Patience.

'If there's anyone you want to approach, just pick up the card,' Mr Keir said. 'Tell them I gave you their name.'

Thomas was relieved when the women came back, though surprised to see Mary arm in arm with her mother, laughing and generally in high spirits. Her Scottish accent seemed stronger in her parents' company. At this point Mr Keir got up and went to load his plate with kippers and fried bread and sausages. There was quite an array of food. Having risen early to drive from Durham, Thomas and Mary went to tuck in.

'It's going well,' Mary said, putting an arm round her young man's waist.

However, the four-star breakfast was subsequently spoiled when an animated argument blew up over the kippers; it began with some lightly mocking observations from Mrs Keir about Mr Keir's eating habits and choles-terol levels, but quickly rippled out into a choppy sea of mutual irritation. Suddenly both fury and hilarity were in the air as one accusation followed another. Mr Keir was ignorant and presumptuous, Mrs Keir claimed; he took no proper care of their financial affairs and left his children to languish unprovided-for. Mrs Keir was a cretin who had not the slightest idea what she was talking about, Mr Keir observed. 'And, quite frankly, the sooner I have a heart attack the better! If I eat like this, it's because food is the only thing that cheers me up.'

'Don't worry, they're always like that,' Mary told Thomas later, when the young couple had waved the older pair away in their Rover 35. 'At least we had a good break-fast,' she added.

'At least we know what to avoid,' Thomas said.

'Oh, I don't know,' Mary took his arm affectionately. 'Deep down they're inseparable.'

Years later, but well before the merciful heart attack struck, Thomas would understand that that was precisely the Keirs' tragedy.

BROTHERLY LOVE

After visiting my mother I feel it's my duty to tell my brother how things stand. 'She's having difficulty moving around,' I email. 'She's in pain. She can hardly get out of the house. I don't know how long this can go on.'

From the other side of the world my brother replies: 'She's a tough old bird. I phoned last week and she sounded very chipper.'

Not that I live nearby. After Father died, Mum moved to London. I have to spend hours on the train to go down there, hence I only tend to see her when work calls me to the city. I add a day on to my schedule and take a couple of buses out beyond Twickenham where she is now more or less imprisoned in her tiny house. 'It takes her a while to answer the doorbell,' I write to my brother. 'She has trouble getting out of her chair. Her left arm is swollen like a balloon.'

My brother often leaves a while before replying to emails, but not these. 'We all have our bad patches,' his message appears in a matter of minutes. 'I've been telling her for ages she should use a stick, but vanity dies hard!'

It irritates me. My mother has had this cancer for some years now. Why is my brother pretending it isn't happening? Why doesn't he accept the testimony of someone on the spot? Worse still, he occasionally seems to be suggesting that I'm some kind of gravedigger; that I'm willing the end to come, out of a macabre love of melodrama. This isn't true. I love my mother, I visit her when I can and I see what I see. 'She has to get her neighbours to do the shopping now and can't eat in the evening. They've given her a morphine substitute to inject herself as required.' My brother responds, saying his daughter, who is on a tour of Europe, visited a few days ago when she was passing through and apparently found her grandmother in good shape. 'Mum took her to an Indian restaurant and ate with gusto, it seems.'

This is strange. I realise my mother must be giving a different account of herself when she talks to my brother or his close family. Is this because he was the poorly one as a child? She doesn't want to scare him. Certainly he loves her quite as much as I do, perhaps more. Or because she fears if she tells the truth he'll feel she's trying to get him to make the expensive trip back home to visit? With me she puts a brave face on things, but if I ask directly, she's all too frank. 'Most days I feel terrible,' she told me on my last visit. 'I'm nauseous and confused and not myself at all.'

I wonder if her confessing these things to me isn't a kind of compliment – a recognition that I'm tough enough to handle it. She's glad of the relief of being able to tell someone the truth. Or could it be that she is equally candid with my brother, but he doesn't want to take it on board? Or he takes it on board but doesn't want to appear to have done so, since his not being aware how serious the situation is is now the only reason for not coming back to see her while there's time. Perhaps he's so attached to her deep down that he can't face the idea of a last meeting. Or I suppose you could even imagine that my brother deliberately makes light of the situation in order to make me feel like a drama queen, thriving on her dying. Meantime, I catch myself looking forward to the shock it will be for him when she actually does go. How is he going to sound relaxed and optimistic then? I've started observing her more closely to find ominous symptoms that I can describe to him: the slightly slurred speech, for example, or the way she puts a hand on the nearest piece of furniture to steady herself as she moves around the room. It's not good. I didn't want to become like this.

'It seems,' I write, 'she can't take a bath any more because once in the tub she can't haul herself out. She has to wait till the nurse visits to do her dressings.' With uncanny immediacy, given the different time zones, my brother replies, saying his wife phoned the evening before and Mother spoke cheerfully of a visit to a flower show.

It's as if my emails were a threat that had to be neutralised at once. But a threat to what, exactly? I happen to know that Mother was bullied by an old friend into accepting this invitation to the Chelsea Flower Show, then felt too nauseous to enjoy the flowers and spent most of the time sitting in the car outside, getting cold. I could explain this to my brother, but I hesitate, because this whole back and forth between us has begun to make me fear I might be wishing her dead simply to prove him wrong. There has always been a certain amount of competition between us. Out of the blue, he writes: 'Spoke to Mum yesterday, who told me she was enjoying a good game of Scrabble with her old pals from the Church Missionary Society. Complained they kept looking up words in the dictionary and ate all the Battenberg. Guess she'll be with us for a good few years yet.' I realise I should feel cheered by this picture of domestic feistiness, but actually it feels like my brother is trying to ram far more than Battenberg down my throat. I didn't reply.

One thing my brother and I have in common is that neither of us believe Mother will be going to heaven when she dies. Or anywhere else, for that matter. We're atheists. Or he's an atheist, I'm an agnostic. Mother, on the other hand, really does believe. She's spent her whole life in the Church, she's an evangelical. Our childhood was full of talk about being born again and giving your heart to Jesus. Still, she doesn't seem pleased by the prospect of paradise now that it's at hand. Last week, on top of everything else, she was dealing with a urinary infection. 'It's hardly worth living, in these circumstances,' she said, shaking her head grimly. 'Apparently she has written down the details of her funeral service,' I emailed my brother. 'The hymns she wants and where to spread the ashes.'

'I have days when I feel like that myself,' my brother replies, 'bar the hymns of course.'

Unlike her brothers, my sister shares Mother's beliefs. She has the same faith, the same fervency. And she lives much closer to her than I do, only an hour or so's drive. But she doesn't visit very often and is somehow never there when I visit. I don't email her, or she me. My brother doesn't communicate with her at all, though there's less age difference between them than there is between him and me. I'm the youngest, my sister the oldest. The fact is, at some point the whole religious thing split us apart. On the other hand, following my mother's recent fall and consequent deterioration it seems important that we children get ready to take tough decisions. I phoned my sister and asked her what arrangements were in place for the time when my mother would no longer be able to look after herself in her own home.

Why, I don't know, but on the very rare occasions I have reason to be in touch with her, I always phone my sister. I wouldn't dream of emailing her, whereas despite being much closer to my brother I never phone him, only email, and he never phones me. He phones my mother. More often, he has his wife phone my mother.

On the phone my sister was extremely friendly and practical and not at all competitive – it was quite a pleasure to be speaking to each other again. (Actually, this is always the case, so that I invariably end up wondering why we don't speak to each other more often.) What took me aback, though, was how critical she was of Mother. 'She's in complete denial,' my sister complained. 'Refuses to sort out the necessary legal documents, doesn't want to accept that sooner or later she'll have to leave the house. And she's such a bad patient, moping about the pain, but not doing anything to keep her mind busy. Why doesn't she listen to music or watch a video?'

I didn't refer any of this to my brother since it really isn't my perception of how Mother behaves. Instead I emailed to say that, since falling down the stairs, Mother needed a nurse twice a day to sort her out and was having problems with incontinence and a sciatic nerve. 'Apparently she has some kind of arrangement with a hospice but it isn't clear when they'll be willing to admit her, or whether Mother will agree to go to a place you only leave feet first.' 'She'll keep the heavenly hosts waiting a while yet,' he replied.

Laptop on my knees on the long train ride home, it occurred to me that my irritation with my brother might have the function of allowing me not to dwell too gloomily on my mother's suffering. Looked at that way, the friction between us seemed positive. Certainly his offhand responses to my unhappy news are sapping more mental energy than her suffering. A little later, though, it seemed that this stupid distraction – the feeling that her dying had become part of a win/lose discussion with my brother – was actually depriving me of a proper relationship with my mother in this critical period, the last of her life. I was wasting the opportunity of being with her by seeing everything in terms of what I would say, or email, to my brother. On the other hand, however surprised I was by my sister's criticisms, I never felt like challenging them, or arguing with her the way I do with my brother. Mother probably behaves differently with all of us is the truth, and even when her behaviour is the same we see it in different ways. That said, the fact that a person is terminally ill is something undeniable, not a point of view.

When my father died, almost thirty years ago now, my brother had already emigrated, but there was no email then and hence this discussion at a distance couldn't be had. Phone calls cost a fortune; neither he nor I had much money, and it must have been my mother who called my brother to inform him of my father's rapidly deteriorating state. His cancer was much quicker than my mother's, a matter of months. In the event, my brother came to visit shortly before the death but then did not return for the funeral. It seemed sensible. I can barely recall my feelings that day, nor a single word of what passed between myself, my sister and my mother. I wonder whether the same will be the case with the funeral to come. All this irritation with my brother will be forgotten, but so too will all these visits to my mother which take the form, I realise now, of two people knowing that they are meeting above all because one of them is not long for this world. No doubt that's why I feel I have to write those emails to my brother the moment I leave her house. I have to get it off my chest. Certainly, if my brother does come to the funeral it will be the last time we three children will ever be together.

Does that matter?

The next time I came down to the city my sister phoned me while I was on the train to say that Mother had been taken to hospital. That day I had a full schedule and then the following morning, just as I was heading out towards the hospital, my sister phoned again to say that Mother was now being taken down to her house: my sister's. Her husband was driving her. Theoretically, I could have made it down to my sister's and back in time for my returning train, just about, but I couldn't see how I could really help, now that my mother was in good hands and had company. Actually, it felt rather pleasant to find I had the day to myself. I did a little shopping and took the train home without seeing her.

'She was in so much pain, she called an ambulance,' I emailed my brother.

'Poor Mum,' came the response. 'Never underestimate her capacity to bounce back.'

My visits to the city changed. I didn't stop tagging on an extra day to my business trips, something my wife and family were now used to; it was just that I spent the time wandering around on my own. Again and again I planned to make the further trip down to my sister's, but a strange reluctance always overcame me. I had rather enjoyed seeing my mother in her tiny house and being useful to her and eating together and playing a little Scrabble, which she always beat me at; but the thought of seeing her with my sister was depressing, especially since there were no signs of her bouncing back; rather the opposite. I wouldn't have minded seeing my sister on her own, if she happened to be in town, but not my mother and my sister together, and neither of them singly at my sister's house. Why? I wasn't sure. The religious texts on the walls? The fluffy white rugs, the many dogs and cats?

Meantime, my sister's husband began to send rather formal emails to both my brother and myself. Mother was unable to move from a sitting to a standing position. Sometimes she was incontinent. Her left arm was now entirely useless. The drugs were quite inadequate to deal with her pain. I mailed back at once offering to share the cost of a private nurse. I noticed that while I responded using the reply-to-all option, my brother did not. But I knew he had replied, because when my brother-in-law responded to him he copied me in. My brother had said that he wished there was something he could do, but he couldn't see that there was. 'Rather gruesome bulletins from Sis's hub,' he commented in a mail to me. Immediately it felt like we could be friends again. I phoned my sister every few days and she again complained what a dire patient Mother was, in particular her obstinate refusal to enjoy any kind of entertainment; but my sister didn't seem unhappy and her voice was affectionate when she passed the phone to my mother, who actually sounded rather cheerful. She had sewn a button on a coat for her granddaughter, she said, and even managed a few rows of knitting.

Perhaps, it occurred to me, putting the phone down, Mother put a different face on things *over the phone*, not just with my brother but with everybody, and hence the key to his whole blasé approach to the situation was her phone manner, which had led him to believe that my mails were alarmist. Why didn't I Skype my brother, I wondered, and enjoy a nice chat with him? Why did I phone, but never email, my sister? Why did I 'reply to all' in emails to my brother-in-law while my brother replied only to him, even if, as it turned out, there was nothing in his messages that couldn't perfectly well have been sent to me too? On another long train ride I suddenly had the intuition that if I put some pressure on these questions, if I really tackled the issue of why each of us contacted the others in the different ways we did, I would eventually find my way back to some defining moment in our childhood when my sister, my brother and I had become who we were. Behind the mystery there would be some scene, or some protracted drama, that explained everything. It seemed an interesting idea, but I felt reluctant to pursue it. Instead I began to wonder how my father would have communicated with us if he had lived into the period of email and Skype. Dad loved gadgets and electronic novelties. He once spent quite a lot of money trying to find the perfect voice recorder so he could record his ideas wherever he was. Mother used to laugh about him preparing his sermons in the bath. And he bought a fax machine at great expense as soon as they came in. Half asleep with the rhythm of the train, I dreamed I received a text message from my father: 'Soon your mother and I will be together in paradise,' it said.

DAY AND NIGHT

By day Thomas puts on respectable clothes and goes to work. His income will pay for the roof over their heads, the clothes on their backs, the shoes on their feet, schools, holidays, teeth, etc. He feels virtuous and rather successful.

By night Thomas dreams that a violent wind has blown through their house, sweeping up all his and his wife's underclothes and scattering them across the gutters of the suburb where they live. He wakes up anxious and excited.

By day Thomas works in the garden, digging the flower-beds for spring, or pruning the roses, or mowing the lawn, or cutting the hedges to keep things in order for other members of the family to enjoy, if they should so desire. Resting on his spade amid strong smells of soil and yew, he feels that perhaps something has been achieved.

By night Thomas dreams an earthquake shaking the hillside and his wife transformed into a unicorn galloping madly around stones and clods and broken fences. He wakes in a sweat.

By day Thomas and his wife go to a furniture warehouse to order a fitted kitchen. It is a pleasure to examine the smooth stone and steel of the work surfaces and open the heavy doors of quality appliances with their padded rubber insulation and shiny interiors. Installed at home, these items will be handsome and practical. Signing an expensive order, both he and Mary feel quietly satisfied.

By night Thomas dreams a strange strong humming sound. He goes down the stairs from bedroom to first floor, from first floor to ground floor, from ground floor to basement, then down more stairs, narrower and narrower, and still more stairs, deeper and deeper, a pitch-black staircase, leading down down down into the belly of the earth. Now the hum is a roar and suddenly he is standing on the brink of an underground river that runs swift and black through a mass of stone beneath his well-appointed house. Preparing to dive in, he wakes with a start.

By day Thomas reads newspapers and magazines. He is concerned about the economic crisis. He is concerned about youth unemployment. He is concerned about levels of immigration. He is concerned about global warming. And about the fate of Bristol Rovers, his old home team, who are fighting relegation. Over breakfast, lunch and dinner he and his wife and children discuss these things and his mother's cancer and listen to on-the-hour radio bulletins. It seems life is a constant battle to preserve the wealth and security they have accumulated.

By night Thomas dreams a gypsy boy running off with his laptop. After a long chase, he catches the boy and is amazed by his beauty, his long black ringlets and friendly, seductive smile. After the boy hands back the laptop, Thomas can't find his way home. He is lost.

By day Thomas works out, running or swimming or rowing, to make sure his body is fit enough to keep doing all the work he has to do to make his income and pay for the new kitchen and keep the garden in order and worry about everything he has to worry about. Sometimes he pushes himself very hard, especially on the running track, checking his heart rate regularly through a device on his arm. Later, after a shower, he feels a welcome glow of self-righteousness.

By night Thomas dreams excavators toiling around a simply enormous boulder that is blocking the flow of a major river. It seems impossible that man-made mechanics could ever shift such a huge obstacle and he wakes with an angry energy on his skin.

By day Thomas plans advertising campaigns and contacts clients and writes letters and lunches with business associates and takes his car to the mechanic and has his blood tested for PSA and cholesterol levels and generally feels life is a hectic treadmill. But once every few weeks, by night, if he is lucky, he sleeps with his girlfriend and then there are no dreams because actually they hardly sleep at all, though after lovemaking Thomas tells her about his quakes and gypsies and tumultuous waters and wistfully she wonders why he doesn't come and live with her since they are always so happy together.

He can't, he says.

Returning home, Thomas guides his newly serviced Audi down the ramp to the impressive three-vehicle underground garage beneath the well-kept garden. A remote raises the big door and as the car enters a light comes on automatically, illuminating stacked firewood against one wall, bicycles on racks on another, a tool cupboard, packing cases, a bobsleigh, skates, backpacks, books, a red and white Vespa, tennis rackets, guitar cases, amplifiers, an electric piano, a broken scooter. Turning off the ignition, Thomas sits and stares at it all. How many reassuring things, he thinks, tokens of past life and pleasures. After a while the light goes off, but Thomas continues to sit and stare. In the subterranean quiet of his garage on the comfortable seat of the dark sedan he might be an Etruscan prince embalmed in his ship of death.

This is a good place to grow old in, Thomas thinks, a safe place to fall ill and eventually to die in, surrounded by loved ones and household gods.

But Thomas is not old. He is not ill. He is not dying. His beloved is not here.

'I am full of life,' he mutters out loud. 'I am brimming with vitality.'

GOAT

Mary was brilliant with names. She had so much fun with them. Coffee had a name. It was feefee. And tea. It was teawee. That was in her younger days when her Scottish accent was stronger, though sometimes she would bring the old words out even in middle age, when she was in a good mood. London was the Dungeon. Paris, for reasons Thomas never fathomed, Old Weepy.

But it was the names of pets, friends, children and partners that most inspired Mary. Her flatmates, when Thomas first met her, Liz and Patty, were known respectively as Shuffle and Sharpie. Mary herself was Cane. One drunken evening the girls had explained to Thomas how each of these names came to be, an intricate series of shifts and transformations that had seen Patty become Marmar, then Shasha, then Shaman, then one day after she had said something particularly unpleasant, Sharp, and finally, with a little more affection, Sharpie. Quite how Liz had become Shuffle, Thomas couldn't remember. Perhaps her surname came into it, perhaps her dancing skills. Mary had been Mayhem, then Hurricane, then Cane. A hint of hurry and a hint of chastisement, Patty laughed, admitting it was always Mary who thought up everything, and Mary, in the end, who decided which name stuck. Thomas also laughed, stroking a cat that had originally been Bilberry, then Berryboo, then just booboo. 'Booboo!' Mary cried delightedly, rubbing faces with the fat black cat. 'Do you like our new friend, Tum?'

Thomas accepted this reference to his healthy appetite with good grace. But in no time at all, perhaps because stomachs do grumble sometimes, and sometimes couples argue, he had become Tomtom, Grumble and finally Grump. 'Grump yourself,' Thomas told her, since Mary was famous for grousing. 'Big Grump and Little Grump,' Mary elaborated, looking to patch things up. So now both had the same name. Then Grump became Gripe and Gripe Pipe and Pipe Pip and for a while this neutral mono-syllable stuck and both were Pip – 'I love you, Pip', 'I love you, Pip' – until the evening someone on television said, 'You really get my goat' and later that evening Mary said, 'I wish someone would get my goat, for Christ's sake', and towards midnight, and perhaps it was their happiest evening ever, Thomas and Mary were in bed calling each other Goat. They would be Goat to each other now for twenty years and more. They wrote letters to each other beginning, Dear Goat. They started phone conversations saying, Hi, Goatie. In the filing cabinet under the stairs there was a file entitled Big G and another entitled Little G. When mobile phones arrived, each entered the other in the address book as Goat.

Sometimes it was embarrassing. At some formal dinner party Mary would say, 'You do the honours, Goat', or 'Goat, do you think you could go and check the potatoes?' and Thomas would reply, 'No worries, Goat', or if he was in a bad mood, 'Yes, Goat, no, Goat, three bags full, Goat.' 'No Goat, no go,' Mary frowned.

Then everybody laughed and wanted to know exactly how this Goat thing had come about, and Mary would tell a different story on every occasion. Her favourite version was that goats, in popular tradition, were supposed to calm other farm animals down. 'You've got my goat actually meant you've taken away my calming influence. So, being goats, Tom and I calm each other down.' 'What nonsense, we wind each other up,' Thomas protested. 'Nothing to do with sexual performance?' one of the guests would always say. 'Alas, no,' Thomas confessed. 'Or demonic forebears?' suggested another. 'You'd have to ask the Reverend Paige about that,' Mary observed, meaning Thomas's father, 'wouldn't she, Goat?' and Thomas answered, 'She would indeed, Goat, darling, and the response would be: negative.' Sometimes a guest, Mary's sister for example, might join in and start to call them Goat herself, thinking this was fun, but Mary discouraged it. Goat was their name for each other. It was a oneness. Thomas and Mary are Goat. A single identity. But for others they must be Thomas and Mary.

'What about switching to Kid?' Thomas once suggested. 'It's a little cuter, isn't it? It sounds a bit more mainstream.' 'Don't be a silly billy, Goat,' Mary laughed. 'Our kids will be kids!' It was then that Thomas guessed that this name they had for each other needed to be slightly outlandish, slightly awkward in company; that way it became a declaration of love, of dignity forgone; before the world of sensible people they would acknowledge that they were one Goat. They would go out on a hairy limb. For Christmas and birthdays Thomas invariably received presents with images of goats: a mug, a pair of underpants, a key ring. In return he would pick up cards, or posters, or even paintings for Mary with images of goats: Emile Munier's cute *Young Girl with Goat & Flowers*, Kimberly Dawn Clayton's droll *Yuppie Goat* showing a goat's head, painted Matisse-style with a bow tie and an air of comic melancholy. Years later, in a different mood, he bought an original gouache by John Scott showing a mountain goat with horns leaping threateningly to butt an invisible target.

'Ever the romantic Goat,' Mary commented.

However, the most fertile naming came with the children. Here Thomas was allowed his say, for the registry office. 'Sally' and 'Mark' were the fruit of happy negotiation. Then Mary set to work on infinite permutations. Sally, Alley, Miss Bowls, Lorry, Stardust; Mark, Muck, Cluck, Chuck, Chuckles. Here it was not so much, as it had previously been with old friends, a question of the music stopping with a name that worked better than the others, at least to Mary's ear. Rather, as the years passed, different members of the family came to have different names for each other, though all generated by Mary. So Thomas and Mary together called Mark Chuckles, but when Mary was with Sally they called him Cluck; however, Thomas was soon aware that he wasn't supposed to call Mark Cluck since this was the girls' name for him. Likewise for Sally. Thomas and Mary called her Stardust, but Mary and Mark called her Lorry. From time to time Thomas became half aware of names he wasn't supposed to be privy to, in particular for himself between Mary and the kids. Rambo, for example, and Old Stoat. Finally, Old Squeak. They giggled among themselves. Thomas let it ride. When he spoke to the kids of their mother, he just said Mum. Or later still, your mother.

In adolescence the rebellions began. First Sally wouldn't reply to any name but Sally. 'Both syllables, please, Dad.' If you called her Sal she wouldn't so much as raise her head. If you called her Stardust at dinner with guests she stood up and left the room. Mark was more amenable. He allowed them to call him Chuckles right into his late teens. But he put an abrupt stop to it when he found a steady girlfriend. 'It's over, Mum,' he said one lunchtime with his girlfriend present. 'Mark is my name and Mark is what you call me.'

'You're both so damn touchy!' Mary shook her head, 'Aren't they, Goat?'

'They are indeed, Goat,' Thomas replied, and realised as he spoke how he envied his children, who were being

55

allowed to grow up and decide what they would be called. Already he foresaw the day when he would say to his wife, 'I want you to stop calling me Goat, Mary. I can't deal with it any more.'

'But it's so cute,' she objected when that conversation finally happened. She couldn't seem to get it into her head that he was serious. She couldn't see his problem. 'It's us, Goat, isn't it, it's our story? We're Goat.'

The two of them were in bed, in the half dark.

'It was our story,' he accepted. 'It was fun once. But not now. I'm Thomas and you're Mary.' When she was silent, he repeated, 'Our Goat days are over, love.'

'Love' was a coward's mockery.

They had the dog by then of course, and Mary called him in the quiet of the bedroom that night. 'Ricky, Ricky, love.' The dog pattered over to her. 'KiKi,' she fondled his ears. 'Yikyik,' she let him lick her mouth. 'Will you call me Goat?'

'For Christ's sake!'

'Baah,' Mary muttered to the dog. 'Ba-a-a-aah.' Ricky pranced around, excited.

'Mary, love.'

'Don't call me love,' she said sharply.

Moments passed. The dog whined.

'Bleat,' Mary said, her voice resigned. Very softly, she began to cry. 'Is it all right if I bleat a little from time to time?'

'Damn.'

Thomas went downstairs to pour himself a whisky.

56

PROMOTION

Four years ago Thomas was denied the big promotion he
expected, the final elevation. The MD gave the post to
Ms Cavanaugh. It would be hard to find anyone in the
company who does not believe that Ms Cavanaugh is the
MD's lover and has been for many years. It is a relationship Thomas does not understand, since Ms Cavanaugh
is rather mannish and the MD rather effeminate. He lives
with his blind and ancient mother, Ms Cavanaugh with
her schizophrenic brother. Go figure, Thomas thinks.
The fact is that for the foreseeable future he will have to
take orders from a woman ten years younger than himself
who knows nothing about their line of business but is
unwilling to expose her ignorance by asking for advice.
When things go wrong he can hardly appeal over her
head to the MD, since in that case he would be appealing
against the man's mistress, not to mention questioning
his judgement in appointing her. Why the relationship is
officially secret is a mystery, as there is no spouse on either

side to feel betrayed. Not even a dog, Thomas thinks, smiling.

But he is not smiling now. He has just received an email in which Ms Cavanaugh invites him to come to her office to discuss precise allegations: that Thomas, in conversation with Sue Peers, misrepresented the motives behind the latter's removal from the important account she had hitherto been handling. The appropriate moment for them to clarify the situation, Ms Cavanaugh writes in this email, will be immediately after the meeting of department heads on Monday afternoon. Since it is now Tuesday morning, Thomas is at once aware that he will have to spend six full days being extremely anxious.

Returning home, he tries to explain the gravity of the situation to his wife. Having requested, more than a month ago, a private meeting with the MD to discuss issues in his faltering department, he had found Ms Cavanaugh unexpectedly present, apparently affable but no doubt concerned that Thomas was trying to go over her head. One of the dozen or so issues Thomas had discussed was the removal of Sue Peers at least from the Bullard account, which he had always said she did not have the experience to handle and which he felt they were now in danger of losing, along with 23 per cent of his department's income. Since Sue Peers had been rather hurriedly handed the account when, shortly after her appointment, Ms Cavanaugh had clashed with the rather brilliant Mike Dillon, who laughed in her face, told her she was brainless and immediately found himself a job elsewhere, it was quite possible that Ms Cavanaugh saw Thomas's request as an indirect criticism of her management, though he had been extremely careful not to present it that way. Nor had he actually expected that Sue Peers would be removed from the account, since no one was more assiduous than Sue in flattering her superiors, Ms Cavanaugh first and foremost, and no one more used to seeing his requests turned down than Thomas. In fact it was to his great surprise that he discovered at the next department meeting not only that Sue Peers had been removed but that the Bullard account had already been allotted, somewhat unexpectedly and without his having been consulted, to Karl Quentin, a promising member of staff recently brought in from another company of which the MD was a non-executive director.

'However, when I spoke to Sue,' Thomas explained to his wife, 'after the meeting . . .'

Suddenly he found his voice drowned out by the roar of the liquidiser. Mary was preparing pumpkin soup.

'You're not listening,' he remarked when the noise stopped.

'Because you're not really talking to me, are you?' she replied. 'You're just worrying out loud. You're always getting yourself into these messes, Goat. Resign if you don't like the place. Go somewhere else. You're supposed to be so smart, aren't you?'

Thomas would have liked to resign, but his present job had the advantage of putting him in regular contact with his own lover, who was a junior in Personnel. It was also true that the money was good. Later that evening his wife relented and, while Thomas was on the sofa with his laptop and she at the sitting-room table with hers, asked him to explain exactly what had happened.

'Oh, nothing much,' he told her. 'I wouldn't like to stress you unnecessarily with my work problems.'

'Suit yourself, Goat,' she said.

'However, when I spoke to Sue,' Thomas explained the following day to Cathy, 'she was absolutely furious since the Bullard account was the main thing in her career, a make-or-break job for her. So I told her that the decision had been Cavanaugh's and the MD's, that I simply didn't have the power to make these decisions, even assuming I wanted to. The fact is I still have to work with Sue, and of course pretty much everyone in the department loves her since she's always doing favours for everybody. She's that kind of person.'

Cathy was drumming a beat on the pub table. There was rarely a moment when Cathy was not drumming a beat. 'You must have said more than that,' she objected. 'Who went and told Cava?'

Thomas admitted that he had told Sue these out-of-the-blue reshufflings were typical of the way the company was now being run; capricious displays of power that made everything difficult for everyone. The truth is he had been in a hurry to get away and unprepared when Sue had confronted him. As for the spy, feasibly there had been three people within earshot, but he felt pretty sure it must be Frank Law, who always complained that Thomas was dictatorial and hypercritical.

Cathy stopped drumming and took his hands across the table. She looked into his eyes with such intensity that for a moment it seemed to Thomas she was fighting her way across the twenty-five-year gap between them.

'Let's do a runner,' she said. 'The hell with it. You're worth so much more than these shits. It's a sin somebody as smart as you having to toe the line to someone as dumb as Cava. And I was never made for office life. Let's just vamoose.'

The young woman had spoken urgently, her body swaying a little as she did so. Thomas smiled. Then she had to go to a practice session with the band. That night Thomas woke in the early hours to find his brain absolutely ungovernable, between the acute awareness that his girlfriend would soon leave him, the acute awareness that he would not leave his wife, the acute awareness that the meeting with Cavanaugh would be unpleasant and their relationship soured beyond repair, and the very acute awareness that this was largely his own fault for having spoken carelessly to Sue Peers when other staff members were nearby, not to mention the possibility that Sue might actually have told Frank what Thomas had said to her and that Frank might then have pointed out that if he now told Cavanaugh that he had *overheard* Thomas saying what he had it would cause all kinds of trouble for a department manager who had been highly critical of both of them and was probably pushing to have both of them removed from the company altogether. Yes, Sue Peers and Frank Law, Thomas reflected, had long formed an alliance of losers. Until they were fired, his department would be unmanageable.

So the night passed. His body was rigid. He didn't sleep. And again the next day and the next night. Two hours' sleep, then hour after hour fiercely awake, running through all the possible scenarios of what he might say when the famous meeting occurred, and all the possible ways a peeved Sue Peers might respond to whatever line he took, and how Ms Cavanaugh might react to both of them. Certainly if Sue repeated word for word his remarks that Ms Cavanaugh couldn't manage a Women's Institute muffin party and cared even less about the staff than she did about her sickly deodorants, things would grow heated indeed. Sitting on the sofa in the dark, drinking camomile tea, Thomas couldn't understand why he had made himself such a hostage to fortune. He was a stupid, careless man. Did he want to be fired? Perhaps he did, just as he often wished his wife would chuck him out of the house. On the other hand, he was doubtless the most respected, experienced and creative member of his company's staff and the MD would be almost as loath to lose him as he would be to see Ms Cavanaugh humiliated. Almost.

By Friday, Thomas had understood that no useful work of any kind would be done this week. Various appointments had to be cancelled and deadlines postponed. His mind was running riot. He was distracted with the children, distracted with his wife, distracted with the dog. 'You are hell to live with,' Mary informed him. 'For Christ's sake, snap out of it.' At a concert with Cathy on Saturday evening he found it impossible to concentrate on the bands that were playing, impossible to lose himself in even the wildest rhythms. Heavy drinking only fuelled his anxieties. He imagined telling Cavanaugh *exactly* what he thought of her. That she was a complete incompetent whom the whole world found ridiculous. That without the MD behind her, or rather between her legs, always assuming he was still up to it after heart surgery and prostate cancer, she would be a complete nobody and when the old bastard finally kicked it, as very likely he soon must, given the way he was forever yelling at others for mistakes that were all her doing – when he finally kicked it she would be out on her neck in no time and the board would almost certainly appoint him, Thomas, in her place as they should have done four years ago. It was hard to exaggerate, he might tell her – no, impossible to exaggerate – what an utter nullity the rest of the world considered her. An utter utter nullity.

Thomas imagined his satisfaction on saying these words. He imagined the consternation on Linda Cavanaugh's face, the quiver on her pale lips. She would be wearing one of her silver-grey trouser suits, a look of crisp efficiency, which was exactly that – a look and nothing more, some-thing cultivated to cover up for the nothing behind it – with the kind of flashy cufflinks young male executives wear, the kind of glasses a young man chooses if he wants to give himself an authority he doesn't have. The truth was that Cavanaugh was fragile. If she didn't actually know she was a fraud, she was certainly afraid she might be, afraid of any kind of criticism and exposure. And this was exactly what made her so dangerous, so unwilling ever really to discuss anything, ever to take Thomas's advice on anything.

Then Thomas imagined confessing instead, and asking forgiveness. Yes, he would admit to Ms Cavanaugh, he had spoken out of turn. His private life was not going well. He was feeling frustrated in various ways. Stupidly and absolutely unjustifiably he had allowed these frustrations to cloud his vision and make him say the most unpleasant things to Sue Peers, partly because he would have to go on working with the woman despite her losing the Bullard account and partly because of the way she had confronted him so heatedly when he had least been expecting it. He hadn't actually been warned that she had been taken off the account. But these of course could hardly be excuses and he had been criminally disloyal, not to say injudicious, in speaking like that about a superior.

Thomas found the confessional approach easier to imagine than venting his spleen. He could very easily see himself leaning forward over Cavanaugh's outsize leather-topped desk and speaking with great intensity and earnestness. He was good at confessions, good at apologies. From the earliest age his puritanical parents had schooled him in the habit of contrition. Nor was this version without its elements of truth. Immediately he spoke, he would begin to feel he really was guilty, even sorry. Or part of him would feel that. The performing part. Performance would make him feel what he had chosen to perform. Hadn't he experienced that often enough with his wife? Or the other way round with his girlfriends. Romance was also a performance. And Cavanaugh was bound to fall for it. It would be such a relief to that brittle lady to receive this confirmation of her own rectitude and competence. No doubt in her own mind she was rightfully his superior; in her own mind she wasn't where she was because she fucked the MD; rather, the MD fucked her because *as well as* being brilliant and efficient she was *also* seductive and affectionate and loyal. Thomas imagined Ms Cavanaugh becoming suddenly affable and generous, demurring, calling him Tom, telling him please to stop, no problem, not to worry, we all have these disheartening moments when we say things we shouldn't. Now he had set the record straight, she would be the last to hold it against him.

So, yes, perhaps this was the way to play it, Thomas told himself in the thick of the concert while an American punk band belted out inanities and Cathy grinned over a bottle of Beck's, head swaying from side to side.

Except of course that Sue would be present, Thomas now remembered. And Sue had heard a hundred times what he *really* thought of Cavanaugh. Sue would see through his abject opportunism. How could she not? And later she would enjoy a good snigger with the other members of the department over his pathetic capitulation. His authority would be utterly diminished. The situation would be unworkable, unliveable. She might even contradict him to Ms Cavanaugh's face. Perhaps she imagined that if Thomas was fired she would get the Bullard account back, or might even be appointed to his position. Long experience warned Thomas that there was no end to people's overestimation of themselves.

Then how miserable, Thomas went on thinking as the band launched into a new cacophony, to humble himself like this, as he had humbled himself a thousand times with his wife, acknowledging that he was the guilty party in battles of every kind, when he didn't feel he was guilty at all, or not of the things he had confessed. Yes, he had eaten humble pie simply in order to return to a state of peace, to stop the fight and concentrate his mind on the things he preferred to concentrate on. If I'm guilty of anything, Thomas thought, it's of too often choosing to declare myself guilty. It's the coward's way out.

'Ground control to moody Tom!'

Cathy was laughing at him.

'Wake up, spaceman!'

The music was over. The band were unplugging their guitars. People were dispersing.

'I'm sorry,' Thomas said.

'Don't say sorry,' she told him. 'Say I want to fuck you.'

Routinely, they made love in Thomas's car before he drove her on to her boyfriend's. Cathy was a wonderful lover.

'I can never figure out,' Thomas said, driving now, 'why they don't simply admit that they're together, since neither of them have partners.'

'She really has got under your skin, hasn't she?' Cathy said. 'I'm getting jealous. You never worried this much about me.'

'Because you don't make me worry, Cathy. That's why I like you.'

'Perhaps I should,' Cathy laughed. She frowned. 'Maybe they like to be secret. They like to be a conspiracy.'

'Fun for a while,' Thomas agreed. 'But hardly for years and years.'

Cathy sighed. 'What if Cava's actually a transvestite? There is something pretty odd about her, isn't there?'

Thomas tried to smile. 'Maybe they feel they can't have a regular relationship because of their home situations. I've heard her nutty brother can be violent. Perhaps I should feel sorry for her.'

'Fuck that,' Cathy said. 'Why do you always want to feel sorry for people?'

Cathy was smoking in the car, which he knew would be a problem.

'Why don't you feel sorry for me?' she demanded.

'Maybe I chose you,' Thomas laughed, 'because you're the kind of person I never need to feel sorry for. You're so full of life.'

'You wait,' she warned. 'The rate we're going.'

Driving home with freezing air pouring in from open windows, Thomas wondered how it would feel when his complicated life finally became too much and he cracked.

Monday lunchtime, before the department meeting, Thomas met Ms Cavanaugh in the corridor and found her in cheerful mood. She greeted him as though they were friendly colleagues and asked about a presentation he was planning with young Quentin. Replying, Thomas explained the essentials of the strategy and the part their new recruit would play in it. Everything in his manner suggested that he was eager for her approval while everything in Ms Cavanaugh's manner suggested she was granting that approval. It was a promising start, Thomas thought. At the same time he hated it.

The meeting of department heads went on longer than he'd expected. Presiding over a long oval table, Ms Cavanaugh was embarrassingly disorganised. She constantly had to bend towards her secretary for prompts. She seemed to have forgotten the day's agenda. She read out progress reports that could have been emailed to people, enthused over small successes, skated over major problems. When Barker objected that the decision to pass two accounts from his department to Thomas's was ill-judged, she came down on him with icy coldness. The

MD had decided this, she said. If Barker wanted to protest directly to the MD he was welcome to do so, though it might be worth remembering that the great man was already overstretched.

'I thought we had these meetings in order to discuss the appropriate allocation of the accounts,' Barker suggested.

'These meetings are to discuss how best to put the MD's decisions into practice,' Ms Cavanaugh replied.

Keeping his head down, Thomas watched the woman. She had that slightly sinewy look of the forty-year-old who hasn't had children and is frequently in the gym. There was something at once measured yet tense about her; the wrists in their smart cuffs seemed taut. Her hair was a black helmet, her bosom flattened in a double-breasted jacket, her trousers smoothly cylindrical. Throughout the meeting she tapped a sharp pencil on the notepad in front of her, and after every contribution from the department heads around the table she leaned down to tell her secretary whether this or that comment needed to go in the minutes. He had been absolutely right when he had spoken ill of her, Thomas thought. Which did not mean it was not a mistake.

Then this meeting was over and the other smaller, more dangerous meeting could begin. Now whatever was to happen would happen. Thomas began to feel calmer, but at the same time extremely vulnerable, like a canoeist accelerating on the flat steady water that precedes a rapid. Leaving his colleagues, without staying on for the customary coffee together, he took the lift to the fourth floor and waited outside Ms Cavanaugh's office. There was a window here that gave on to a quiet courtyard and Thomas stood at the sill, looking out. He would pretend not to hear her arrive and so she would have to call his name. In the courtyard was a tree in fresh leaf, a flowerbed, and a bench where a young woman wrapped in an overcoat was forking a late lunch into her mouth from blue Tupperware. It was hard to tell from here, but she seemed an attractive young woman, at ease with herself. Why am I never at ease with myself? Thomas wondered.

'Tom,' Ms Cavanaugh said. 'Thanks for coming.'

'Hello, Linda,' Thomas responded. 'I thought Sue was supposed to be here too.'

'That's right,' Ms Cavanaugh said. 'It's not like her to be late.'

'Very unusual,' Thomas agreed.

Ms Cavanaugh's office was more generous than his own. The desk, the carpet, the window, the chair all spoke of comfort and corporate authority. Yet there was something impersonal about the room too, as if the woman hadn't quite dared to inhabit it fully, or had feared that if she did so it might lose some of its power to intimidate. The only personal touch was a large box of chocolates on the desk. In affable mood Ms Cavanaugh would immediately offer these, then take one herself and make some twee remark about her sweet tooth. Today she did not. She began to fire up her computer, presumably waiting for Sue Peers's arrival. Thomas decided to go first.

'So what is all this about? I'm afraid we have two people coming in from Courtney's shortly. I'm a little pushed for time.'

Ms Cavanaugh looked at her watch. They were running forty minutes late.

'She couldn't have waited a while then left, do you think?'

Thomas shook his head. 'She would have put her head round the door,' he said. 'Can't we proceed without her?'

Ms Cavanaugh looked up and her manner changed. Her features rearranged themselves in a concerned, even pained look. She put her hands together below her sharp chin.

'I wanted you two to confront each other so that I could get to the truth of the matter.'

Sweating though he was, Thomas raised a wry eyebrow. He was on the brink of the rapid. From here on, it would all be instinct.

'That serious?' he said.

'The fact is that someone has told me something that, if true, would leave me enormously disappointed.'

Thomas waited. Evidently 'disappointed' meant 'disappointed with you'.

Ms Cavanaugh picked up the phone and called her secretary. Could she contact Sue Peers and find out why on earth she wasn't here as she was supposed to be?

Of course, Thomas thought, they both had Sue's mobile number, but a secretary had to be brought in to avoid any notion that they were communicating as equals. He felt weary with all this.

Covering the mouthpiece of her phone, Ms Cavanaugh said, 'Apparently her mobile isn't answering.'

Madly, it occurred to Thomas that Sue might have killed herself. She cared that much about the Bullard account. She wanted to make them feel that bad. Simultaneously, he was aware that this was a stupid idea and the merest projection of his own anxiety. 'In that case,' he said, 'perhaps we had better leave it till after Easter.' In reality the last thing he wanted was to have this nonsense hanging over him during the Easter break.

Ms Cavanaugh put the phone down, frowned. 'No. This needs saying now. Tom, the fact is, I have it on good authority that you gave a completely false and unpleasant account to Sue of the reasons for her removal from the Bullard account.'

Thomas sighed and seemed to cast about for a proper response.

'Good authority from whom, Linda?' he eventually asked.

'Let's say someone was in the vicinity when you had this conversation.'

'Someone?'

'Someone I trust.'

He shook his head. 'I really don't recall anything very special being said.'

'It seemed special and ugly enough for someone to warn me.'

Thomas drew a deep breath; he felt perfectly poised between the two approaches that had been hammering away in his head for the past six days and nights. He opened his mouth to speak, wondering which would come out, which decision he would take. Then hesitated. He was lost. He simply didn't know which way to jump. I don't know who I am, he thought.

Finally he said: 'Honestly, Linda, I can't remember anything out of order being said. Sue was very angry and, not having been warned that she had in fact been taken off the account, I was a little at a loss. I think I told her that there had always been doubts surrounding her appointment and that anyway these were decisions taken at the highest level. After all, authority lies with the MD.'

'I'm very disappointed,' Ms Cavanaugh said. She removed her glasses and rubbed the tips of her fingers into her eyes. The massage went on for some time. Eventually she came to herself. 'Tom, I can't understand why you didn't tell her that you brought up the issue yourself with the MD. It was you who insisted on replacing her.'

'It's hardly my part to relay confidential conversations with the Managing Director,' Thomas said. 'And, of course, I have to go on working with Sue.' He added: 'Did you actually have a meeting with her to explain the decision?'

Thomas imagined the answer to this was going to be no. Cavanaugh was famous for simply announcing major changes through her secretary with no explanation. And otherwise why would Sue have come at him so angrily after that department meeting?

'Of course I did. What kind of manager do you think I am?' Ms Cavanaugh looked genuinely shocked. 'I brought her in to tell her what we'd decided and explained that it was part of a general strategy we had worked out for your department with the MD, at your specific request. And that these changes would include Frank's being moved at some point too.'

Thomas was startled. 'You told her that?'

'Of course I did. You can't just go changing people's lives without giving them some explanation. It has always been my policy to be entirely transparent.'

All Thomas's preparation was now swept away. How incompetent could one be? Ms Cavanaugh had not only put all the blame on him, the man who had to manage her, but had given Sue the chance to alert Frank that he would be next in the firing line. With the result that Frank would have had an even greater interest than before in telling tales to Ms Cavanaugh. Above all, it was clear that, while needing total power to feel safe, Ms Cavanaugh also expected to be loved, so she passed the buck.

'The fact is, Tom, I have to be able to trust you to back me up and give a fair representation of how we go about things here. I can't have you giving entirely different and disparaging accounts of events.'

Thomas sighed. He wanted out of his job and out of his marriage. He wanted to sit in the courtyard wrapped in a thick coat eating vegetarian fare out of Tupperware.

Rather boldly, he got to his feet. 'Linda,' he began, 'I'm truly sorry if anything I said to Sue was inappropriate . . .' but at this point the telephone rang.

Ms Cavanaugh now spoke in a lower voice. All the same, it was immediately clear it was the MD calling her directly to ask when she would be ready to leave. They must have some appointment together. 'I'm afraid that idiot Barker dragged things out,' Ms Cavanaugh explained, 'complaining about your moving those accounts out of his department.'

That idiot Barker! Did the MD appreciate, Thomas wondered, that his lover was speaking in his, Thomas's, presence? What if Thomas now told Barker that Ms Cavanaugh had referred to him as an idiot in conversation with the MD?

'Oh, he seemed ready to back down at the end,' she was saying, 'but it made the meeting longer than it needed to be. Just give me five minutes.'

She put the phone down. On his feet, Thomas said, 'You look tired, Linda.'

'Can you believe that conversation with Barker?' Ms Cavanaugh asked, as if the phone call had reminded her, as if despite what she had said immediately before the call she was still looking for solidarity from Thomas. She shook her head and again removed her glasses to rub her eyes. 'This place is such a snakepit. I really need a break.'

'I know what you mean,' Thomas said carefully. 'Strange that Sue hasn't come.'

With suddenly renewed severity, Ms Cavanaugh said, 'I'll write you both an email to clarify once and for all how this situation came about. After which we shall hear no more about it.'

Leaving her office, Thomas thought: I worried all week over this. I lost sleep. I upset the people around me. For nothing.

On the train home he was surprised to find that an email had already arrived. The woman must have written it, he thought, while actually in the MD's company, since the two had clearly been planning to leave work together. Perhaps in a taxi. He clicked it open: the gist, in her usual absurd formalese, was that the planned meeting had been held despite Sue's absence, an absence Ms Cavanaugh hoped could be explained and justified as soon as possible, that Tom had admitted he had spoken unwisely and in circumstances ill suited to a delicate discussion of this kind and had apologised for it; that the real explanation of the change in company strategy re Bullard was as previously described in the earlier meeting with Sue, and that it was now time for them all to put the past behind them and make a success of these decisions that had been taken for the good of the company.

Thomas shook his head.

Soon after this, another mail arrived, this one from Sue Peers. She apologised profusely for her absence but pointed out that the original email from Ms Cavanaugh had mentioned the meeting of department heads as being in April, not March. Since she was not a department head herself and hence not invited to the meeting, she had had no way of supposing that it was really this Monday. In the event, she had been away from work, visiting her dying father.

After reading this Thomas went back and checked the original email to both of them from Ms Cavanaugh and saw that she had indeed spoken of April, not March. Knowing perfectly well when the meeting of department heads would be, he had barely noticed the actual date. On the other hand, how could Sue have imagined that Ms Cavanaugh would fix a meeting like that five weeks hence in an environment where the people involved saw each other at least weekly, if not daily? Either she was even more scatterbrained than he imagined or she had decided to exploit this loophole so as not to have to confront Thomas, of whom, quite possibly, she was afraid.

What am I doing working for this bunch of losers? Thomas thought.

An SMS arrived. Cathy would be playing drums in Berlin at the weekend and wanted him to join her. 'Do it do it do it!' she wrote. 'Let's get wasted! Let's live!'

Thomas texted to say he would move heaven and earth to be there. Picking up the car at the station after his train journey, he at once found himself stuck in heavy traffic. His wife would complain, he thought, that he hadn't come early enough to pick up the groceries they had ordered from the supermarket. Should he bother to explain about the overly long meeting? Perhaps mention Barker's irritation over the reallocation of two accounts. In the event, however, his spouse was in a cheerful mood and when Thomas invited her to a restaurant she, rather unusually, agreed.

'So how was the meeting with the MD's lay?' she asked.

Thomas recounted.

'So you're relieved, Goat,' she smiled, 'after making our lives miserable for a week?'

Thomas reflected. He looked at his wife eating her salad and waited. At last, with the growing silence she looked up. For a rare moment there was eye contact.

'No,' he said. 'I'm not relieved. I wish it had been conclusive. I wish we had shouted at each other and all the filth had come out and she had chucked me out of the company. It's the paralysis that's driving me crazy.'

Mary looked down at her food. 'Filth?' she enquired softly.

ZONING

Thomas stands accused of not closing the fridge door properly. The kitchen is not his territory. Apparently the appliances do not belong to him, even if they were bought with money he earned. Thomas has committed other crimes in the kitchen. He has dropped sticky marmalade on the floor. Cleaning the top of the oven once, he used an abrasive product that blemished its brushed-steel surface for ever. His kitchen duties involve rinsing off the dishes and putting them in the dishwasher; also, freeing the blocked sink from time to time. Sitting at his place, back to the French window, with the cat standing sentinel outside, he waits for his plate to arrive. He was not involved in its preparation. Beside and opposite him, his children are also passive presences. Mary presides. 'What a great cook you are,' Thomas says appreciatively. She eats on her feet while the others sit. The dog pads from one to another with beseeching eyes and bushy tail.

The downstairs toilet is also Mary's.

The upstairs toilet and bathroom are shared by Thomas and his son, Mark.

There is a toilet en suite in their daughter Sally's room, though she is rarely home these days and the toilet rarely flushed.

Thomas would like the garage to be his, but can't persuade Mary to park her car where he thinks it should go. He has to squeeze his against the wall.

Each child has his or her own room and of course Thomas and Mary have their bedroom, though this is divided up, as it were, down the middle of the bed: the window side is Mary's, the stairs side is Thomas's. He cannot remember the last time he visited her bedside table and presumes the same holds for her. It has been some years since anyone sat on the armchairs at the foot of the bed. They are used for draping clothes: Thomas's clothes on the chair nearer the wall, and Mary's clothes on the chair nearer the windows. The cleaning is done by a cleaning lady. Polished and tidied, it is a beautiful, rather empty room. The bright light from the window mills with dust.

The playroom, built as an extension at the side of the house, belongs to the children. Here there is the TV. There is space. There are guitars and amplifiers. In the old days there was the family computer. Once a ping-pong table. Once a railway set. A doll's house. Now it is rather dusty, rather messy, with a beer bottle or two and blankets heaped on the sofa. There are remotes and game consoles.

Dog hairs everywhere. Peeking in, Thomas smiles and thinks he should tell the kids to tidy up.

The garden is Thomas's duty but, duty done, no one takes advantage, save the dog, which ruins the flowerbeds scrambling after the cat. It would be hard to say exactly what the family gains by having a garden, unless it is a place where Sally's boyfriend can smoke his Marlboros when she's home. Thomas digs the stubs into the earth without complaint. He likes the boy.

The washroom with its powerful machines is Mary's. She knows the codes and programs of the washing machine as she knows the settings and times of oven and microwave. These are all Greek to her husband. The children hang out the damp clothes to dry, after some prodding.

But the sitting-room fire would never be lit if Thomas didn't light it. This means going down to the garage under the house and bringing up a box of logs. It's a chore. Nor will the sitting-room curtains be opened unless Thomas opens them, as if only he cares about light and warmth here where there are sofa and armchairs and carpet around the pleasant hearth.

Thomas loves the fire. He loves to stretch on the carpet before the fire, even though it is not really comfortable. He loves the idea of a man stretched on the carpet before the family fire. He doesn't mind the dog joining him with its doggie smell. He loves it if his children join him, though they rarely do. It's hard staying long on the carpet alone, in discomfort, however mesmerising the flames and reassuring the thought of his being stretched out there. Occasionally Mary joins him, she on the sofa, he on the carpet, or he on the sofa with his computer on his knees, working, and she on an armchair with a book in her lap, reading about cocker spaniels, perhaps. But very soon one of the two will get up again, rather like a fire that hasn't caught, or two sticks that won't make a spark. More often she sits at the sitting-room table. There is a place, back to the window, that is her place, with her computer and her papers. No one else would ever dream of sitting in this place.

It is not finally clear, then, Thomas reflects, who presides in the sitting room. At the same time it does not feel as though the space is really shared. Perhaps it's a question of timing. Often, when his parents are not there, for example, Mark will take over completely, rolling around the floor with the dog, tossing a slipper right across the room, perhaps, or in a tug of war with a rubber bone. Thomas has seen him playing like that through the window on returning home. And when no one is around it is the dog that relishes the sofa's soft cushions, snuggling its golden fur into the green upholstery. Perhaps the dog presides, Thomas thinks, returning to find the house empty one day. Guiltily, the handsome creature sits up, wags its tail, sniffs the air, pants from a pink mouth, but doesn't climb down. At the absent heart of the family is a dog. If only, Thomas thinks, it could learn to play the piano.

BLACK TIE

My lover looks great in a tie, though it's not really him. He asks me for advice about shoes and shirts. What do I know? I could never have imagined someone in his position being so insecure. My father isn't. My boyfriend would never ask my advice. He takes it, too. He wore the orange tie I chose. It felt like a pact. Something we knew that no one else did. I was filled with tenderness when he stood up to speak. He's got charisma!

My lover should get in touch with who he really is. He doesn't fit with suits on a dais, conferences and the like. He's so much more himself with his hand round my waist swaying to music. People look at us, but who cares? You'll leave me, he says. He says he can't do family again. In the evening we walk round town with a half-bottle of Bell's, looking for places with live music. If I need a pee, I squat between cars. He loves to put his fingers in the flow. He says he's never been with someone so alive.

It's not easy for me to make love to my boyfriend now. My lover says he doesn't have to make love to his wife. They stopped years ago. Mum likewise with Dad, I reckon. Maybe not. They're still in the same bed. My lover sends beautiful messages to me before he falls asleep. I read them after practice sessions. Your hair, your eyes, your skin, your smell. My boyfriend is inspired on keyboards, but not in bed. He wants marriage and children. Soon. Dad says he was smart not to give up his day job.

In bed with my lover I go liquid. I go mad. It's like dancing in a frenzy. He's a wild man who shouldn't be wearing stuffy clothes and wasting his charisma on brand awareness and impact tracking. We should be dancing together every day. *I'm* your brand, I told him, track my impact. He likes to get me on top to bring him off. Afterwards we talk. We talk about my family, my brother. My mother is seeing an analyst. He laughs. He understands everything very quickly. Why my brother is so angry. Why my father is so frustrated. He thinks it's crazy my boyfriend is bailing out of a holiday with me because the family dog can't be left alone in the house. 'He's not alive enough for you,' he says. 'You're dynamite.'

'You write those messages in bed beside your wife,' I tell him. 'Why do you stay if you'd rather be with me?' He says he's tied. Family tied. He can't change. He smiles: 'And that's a black tie! I prefer orange, but there you go.' Sometimes I bring him off in my mouth with a finger in his arse. You should see his face then.

My lover says I started the affair with him because I'm dissatisfied with my boyfriend, but I'll leave him (my lover) when I want to get serious because he can't do children again. I hate this sort of talk. What's the point? It's freezing and we came into a café to get warm. He pours whisky in the coffee on the sly. Later he talks to a barman in the Cayenne, and later still to one of the singers in the evening's band. People always want to talk to my lover. He has that. I tell him if he says this stuff to me again about me wanting to settle down and have children I'll leave him that minute. I started the affair because I was curious and I'm going on with it because I'm in love.

'In love, get it?'

My lover has to stay at home at the weekends, or says he does. Which is when I travel and play. Sometimes with the band, sometimes standing in for some other drummer. In Düsseldorf last week. Dublin next. I send him texts about other men making moves on me. It happens all the time. 'Because you're beautiful,' he texts back. 'Because you're so peppy.' I send the same texts to my boyfriend. 'There's this Indian guy tried to follow me into the loo.' My boyfriend gets furious. He drives fifty miles to come to my rescue. My lover lets me breathe. I want to breathe with him.

My lover doesn't look as old as he is but he should learn to straighten his shoulders. And the way he walks. He forgets to do up his zip. Sometimes he's distracted, like he hardly knows you're there. When I was still at work, I told him one day, 'You're at half mast, Mr Paige.' He laughed and pulled up. A few days later we emailed. I told him I was determined to be a successful musician. It was the only thing I believed in. Not love, no way, but music. He said if I believed in something I should risk everything and go for it while I was still young and there was still time. I left work and fell in love with him.

My lover has a sort of dazed look about him when we meet sometimes, as if he can't believe how lucky he is. We went on a camping holiday together. Crazy, I know, *camping*, when you think of the money he has. We could have done four-star hotels. But it was very us. We're kids, really. You can see he wants to be a kid. He wants to shake off his solemn life. I took my bongos. We arrived at one campsite in the small hours and had to climb the gate and put up our tent in the dark. Without torches. We'd forgotten to bring them. It's amazing how well we work together. Next day the site manager was furious. We could have scared his family clients, he said. We slept two nights on the dunes and I played the bongos, looking into my lover's eyes. He gazed into mine and there were tears on his cheeks. We had a bottle of Chablis. The second night three black guys turned up and danced. They thought he was my father.

I felt fantastic on that camping trip. We slept in each other's arms. On the Saturday he left me at the station where he was expecting his wife and children. 'Let's escape together,' I texted. 'I'd love to, but I can't,' he answered. On the train I felt empty. 'Why not?' I texted. 'In the end what's stopping you?' He didn't reply. Maybe he was driving. I began to feel angry. 'Why not?' I texted again. Over the next twenty-four hours I texted him about two hundred times. 'I can't bear this. We've got to be together. We love each other.' I texted him from the train and then from my boyfriend's car and then from the room my boyfriend had booked for our holiday with the dog as well and then all night from the bathroom when I vomited and then from the beach when I got up and went out to walk all night, up to my knees in the sea sometimes, texting and texting and texting, freezing cold.

'How can you still sleep with your wife?'

'Why aren't you awake?'

'You must care so much about your damned reputation to throw up what we have together.'

'You'll never find anyone else like me.'

'You look like such a winner in your suits and ties, but really you're a loser.'

'You're a loser to live with someone you don't love.'

'How are you this morning, Mr Loser?'

'Met any cute girls lately, Mr Loser?'

'I mean girls that you can fuck on the side before going home to your wife, Mr Loser?'

'Please tell me you love me, Tommy.'

'Tommy, I'm in hospital. I nearly drowned. Come to me. Please come to me.'

'I went swimming in a storm. I was drunk. Why don't you come to me?'

'Seems I was unconscious. I banged my head.'

'I love you, Thomas. Feels like my brain is exploding.'

'There's a nice doctor fancies me and sits with me. Says they won't know if I'm out of danger for another forty-eight hours.'

'My boyfriend is so tender. I can't bear him.'

'My boyfriend sits by my bed all night. I could kill him. But he's not so much of a loser as you are. How can you sleep while I'm in trouble like this?'

'Answer me!'

'You're a coward. You'll never find anyone else like me.'

'You'll never have anything halfway so beautiful as what we have.'

'I hate you.'

'You should be scared of me. I'll make your life hell.'

'I should never have listened to you. You made me leave my job. You've ruined my life. I'll never make a living as a musician. It just doesn't happen that way.'

'When I die, be sure it's your fault, Mr Loser. You'll have me on your conscience the rest of your days.'

'Loser loser loser.'

My lover and I met at the end of summer in our usual pub and went back to my room. He was in a suit and tie after a board meeting. I let him feed it way into my pussy. I mean the tie. He'd gone back to black. Knotted. He was getting very excited, licking round the tie inside my pussy. 'I wish it could all dissolve in your juice,' he said. 'And all the things that hold me back with it.' When he was completely crazy to fuck, I told him he'd have to leave quick because my boyfriend was coming. He pulled his pants over his erection and left. Later, I put his smelly tie in an envelope and mailed it to him. I wrote: 'Go hang yourself, loser.'

HARRY

Harry's wife died recently. Now his sister, Martha, is dying. She is ninety, almost ninety-one. The only good thing is that since the pain got too much they have moved her into a hospice five miles from his house. This means he can see her pretty much when he likes. Before, he had to get in the car and drive for more than an hour in heavy traffic. And he needed an invitation. His sister wasn't someone you could just drop in on. She always had things to do. While his wife, Eileen, was alive, there was no question of visiting. Eileen wasn't mobile and demanded all his attention. It was rare that Harry could get away from Eileen for more than an hour or two. Since Eileen's death, Martha has only invited him a couple of times – she has her own circle of friends – but she did accept three invitations to come to his place. That was actually better than going to hers because first he had to cook, then he had to drive to hers to pick her up. They would have a cup of coffee together in her sitting room so he could rest. Then they'd drive back to his place. They rested again, maybe with half a glass of white wine. Then he finished the preparations for the meal and put it before them on the big table. Martha had to be helped to her feet from the armchair and he held her elbow as she steered towards the table, though she said this wasn't necessary.

They ate. They didn't talk much. There was nothing particular to be said. She was careful not to speak of her Christian faith and he could hardly hope to interest her in rugby results. Politics had long since lost any attraction for either of them. Their brother Walter was dead. Walter had lived it up, he was the youngest. They were a family who died of cancer, in pain. But Harry's cancer was slower than his sister's and she was seven years his senior.

After lunch he cleared things away while his sister dozed in the armchair again. Later on, he drove her home. There was post on her doormat and as soon as they were inside, the phone rang. Her daughter in Swanage. While she made some tea, holding on to the kitchen surfaces, it rang again. Her son Thomas, in Manchester, or her son James, in California. Then while they drank the tea the local vicar phoned about helping with a church event. Martha scribbled a note inside a book she had been reading. The local vicar was a woman.

'You should conserve your energy, love,' Harry warned.

On the way home, he listened to stock market reports. His sister had a tiny home, a sort of bedsit on two floors. But he could see she felt good there. She felt protected and busy. She drew energy from the place. The garden was a concrete patio with soil round the edge. She grew raspberries and fuchsias. Harry admired her. He envied her. He and Eileen had moved out of their big home a year before her death but it had seemed important to find a flat in line with their aspirations. His big bay windows now looked out over the sloping lawn of a rather grand residence. There were rooms he never used and an underground garage with a lift. In the evening his son called from Cork, but his daughter never would and didn't always answer if he called her. Disappointed, Harry settled in front of his plasma screen. None of the programmes featured people his age.

But he cheered up when Martha was moved to the hospice. Now he could see her every day. Sometimes twice a day. He phoned the director of the hospice and told him they must look after her with immense care. She was a special person. He took her flowers and fruit and chocolates. Sitting on the chair by her bed, he looked around. 'Would you like some tea, love? Can I get you something to cover your shoulders? Or your book?'

His sister looked frailer. 'I've got everything I need, thanks,' she said. She had fallen down the stairs. She had damaged her back. Or maybe the cancer had got in there. A few days later they drove her to a hospital for tests. She came back exhausted.

'Are you all right, love?' Harry asked, leaning over to kiss her.

She lay with her eyes closed. He put the *TV Times* on her bed and sat down.

'Are you okay?'

'Harry,' she said softly. She opened her eyes but didn't move.

'I'm going to ask the doctors what's going on,' he announced, and pulled himself to his feet again. 'I get the impression they've taken their eye off the ball.'

She half raised her right hand to signal no. 'I'm fine, Harry. Just tired.'

'You're not fine, love,' he told her. 'I'm going to go and talk to them. They need to do something.'

'I'm as fine as I can be,' she said. 'They're doing what they can.'

She lay in the bed, saying nothing. Harry was fretful.

'Did they say anything about when they might get you on your feet and mobile again?'

After a pause she said, 'Not soon.'

The phone rang and it was James in some airport or other. Harry passed her the receiver. She activated the command that raised the head of the bed and they talked for a few moments. 'It's just the fallout from the fall,' she joked. Harry was surprised how much energy she got into her voice. She sounded in good spirits with her son. He felt jealous.

'Otherwise he'll feel he has to come over,' she said after ending the call.

'He should come over.'

'No doubt he will, at some point.'

The energy was gone.

Harry visited more and more often. Their mother had died while they were still children. Martha was thirteen then and had played mother to her younger brothers. Eventually there was a stepmother who made baby Walter her favourite. That brought Harry and his sister closer. Even with his subsequent career successes, marriage and family, the big house, the yacht and all the powerful cars, that relationship and its peculiar mother–sibling ambiguity had remained. She was the adult, the tough one. Now Harry sensed this protection slipping away. His big sister was letting go. Soon there would be nothing between him and . . .

Harry did not allow himself to think the word.

When she had to use the bedpan, he went to talk to the doctors. There was only a nurse in a small room with a glass screen. He demanded to see the doctor. Then it turned out she was the doctor. She didn't seem offended that he had imagined her a nurse. But this not being offended struck him as proof of his insignificance. Nobody's afraid of an eighty-year-old. Nobody expects you to understand anything. He felt he would explode.

'What exactly is my sister's situation? There must be something you can do.'

'We're still waiting for results of the scans.'

'But a scan is instant,' Harry protested. 'A scan shows what it shows what it shows.'

'A magnetic scan requires expert interpretation,' the doctor explained.

'But when will she be mobile again?'

'Much depends on what the scan tells us.'

Harry felt he was being stonewalled, but he did not have the authority he once had to force people to come clean. Folding his arms, he hugged his chest tightly. The doctor watched him sympathetically.

Returning to his sister's room, Harry found her pale, her nightie crumpled.

'I'm sorry,' she said. 'The toilet routine is excruciating.'

'Don't say sorry,' he told her.

She didn't reply. He asked her if she would like to watch some television.

She didn't move.

Harry sat a while watching her. She had closed her eyes. Her lips were puckered and moved very slightly. Her grey hair was uncombed.

'Are you asleep, love?'

She sighed. 'No.'

He waited. But he couldn't be still. He felt agitated.

'Are you in pain? Is there anything I can do?'

She didn't speak. One hand was slowly opening and closing as if to test something. Harry felt he would go mad.

'I'm all right,' she said at last.

Harry stood up to look for the TV remote. 'I thought there might be something on the box. A comedy or something. I brought the listings.'

Her mouth was moving very slightly, but she didn't answer.

'There's that American thing about modern alternative families.'

She breathed deeply. He waited, fingering the remote.

'I have to concentrate,' she said at last. 'It takes all my energy.'

Harry didn't understand.

'The pain. It takes concentration.'

Three days later, coming in, Harry met his niece going out. He drew her aside.

'How did you find her?'

In her early sixties, the dying woman's daughter was pleasantly solid and practical. 'She seems comfortable,' she said. 'I mean, for someone with cancer in her spine.'

'The cancer's in the spine now!'

'That's what the scan showed.'

Harry looked at her. 'But why didn't they tell me? I asked them and they wouldn't tell me.'

His niece smiled. 'They didn't tell me either. They told Mum. She told me.'

'But why didn't she tell me?'

His niece didn't know what to say. 'Maybe it didn't come up.'

As she was going, Harry called back to her and invited her to dinner; with her husband, of course. 'If you can.' But she had to drive back to Swanage.

Harry went to see the doctor on duty, who this time was a man.

'I hear the cancer has got into her spine,' he said. 'I'm surprised I wasn't told.'

The doctor consulted a computer on the desk. 'You're not registered as the next of kin, Mr Marshall,' he said. 'We have the daughter's name. But I believe on this occasion the patient was given the results of the scan herself. In such cases we would not necessarily refer to relatives. Is there anything particular at this point that you would like to know?'

The doctor looked up squarely and frankly at Harry. He was a quiet but alert-seeming man in his early forties. Harry felt his age. Obviously there was only one real question, but he could not ask it. His knees were trembling. His hand found the handle of the door and held it.

The doctor watched. Harry couldn't speak but couldn't leave either. Then he said: 'My wife died six months ago, doctor. It was completely unexpected, there was no warning.'

The doctor thought for a moment.

'That will not be the case with your sister,' he said.

In her room, Harry found her quietly awake, her hair combed and bedclothes smooth. She was smiling.

'It's good of Elaine to come,' she said. 'With all she has on her plate.' There was a half-eaten bar of mint chocolate on the bedside table.

Harry sat on the chair. He felt shackled, as if the chair were stopping him from doing anything – anything but being there. Perhaps he should stand up.

'She always combs my hair. She has such a gentle touch.'

He leaned forward and picked up the TV remote, but knew she didn't want the TV on. She never did. Eventually, looking out of the window, he said: 'It's October.'

'My poor garden,' Martha said.

'Just a month to your birthday.'

They were silent a while.

He tried to sound bright. 'What do you want me to get you for a present, love? You know I never know what to get. We should celebrate.'

After a few moments' silence she said: 'A month is a long time, Harry.'

'But time flies,' he said.

She had closed her eyes. They could hear the evening food trolley moving down the corridor.

'What could I possibly want?' she asked at last. 'I have everything here.' There was a hint of a smile. 'I don't even have to cook.'

'There must be something, love.' Again he added, 'We should celebrate. A birthday is a birthday.'

Martha was to be ninety-one. He stood stiffly and went to the window, then turned and looked at her, but her eyes were closed. He went and sat down again, and stood again, and sat again. He sat watching her for a long time, turning the remote over in his hands, listening to the food trolley drawing nearer down the corridor. The minutes passed, not flying but inching forward, on a Zimmer frame.

'Dinner!' a voice said cheerfully.

Martha opened her eyes, turned her head to the door and shook it very slightly to indicate she wasn't hungry. She would wait for her medicine, then sleep.

'Not even a bite?'

She wasn't hungry. 'Sorry.'

More agitated than ever, Harry got up to go. He couldn't bear it.

'I'm off then, love,' he said.

But now his sister smiled. 'Actually, I was thinking,' she said softly.

'Yes?'

She buzzed up the bed a little and struggled on to her elbows. 'For my birthday.'

'Ah?' he turned hopefully.

'My present.'

'Yes?'

The two ageing siblings looked at each other. It was clear she was in pain, but perhaps still able to pull his leg.

'A little bit of peace.'

He didn't understand.

She smiled and lay back. 'You can give me a bit of peace, Harry. Just a nice day, sitting quietly together.'

DENIAL

She called the movie dumb, and him with it, for inviting her. They were twenty-two years old. This is over before it started, he thought. So he was surprised when she phoned and asked him to share a bottle of champagne. The lovemaking was fun. She took the initiative. There was perfume. Later, he told her it would be over if she went off as planned with an older man who had invited her to London for the weekend. She said that relationship was not about sex. 'For me it's over,' he insisted. When they lived on Church Street she pampered him, she was good with cocktail snacks, but said a relationship where one person did all the domestic work had no future. He told her it irritated him when she spoke affectionately of past lovers. It wasn't her fault he hadn't got up to much, she laughed. Two attempts were made to play tennis together. Jogging was easier. Walking even more so. Wherever they lived, they walked the place inside out: parks, canals, shopping streets, even slums. Out of town along the river, up into the hills, through fields and farmyards. They walked side by side, not quite touching, she perhaps half a pace ahead. They were in love and they walked like this for more than twenty years. They fell into a rhythm. Particularly towards the end of a long walk, say three hours, it would seem to Thomas that they had settled into silent synchrony. The faster they walked, the more in synchrony they were, as if escaping, as if going somewhere. Sometimes it seemed Mary used that half-pace ahead to step into his path a little. He felt slightly blocked. He moved further right. He almost always walked to her right. She almost always walked slightly ahead, slightly blocking, or so he thought. He wanted to stop for beers, meals. She liked to keep going. She didn't drink beer. 'Wait till we get home,' she said. 'I'll prepare you something nice.' When he had to leave for the job in Manchester, she said it would only make sense for her to follow if they married. On their wedding night she was tired, she turned away from him to sleep. The day had exhausted her, she said. The hotel was not what she'd hoped. A discotheque kept them awake. Next morning they walked for miles along the dunes. Man and wife. In Manchester she fell out with his old friends. He fell out with her family when they visited. They were kind of mad, he felt. She fell out with his family. She made fun of them. They were kind of dumb, she thought. 'We're a conspiracy against the world,' he told her. They had fallen out with everybody. 'We're a team,' she said. Now she was pregnant. They fell out with each other when he couldn't see the need to drive her twenty miles for her second scan. Why had she got herself a driving licence if she wasn't planning to drive herself? 'I'll never forget this,' she told him. He was making serious money now. She didn't go with him when he travelled for work. She had the baby. He went to London and New York. It was many years since they had spent time apart. For ten years they had never spent a single evening apart. Because they were in love. Nothing was said about the change. All the talk these days was directed at the first child, then the second: they had to learn how to speak, how to talk. They had to be got through school and driven to extracurricular activities and taken on holidays, and more generally for treats. Usually, it was Thomas who took them for treats, treating himself to beer. Mary said it was good for them to spend time with their father. She went through a knitting phase, an embroidery phase, an aerobic phase, a vegetarian phase, and a yoga phase, then a dog phase. Also a swimming-pool phase. She found a lovely thoroughbred cocker spaniel which would feel alone if it did not sleep in their bedroom. She did not question his need to travel. She did not phone or pester him. She was loyal. He was concerned she would see he was in love with someone else. He didn't have time for phases. Then he was concerned that she did *not* see he was in love with someone else. How? Was it the dog? Was it the yoga? He was amazed one partner could fall in love, out of love, and the other not be aware. The other just went on. He was heartbroken now. It had been a long affair. Now it was he who just went on. Life was dry, willed, forced, false. Nothing moves, he thought. He was heartbroken and still taking the kids out for treats. He treated himself to whisky. Eventually the younger child spoke to Mummy about what he had seen on Daddy's phone. The boy had learned how to talk. In the garden, Thomas told Mary he hated her. She told him he had behaved despicably but this kind of crisis was inevitable in a long marriage. 'We'll get over it, Goat,' she said. The children would get over it. Despite his despicable behaviour. And she was right: soon they were back to normal. Soon they were taking long walks again. Maybe they still loved each other. Accompanied by her faithful dog. Your trophy dog, he called it. However much you talked to it, the dog would never learn to talk. The dog was not interested in Thomas's phone messages. Soon Thomas had another girlfriend. He was elated. The second girlfriend would leave him when he didn't leave his wife. And the third. Why does nobody intervene? he thought. Why does nobody help us? Why are we incapable of helping ourselves? Some years later twenty-five red roses were tossed into the bin, still fresh.

LIST

Susan would not step on grates. One day, one would give. Walking Manchester's streets he learned to move this way and that so she would always have solid ground under her feet. She was not afraid of smoking, though. Or drinking, quite a lot. Or unprotected sex, so long as he pulled out in time. She would not be seen without her make-up, however great the hurry. She would not wear skirts with the calves she had, though they looked fine to him. She could never ask an employer for more money or better conditions. Her clothes were always jeans and jacket. Both black. A simple sweater. The bra must hide the nipples. She never wore a hat. But she must never get her hair wet. Umbrellas were important. He steered her round the grates and covered her with his blue umbrella. She would not eat any sauce with a tomato base; she did not like minced beef. But she was at home with whisky. And tapas. And she liked to chew gum. Her mouth was always round and red and pursed. When she was anxious, her periods

104

came early. In form, her humour was acid. Mostly directed against herself, with a wry lift of well-defined left eyebrow. When finally it all became too much she told her mother, and her mother told her to bail out, and bail out she did. He was distraught. I was a grate she shouldn't have stepped on, he thought. I couldn't be her solid ground.

Cathy played drums. In a band. On the table. In the pub. On his buttocks. On her own buttocks. A small girl with dirty fingernails, she made life difficult but took the pill. Her mouth was full, but twitched nervously. It was hard for her to eat with someone, she said, or sleep the night together, but sexually she had no inhibitions. She had a boyfriend whom she kept throughout and even wanted him to meet. 'Graham really loves me,' she said. 'Graham would do anything for me.' He demurred. She liked a ragged bohemian look, a black T-shirt that exposed sharp shoulders, a feathery green scarf around the neck or a man's cravat falling loosely tied between her breasts, baggy jeans, or loose old cardigan. In her pocket perhaps a flask of whisky. On her tousled hair a black fedora at a cocky angle; with a white ribbon, maybe. She smoked roll-ups and texted constantly, teasingly, passionately. She loved him to distraction, she texted. Another man loved her to distraction, she texted. A man had tried to molest her on the Underground, she texted. He didn't know how to respond. He felt like a heavy old stone some crazy tourist was trying to roll from its place. With love. With violence. Her movements were swift and nervous and furtive. Repressed, then released. Timid, then bold. Mouth and hands were never still, even when nothing was said, nothing done. Eating, she was wired up, rabbity, alert for predators. Her bright eyes darted here and there, as if on the lookout. In the mood, she loved to flash. She lifted her T-shirt in a restaurant in Newcastle. A split second. She boasted breasts that didn't need a bra. And she did boast. Nipples hard as coins. They sprang out. He adored her. He was overwhelmed. At the pool she dropped bikini bottoms. Fleeting black fur. Once she fucked him in the cinema. And in the lavatory of the pub. And on the damp shale of Brighton beach. 'I won't wait long,' she whispered. In bed she turned her back on his desire. 'I won't wait long for my old stone to budge.' He didn't and she didn't. When the texting stopped he was distraught. I couldn't be the music for her beat, he thought. Cathy's wild beat.

Patricia wrote. Taught journalism. Had money, had style, had experience, had husband. Patricia was also beautiful. Very. Handsome cheekbones. She was haughty and girlish. For a mature woman. She was sassy. She gave good advice, made good conversation. She had a life, a track record, a following. People were impressed. People were polite. She was contained and judicious too. She would never, for example, allow him to put an arm round her waist on the street. Even when they drove down to London. Her shoes had high heels, her skirts were boldly coloured but below the knee, her underwear expensively feminine, her blonde hair held with bright clips, ivory clips, jewelled clips. She was sophisticated and sure of herself. But lost it completely at a touch. The merest physical touch, the slightest brushed caress, of downed forearms, or bright cheeks, and Patricia lost it. Her body melted and trembled, melted and trembled. In his office she wanted him to come in her with no protection. Then her mobile rang. She would never turn off her mobile. What would her husband think? She bought a second secret mobile to call him, to text him. Her husband called almost hourly. Her husband checked her phone, she said, and had the password to check her phone account online. Patricia was oppressed, she was flattered. He touched her and she melted. Even while speaking to her husband, on one occasion. In an empty compartment on the train, she let his hand up her skirt. She was reckless, animal. Afterwards she laughed like a child. At the station she had a BMW. He couldn't understand the gap between her normal self and the woman who responded to his touch. He felt it couldn't really be his fingers she was responding to. Once they spent an afternoon in a hotel but only after he figured out how not to check her in. Then she was a tempest. He felt he could not have been responsible for this meteorological event. When she showered she took the phone into the bathroom. She was worried her husband hadn't called. After she fell pregnant she told him she would have to stop. He was distraught. But this time he couldn't feel that all this emotion depended on losing her. Nor could he feel he had let her down. She hadn't allowed him to be in a position to. In his unhappiness now he wrote out the list. Liz who was terrified of dogs. Ann who could never decide. Marsha who pretended indifference. Isabel who regretted betrayal. Elaine who had been abused. Rachel, obsessed with hygiene. Judy who spoke of her children. Claire who broke off to smoke. Claudia who phoned him at home. Ruth who tried to kill him. Sophie who almost killed herself. There were others, less memorable. There was a general disturbance of names and perfumes and smiles and tears. If I was looking for something, he thought, I haven't found it.

MRS P

From being someone with time on her hands, happy to get company when she could, Mrs P has become rather difficult to get hold of, a person you need to make an appointment with. She has even turned down a number of meetings, refusing to see people who came explicitly to speak to her. I myself had been wondering for some days when would be the right time for me to make the journey to see Mrs P, if only because it appeared that the time when she would not be seeing people at all might not be so far off. I made frequent attempts to phone her, but she was well defended by administrative staff. On two occasions I was told I could speak to Mrs P if I were willing to accept responsibility for waking her up, but, given her increasing reluctance to respond favourably to the demands made on her, I decided this might be unwise.

Eventually, fearing that a window of opportunity was narrowing and that someone it had once been all too easy to talk to had now become remote and was threatening to become infinitely more so, I booked a flight and made all necessary arrangements to reach Mrs P's new place of residence. My ticket paid for, I tried again to phone to fix an appointment and, as always, was told by a young female voice that she would have to check whether Mrs P was able to take my call. What euphemisms! And of course it appeared she was *not* able. I was invited to call back in an hour's time, which I did. And then in ten minutes. It was frustrating. But at my fourth or fifth attempt, Mrs P's guardians finally told me she was now willing to take my call and so I spoke to her for the first time in quite a while.

'Thomas,' she said. Her voice sounded odd. Posher than I remembered it, more formal. Perhaps due to her changed circumstances, I thought, and the increased pressure on her agenda.

'I'm coming to see you tomorrow,' I informed her, perhaps presumptuously.

'Oh, you are coming, are you?' she said. 'Tomorrow?'

It was difficult to judge her mood. On the one hand she seemed relieved, even pleased perhaps, but on the other perturbed, as if this information – my peremptory decision to come and see her after an absence of some six weeks – were rather ominous.

'At what time?' she asked, continuing with this curiously correct Queen's English she was adopting.

I told her around two.

'We shall see each other tomorrow, then,' she said and ended the call abruptly.

The following day I boarded a morning flight, landed at Heathrow, found my bus stop and bus and alighted forty minutes later at a small railway station, whence on foot the half-mile or so to where Mrs P had recently moved her residence and was receiving the few visitors she was now willing to grant time to. Needless to say, I had to sign in and declare my intentions and relationship with Mrs P, which I duly did, feeling at once how powerfully defining that relationship was for me, and how the forthcoming meeting, whatever its tenor, could only reinforce the importance Mrs P had always had in my life.

I should go to room 3, I was told.

The door was on the left, a stained-wood double door in a corridor typical of certain institutions, neither attractive nor drab, but determinedly functional. Her name was posted on the door – a printed card in a nameplate holder – in very much the manner that my name is posted on the door of the office in the organisation where I work. This was a novelty, I thought, for Mrs P, and indicated she had moved into a different league. When had I ever seen her name on a nameplate before? I knocked on the door and after a brief, respectful pause, during which there was no perceptible response, pressed down the handle and entered.

Mrs P was much changed, and at once the reason why she had not reacted to my knocking was apparent. Half seated, half reclining, she was asleep. It seemed a troubled sleep of uneven breathing and sharp twitches, in particular of her naked left arm, which, mottled and flaccid, was looped about by a white wire, at the end of which a small plastic box with a red button presumably enabled her to call and command the administrative staff. What most, however, attracted my dismayed attention was her mouth, which had sunk drastically into her face. Wrinkled and bloodless, the lower lip appeared to have been sucked back over the gums and down into the trembling darkness of her deep drawn breath. She was not wearing her lower denture.

Dutifully, I sat beside her bed, which was clearly an expensive item complete with various gadgets of advanced technology. I stood, removed my coat, hung it on the back of the seat and sat again. Waiting for her to wake, I took in the room that her changed status had assigned her. There were three or four chairs, of which one was an elaborate recliner. There was a French window and beyond it a patch of patio complete with a modest fountain, whose soft splashing mingled with the sounds of Mrs P's breathing. It was by no means an unpleasant place to be.

For a while, then, I sat still, absorbing all the transformations that had overcome Mrs P since our last, rather happy meeting, in her tiny terraced house. I should let her sleep, I thought. She looked in need of a long rest. Then I remembered that I would not be the only one with an appointment this afternoon. It was already 2.45. Very soon other people would appear on the scene and this privileged moment would be gone, perhaps never to return. I stood and leaned over her. I was intensely aware of a new whiteness, wanness rather, in her skin, and of how thickly pleated it had become at the corners of lips and eyes. I shook her shoulder through the white nightdress, noticing that the blanket covering her legs, waist and lower chest was a rather improbable fuchsia colour. Indeed, its intensity made everything else in the room seem colourless, as if it were drawing all life and warmth into itself to keep Mrs P cosy.

'Mum?'

For some reason I had assumed it would be difficult, perhaps impossible, to wake her; I am prone, I believe, to what psychologists have dubbed 'catastrophic thinking'. But the eyes opened at once. And how blue they were and clear, an immediate reminder of the charisma that had always hung around Mrs P and made her, in her modest way, a rather formidable person. Her lids fluttered open and the eyes focused.

'Thomas.'

Mrs P is the only person in the world to call me Thomas, rather than Tom, or Tommy, perhaps the only person who feels, without even being aware of it, that she has the right to call me what she likes, without negotiation.

'Good heavens. What time is it?' Her eyes went to the clock on the opposite wall. She squinted.

'Two forty-five,' I said. She seemed perplexed. Realising she wasn't wearing her hearing aid, I repeated, 'Two forty-five, Mum!'

'But it can't be. Did I fall asleep?'

She smiled, and the transformation was remarkable. What had seemed the face of a breathing corpse was now full of warmth and mobility. Clumsily, I bent down and embraced her white hair.

'Thomas,' she repeated. 'Thomas.'

It was the missing denture that gave her the posher accent.

'Mum,' I told her.

'Is Mary with you?'

'She couldn't make it,' I said.

'Ah,' she frowned.

Sitting beside her, smiling, I demanded that she explain these drastically altered circumstances. What had happened? And she told, albeit with some effort and failures of memory, the same story I had already heard from other sources: namely, her fall on the stairs at home, the days of increasing pain and immobility that had ensued, her eventual removal to hospital, the doctors' difficulty distinguishing between creeping cancer and immediate back injuries, a period staying at my sister's house that, despite everyone's goodwill, had been neither easy nor happy, then her eventual transferral to this charitable institution.

'They are wonderful here,' she told me with a sigh. 'They are so kind.'

'That's great,' I agreed.

'And how is Mary?' She spoke with a false brightness, on automatic pilot.

'Mary's fine,' I said. 'Just fine. The kids too.'

She looked hard at me, as if sensing something was wrong.

'I'm living away from home now, remember? While we think about things.'

She hesitated. 'Of course,' she said, but still looked puzzled.

'It's all fine,' I said. 'Things will sort themselves out.'

Then she asked me how long would I be staying, and I replied that I had a return flight the following evening, since the morning after that – the day after tomorrow – I had to be at an important meeting with a new client. She seemed to reflect on this for some time, as if weighing up information of great import.

'I see,' she said at last, and I understood that what she had seen was that if I did in fact catch the plane tomorrow evening, this would almost certainly be our last meeting.

'I'm glad to be here, Mum,' I said hurriedly. 'I'm so glad to be here with you.'

She smiled and again that unexpected vitality rose to her face. Perhaps she would indeed go on for ever, I thought, as my brother had always maintained. I stood and leaned over her. I wanted to embrace her. But there was a railing along the side of the bed and though she struggled for a moment she was unable to sit up. In the end I bowed over the railing and bent down to her white head.

'It's so good to see you,' I repeated. 'You're a fantastic mother, Mrs P.'

Speaking close to her ear, my chest almost smothering her face, I was struck by the size of the lobe, which seemed to have grown quite disproportionately, and by the quality of her grey hair, which had become finer, with a faint and rather mysterious yellow hue.

'What is it? Are you in pain?'

She shook her head under my smothering breast – I was wearing a heavy woollen sweater – but it seemed she had begun to cry.

Rather clumsily I said, 'Don't worry about me and Mary, Mum. We'll be okay.'

I spoke very close to her ear and very clearly. I didn't want her to have to struggle to understand. And I asked: 'Aren't you happy to see me? It's good to be with you again.'

Her weeping intensified. Perhaps it was the fact that my embrace was covering her face that allowed this to happen, since in the normal way of things Mrs P did not cry in front of others, and certainly never sobbed. It had always been important for Mrs P not to impose – for this is doubtless how she saw it – her weeping, her suffering, on others; not to stoop, or perhaps simply give way, to this form of manipulation. Which I suppose suggests that she did feel tempted so to stoop, tempted to weep. But perhaps this was all my interpretation, recalling the moment forty and more years ago when through tears – one of the very few times I had seen Mrs P cry – she had said to me, 'If you go on like this, Thomas, you will bring me down with grey hairs to my grave.' That is how I remember her words, though years later, checking in *Cruden's Concordance*, I discovered that the biblical text she was quoting actually reads 'bring down my gray hairs with sorrow to the grave', and it is hard, honestly, to imagine that Mrs P would ever quote a biblical verse wrongly. No doubt my memory is at fault. Certainly I have no idea now what it was exactly I had done, aged seventeen, to deserve this remonstration, though vaguely I sense it must have had to do with my brother, whose rebellious and unchristian behaviour, as they saw it, had caused my parents much grief, and in fact when I checked the quotation in *Cruden's*, tracking it down through the unusual plural 'hairs', it was to find that the words were spoken by Jacob when he feared he would lose his youngest son Benjamin *as well as his next youngest*, Joseph. In fact the verse begins, 'And if ye take this [Benjamin] also from me . . . ye shall bring down my gray hairs' . . . etc. So in echoing those words Mrs P, consciously or otherwise, was accepting as given the loss of one son, my brother, and expressing the anguished fear that another, her youngest, would go the same way.

This will seem a long digression, but now here I was embracing Mrs P's grey hairs that had indeed been brought down, if not to the grave, then to a hospice bed, which is the closest thing. And she was in tears.

Voices came into the room from the corridor now. Two nurses hurried by the open door and further away a vacuum cleaner was whining.

'Are you happy to see me?' I asked again, and in asking that I knew I was betraying anxiety. I spoke close to her ear.

'Of course,' Mrs P whispered. 'Only . . .'

I held the embrace. I felt very self-conscious; all this had been foreseen.

'Only' – her head was shaking under my chest – 'you don't love the Lord Jesus, Thomas. I keep thinking that, and it grieves me. More than anything else in the world.'

So this was it. Here we were. This was the hurdle that had to be negotiated before Mrs P and I could part. I had agonised for weeks before telling her my marriage had fallen apart, but what really mattered was my not being Christian, my not loving, or even acknowledging, the Lord Jesus, unless perhaps the two problems were the same, since only someone who did not love the Lord Jesus, or only a man who had no faith in God, would end up in this way. A son of Mrs P's should know that.

In any event, this was the problem and the fact that we were confronting it, or she was – since for me there was nothing to confront but her need to confront me with it – indicated that she at least felt sure that this really was our last meeting. Suddenly overwhelmed by emotion, I too began to cry, though in a different way from Mrs P. Tears ran freely down my cheeks; it seemed mad that it wasn't enough for her to suffer the pains and humiliation of her sickness; she also had to worry about my marriage and my soul.

'It grieves me, Thomas,' she repeated. 'It makes everything more difficult.'

My embracing her, I'm sure, hiding her face as I bent over her hair to speak in her far ear, had made this outburst possible; opened, as they say, the floodgates. And the drama had come so much sooner than I expected. After all, I was barely through the door. We had barely said anything to each other. Apparently she felt she had to act immediately. Any waiting would be folly. 'It grieves me,' she said again. And the challenge for me now was to avoid the mistake that I had made when the same scene had presented itself – almost the same scene – with the Reverend P, my father, thirty-two years before and just a few months after he had pronounced myself and Mary man and wife. But his cancer had been more aggressive, more rapid, and he had not enjoyed the same level of care. In fact it was in the vicarage bedroom where he and Mrs P slept together that he had begged me to convert before he died and I had told him, petulantly, that it was unfair of him to use his suffering to sway my mind, thus adding unkindness to the many pains, physical and psychological, he was already dealing with.

Fortunately, I had had more time to rehearse for this appointment. I was older. So now, to Mrs P, I said, 'Life is long, Mum, who knows what I will believe or become in the future. Or even whether Mary and I will get together again. You rest now. You need to rest.'

Mrs P went on weeping, but wordlessly. I was at a loss, reflecting that rather than being shorter than I had feared, this appointment was already beginning to feel longer than I could be easy with. Still speaking close to this strangely large ear, I muttered, 'We each have our own journey, Mum.'

This was false. It was a platitude. It was not the kind of thing Mrs P's son would normally say. And the very falseness prompted me to add, 'Forgive me for being unkind.'

Perhaps Mrs P realised I was floundering, for she rather abruptly stopped crying and somehow communicated to me that the moment was over and that my embrace, hiding her face, was no longer necessary or appropriate.

Stepping back, it occurred to me that Mrs P now felt a little guilty for having pushed me into producing first a platitude then this half-hearted request for forgiveness. The truth is that Mrs P harbours unlimited reservoirs of guilt just waiting to find a breach and gush out. She felt guilty for having invited me to contemplate my 'guilt', my responsibility, as she saw it, for her unhappiness, thus making me guilty of prevarication. I couldn't help smiling through my own drying tears. The sheer conflictedness, if that is a word, of Mrs P's behaviour has often been a cause of endearment. I sat down.

'I'm so glad to be here,' I said more frankly. This was true, I was glad. 'Glad to be with you, Mum.'

It took her a moment to return to herself. She was aware I was now seeing her tears. But her face was unclouding, the unhappy contortion of her weeping was smoothing out, so it seemed to me she too was glad now, glad, as it were, to have got it over with, to have said her piece, her very last piece about my lack of faith. However much grief it brought her, no more need be said on the matter. The business of our appointment was done. She had felt duty-bound to make that play, to reopen negotiations one more time, one last time, in the hope that something in me might finally give; yet no sooner had she made the play than she felt it had been wrong to make it. So now she was relieved that, having done what she had, she was free to stop doing it. This is the sort of sick, messed-up atmosphere you grew up in, I thought, and simultaneously I also thought what a long way Mrs P and I had come from the days of my adolescence when she had talked so melodramatically of grey hair and graves; how civilised we now were, like two countries who still dispute a crucial stretch of border territory and will never renounce their claims – on the contrary: at every crisis those claims will be aired and pressed – yet deep down both have accepted that nothing will ever shift in this dispute, no armies will march or missiles fly, so they might as well get on with the normal trade that makes life pleasurable and profitable, if nothing else because they are neighbours. And we were mother and son.

'It's lovely to see you, Thomas,' Mrs P said.

'Mum,' I cried, delighted.

'No Scrabble, though, alas.'

Here she did something with her face that beggars description. The truth is that Mrs P has always been a good girl. Mrs P has never knowingly broken any rule or law or misbehaved in any way. Yet now she sought to put on a mischievous expression, half wink, half smirk, as of complicity between malefactors, an expression that was meant to amuse: here we are on the brink of eternity, Thomas, lamenting the absence of Scrabble. Aren't we naughty!

I knew the look, of course, knew it of old and the emotions it aroused, though I had never seen it on this new and changed face of hers, this mask of suffering and death, which gave it an unreal quality; all the more so for the intense transparency of her blue eyes, something, I was aware, that had much to do with the operations to remove her cataracts of three and four years before.

'I loved a game of Scrabble,' she sighed.

'So I'll go and get a board,' I said, deadpan. 'I'm sure they have board games here.'

She looked disappointed. 'Bored?' Then she guessed she hadn't heard correctly. 'I'm too tired to be bored, love.'

'I said, I'll go and get a *Scrabble board*. Scrabble.'

She saw I was laughing.

'Perhaps I'll have the beating of you, at last,' I cried.

She looked at me, melancholy and perplexed, and I realised she was too tired for banter. I always lost to Mrs P at Scrabble. Putting my hand through the railing, I took hers, which was whitely fleshy and worryingly cold. I squeezed and she squeezed faintly back and at once her eyes closed and the lower lip sank back into the mouth and she was asleep.

I always lost at Scrabble to Mrs P because she had a sharp mind, was formidably competitive and played a great deal more than I did. The triple-letter and, above all, the triple-word scores were constantly present to her. But the pious person who wishes to compete has to choose her opponents carefully. I'm sure Mrs P enjoyed playing my brother far more than she enjoyed playing me, because he is more or less unbeatable at any board game and so she could compete with him to the very best of her ability without fearing the guilt she would always feel when she won with me. My brother would never grant to anybody a single point more than was necessary. By the same token Mrs P would never have felt the need to challenge my brother on his lack of faith since he made it scathingly clear that he was beyond such challenges. Conversely, with my sister, the eldest of the three, Mrs P would never play Scrabble at all, since it was generally understood – and indeed broadcast to the four winds, above all by my sister herself – that she was not 'brainy' (her word), hence to play her at something like Scrabble would have entailed a massacre. Likewise, there was no need to challenge my sister on her faith, since she had it in abundance. My sister was a pillar of faith; in proportion, my brother had some- times cruelly suggested, as she was not 'brainy'. There was always a great confusion surrounding piety and intellect in our family, to the point that no one was ever really sure if there wasn't a touch of devilry in every intelligence and a touch of dumbness in every piety. All the same, you had to be one or the other, either smart or good. No member of the family could ever have contemplated being neither intelligent nor pious. Only the Reverend P had somehow contrived to be both but he had died shortly after his sixtieth birthday, leaving the field divided.

In any event, whenever Mrs P started winning at Scrabble – and with me this would generally happen around moves five and six as the ramifying letters reached out towards the triple-word scores – whenever the points that separated us, which she diligently recorded with a system of pegs at the top of her letter holder, started to look decisive, Mrs P would step in on my side with generous suggestions: Did I have an S, she would ask, to build a word on the end of 'altar' over to the double-word score? Or did I have a K to create something on the top of 'nave'? Then it was fascinating to watch her helping me out, or trying to, seeking to protect me from any possible feelings of embarrassment at my ineptitude, while at the same time never renouncing the idea of winning, because in the end, as I said, and however much against her better instincts, she couldn't help competing, couldn't help wanting to win, just as she hadn't been able to help wanting to convince me, *in extremis*, to give my hard heart to Jesus. What a victory that would have been! Meantime, back with the Scrabble, I might have sunk half a bottle of wine or more, or the over-sweet sherry she liked, so that the letters I had pulled out of the bag began to seem a little soft at the edges, simply refusing to organise themselves into recognisable patterns, and anyway it was far more interesting following this back and forth of Mrs P's, as she was torn between beating me and protecting me, than trying to follow the growing tangle of words on the board. The truth is Scrabble always bored me.

Now Mrs P slept. I held her left hand. The arm was swollen with lymph; it was heavy and fatty. Below her neck, above her nightdress, were traces of inflammation and patches of dressing. Removing the breasts, some years before, had not prevented the cancer from invading her chest. She had gone to the doctors too late. There were open and 'weeping' tumours, she once told me. 'Ugly and smelly.' Mrs P rarely spoke about such things, but when she did, she was blunt and to the point, so that now, thinking of her poor offended body, I remembered a conversation we had had about a year before, perhaps over one of those games of Scrabble, about the mind and the body. I had insisted, rather zealously, that mind and body were one, only existing as separate entities in the precarious system language is. 'Quite simply we *are* our bodies,' I had declared emphatically. 'And our bodies are us.' But Mrs P had objected that this just couldn't be true. Her body aged and declined, she said, and the more it did so, the more she felt separate from it. She was *not* her cancer. And she felt sure the soul enjoyed eternal life and that her body would remain on this earth until the Resurrection Day, while her soul would be taken up to be with the Lord, in paradise.

I looked at her body now on this hi-tech bed in Woking Hospice; there was an intermittent twitch in her left shoulder and her legs too twitched at the knee from time to time, and I asked myself if Mrs P was indeed to be entirely and absolutely identified with this suffering body. I started to think about this, but the more I did so – the more I tried to bring some lucid thinking to this ancient chestnut, the relationship between mind and body, self and flesh – the more the question seemed completely meaningless, merely part of a will to unhappiness on my part, or to mental troublemaking. Changing changing changing, at every moment Mrs P nevertheless remained Mrs P, my Mrs P, her recognisable self. Now a suffering woman dozing in a hospice bed. To what end pursue the matter further? What purpose would be served by leaning to this or that unverifiable hypothesis? The important thing was to be with Mrs P now in this brief space that remained to us.

My eye moved over her with a kind of wonder at what she had become, what she was becoming; then it moved across the room to the chairs, the swing table the other side of the bed with its plastic baby bottles for drinking without spills, the rose-patterned curtains, a loudly ticking wall-clock, some official notices pinned on a board just a little too far away for me to read but nevertheless conveying a sense of restriction and institutional imperatives. They would be about things one must not do.

Then my eye came back to the bedside table. A radio. A white water jug, the phone, and beside the phone a book:

What To Do When Faith Seems Weak & Victory Lost, by Kenneth E Hagin. This troubled me. Why was she reading this book? Not out of need, surely? I did not want Mrs P to lose her faith at the end. She had wanted me to find faith, something that didn't interest me in the slightest, the Christian story seems grotesque to me. But just the thought that *she* might doubt her faith, and doubt it now, at the end, bewildered me, horrified me. Registering the intensity of this reaction, I was obliged to acknowledge that I counted on her faith. I had faith in Mrs P's faith. How odd, I thought, that I needed someone else to go on believing something I myself not only didn't believe, but couldn't even really rouse any interest in; in order, presumably, that things would remain the same, that the people around me all stay in their proper places. Which was perhaps why others needed me to stay with Mary.

I picked up the book, which was not a slim volume, and turned it over in my hands. I read the title again. The words were printed over a photoshopped image of an iron shield with a sword lying across it. It was a battle, a competition, then. But, unlike Scrabble, a battle one couldn't afford to lose. When faith *seems* weak, I noticed now. Not *is* weak. When victory seems lost, but in fact is still victory. It was a curious title, naming a crisis, but at the same time suggesting it wasn't a real crisis. Only a seems. Defeat wasn't really contemplated. Though of course something needed to be done. Otherwise why read the book? What, though? What did one do to bolster one's faith? I had no intention of finding out. The book wasn't addressed to me, to someone who had no faith that might one day be, or merely seem, weak, to a man, in short, so faithless as to contemplate leaving his wife of thirty-two years. Anyway, whatever it was that needed doing, I thought, Mrs P, could be counted on to be doing it, or to have already done it. She would have read Kenneth E Hagin's advice carefully. She would have taken all appropriate steps. No, the important thing for Mrs P was to take her faith along with her grey hairs to the grave. For my sake as much as for hers. Because it was impossible to imagine Mrs P without faith. She would become someone else and then I too would have to change. Even the erratic course I steered, perhaps, made a little sense in relation to her steadfastness. And as I was thinking these odd thoughts, my sister walked into the room and my privileged time with Mrs P was over.

My sister was also much changed, but then I hadn't seen her for rather longer. Some years. She had lost weight, she had dyed her hair honey blonde and put in pink highlights. She looked well and, with discreetly applied make-up, much younger than her sixty-three years. Mrs P, I immediately thought, had never dyed her hair, or applied make-up. In fact it was even less imaginable that Mrs P dye her hair, than that she lose her faith. For some reason the two did not seem unconnected; although, as I said before, my sister is the most religious of the three children and has always dyed hers, or at least ever since the various calamities that overwhelmed her in her thirties and caused her to go prematurely grey. Now, after briefly but warmly greeting me, she went round to the other side of the bed, leaned over Mrs P and stroked her hair, and assured her in the voice of one speaking to a child that all was well, that the Lord Jesus was looking after her, that He would never let her down and that she mustn't worry about needing to entertain us or look after us. She didn't. We required nothing of her, there was nothing she need do but relax and lie there.

I was a little surprised that my sister felt the need to say all this, since Mrs P had shown no signs of being anxious to entertain us, though it was true that this had been her constant, lifelong concern when visitors came to her tiny house. Mrs P had always been afraid of disappointing, and that fear easily turned into a need to control, to over-perform, to make you eat things you didn't want to eat, to wash and clean things that didn't need washing and cleaning, something my sister had no doubt found oppressive at times when she had urgently needed Mrs P's help but not her smothering anxiousness. And in fact, however patronising my sister's words might have seemed to me, I noticed that Mrs P's face did actually smooth out as she spoke, as though in her sleep – if it was sleep rather than simply exhaustion – she were taking comfort from her daughter's reminding her that God has everything under control, however much, to others of us, it may seem that nothing is ever really under control and that life, even when boring, is unspeakably precarious.

It was 3.30 or thereabouts and thus began Mrs P's last twenty-four hours, since she would expire – the word is appropriate – at 3.20 the following day, at exactly the moment I would need to leave her bedside to catch my bus to the airport, as if in her determination never to be the slightest bother to anyone Mrs P had been willing herself to depart in time for me to watch her go and still arrive punctually at Heathrow for my rather shorter journey, perhaps not appreciating that, having watched a parent die, it would not be easy even for a faithless son to grab his bag and head for the airport.

In any event, the time for private exchanges was now definitely behind us. Already the visitors were flowing thick and fast. First my uncle came, Mrs P's younger brother who had recently lost his wife, followed a few minutes later by his son, my cousin, who had returned to London from Cork to be beside his father in the difficult aftermath of his bereavement, only to find him facing a second bereavement. And indeed the poor man looked needier even than his sister, certainly more troubled, sitting heavily by the bed, wringing his heavy old hands. Now my brother-in-law arrived, my sister's husband, and explained that first he had had trouble finding a parking space for the van, then had had to walk the dogs they had brought with them, since the animals couldn't be left behind with the woman who was looking after their daughter, their seriously disabled daughter, and he fired up his iPad and began to show us photographs of these dogs – a handsome

Irish Setter and a white Pomeranian – and when Mrs P could not raise her head to look at his iPad he told her with no change in his cheerful tone of voice that he could already see her dancing down the golden streets of paradise with the Reverend P, my father, deceased thirty-two years before. But my sister, I noticed, was more careful with the evangelical talk in the presence of my uncle and cousin. My uncle and his son, my cousin that is, I realised, were to be spared the religious rhetoric. They were not part of the inner circle. Then two nurses came for the bedpan and a change of sheets and we visitors were invited to retire and make ourselves instant coffee in the guest lounge.

So it went on for the entire afternoon and early evening – long watches beside the bed interspersed with breaks drinking coffee in the lounge – until another nurse came into the room and said she had my brother on the phone and did Mrs P wish to take the call? Then Mrs P, whom I sometimes suspected was merely lying low so she would not have to waste energy discussing dogs and iPads, imme-diately perked up and said yes, yes, she would take it, and when, a few moments later, the phone on the bedside table rang, she actually raised herself, albeit with some effort, on to an elbow, reached out a shaking hand, lifted the receiver and brought it back to her large ear, as if she were her old self again; and even when she called my brother by the wrong name – by *her* brother's name, that is – none of us considered this a sign of dementia since Mrs P had always mixed up the names of those she loved, though for all other names, and especially for biblical verses, she had a memory second to none.

'Not very well,' Mrs P confessed to this son whose soul she had given up for lost.

'Oh, very comfortable, thanks,' she told the man who always beat her at Scrabble.

'Yes, I know it's a long way to come,' she agreed. 'Yes, of course, I understand, my dear, and at such short notice . . . No,' she said. 'I can imagine. Don't you worry, love. I'm being well looked after.'

She put the phone down, and perhaps twenty minutes later the vomiting began.

So – and this I hadn't foreseen – there was to be one last serious exchange between myself and Mrs P and a last decision for me to take that had intimately to do with our relationship. She had vomited three or four basins of black blood – curious disposable basins, made of that rough compressed cardboard they once used for egg boxes – then fallen into a deep sleep. Given this deterioration, I had decided to stay the night in the hospice rather than with my uncle. There was a well-upholstered recliner in the room. The head nurse seemed rather pleased about this, since it meant somebody would be constantly at hand if Mrs P had another crisis. And so it was. Shortly before midnight she had asked for water. I had given her the plastic cup with the easy-drinking lid, a cup in every way like those I had given my children in their playpens. However, when she tried to swallow, a river of black blood frothed out.

I had not expected to have to show practical skills; all the same, grabbing basins and calling nurses was rather easier than being challenged on one's faith. 'I want to go tonight,' Mrs P cried as the two young women cleaned her up. 'Dear Jesus take me tonight.' The nurses asked me to step into the corridor for five minutes while they changed her soaking sheets, and when I returned and again sat beside her and took her hands and called her Mum, she looked perplexed.

'I thought you had gone to the hotel, dear.'

'No, I'm staying.'

She didn't understand.

'I'll sleep on the chair.'

'Well, goodnight,' she said. 'I hope it's a nice hotel.' Then she muttered, 'I'm not worried about you splitting with Mary, Thomas. I'm worried about you dithering.'

The nurse came in to check her blood pressure. While the pad was pumping up, Mrs P said. 'My son is just going to his hotel. Goodnight, Thomas.'

The nurse raised an eyebrow in my direction.

'I'm staying with you, Mum,' I said. 'I'm staying here. In case you're sick again.'

Then at last she understood and a look almost of panic tensed her drugged lips and cheeks.

'I don't want you to see me like this, Thomas.'

I was holding one hand while the nurse pumped the blood pressure pad around the other wrist.

'But I don't mind, Mum. I'm glad to help.'

'I don't want you to see,' she repeated.

In the corridor I spoke to the nurse, the head nurse. They could prepare me a bed in a guest room, she told me. Obviously they would fetch me at once if there were 'developments'. Or I could lie on the recliner. Mrs P was sleeping again. They had adjusted her medication in response to the new situation. She would probably not even be aware I was there. On the other hand, she had expressed a very clear preference.

I sat in the guest lounge and drank coffee, watched some football highlights. Why did I want to stay in my mother's room? Did I think I could help her, protect her, reassure her? Did I want to be a hero, want to tell people I had spent the night beside her, the night she died? She is not reassured by your presence, I told myself. On the contrary, she is perturbed to think that her son, her younger son, is seeing her in this state. Mrs P wants you to find faith and love for Jesus, she wants you to be decisive about your marriage, but she does not want you to show your love for her in this way. Perhaps she was afraid as much of what I might hear as see: some outcry perhaps, some doubt, some moment when faith seemed weak and victory lost. She wanted to protect me from that, protect me for one last night from death. All at once it was easy to see that I must respect her wish. I must protect her from realising she had lost her protecting role towards me.

I slept soundly in the guest room. Mrs P had three more bouts of vomiting during the night. She had been lucid then, the nurses told me, and calm, but when I went to her around eight she was not speaking and would not speak again; there was a slight squeeze of the hand, perhaps, before ten o'clock, the trace of a smile, maybe, until midday, after which it was left for those friends and family members who came to stand and sit in silence, waiting and watching and listening and wondering whether each quavering breath would be the last until, at last, around 3.20, it was. Half a dozen of us were present, holding our breath to hear if Mrs P was merely holding hers. But when we breathed again, she did not. I had her hand in mine and after some minutes, leaning my head on the bed rail, my eyes, though full of tears, finally focused on the notice on the opposite wall:

Visitors are warned that all doors, including patio doors, will be closed and locked before 10 p.m. in order that the security alarm system can be turned on for the night.

I looked at my watch. That moment was six and a half hours away. It would come. There was no need for faith.

THE WEDDING PLANT

Someone had given them a plant for their wedding. Neither Thomas nor Mary could remember who. It was there with the other presents when they collected them from his father's house after the brief honeymoon: a slim grey tropical trunk with long thin leaves radiating outwards then drooping under their own weight to pointed tips. The leaves were dark green but edged with a purple red. It was elegant and quietly exotic. They called it the wedding plant.

Thomas looked after the plants. This was partly because, having only to walk to work at that point, he had more time morning and early evening and partly because he loved anything to do with gardening. Both of them felt plants were important. So their window boxes had petunias, fuchsias, geraniums, forsythia and various ivies, while in the flat itself they brought together all the usual suspects: spider plants, a wandering Jew, dieffenbachia, philodendron, a rubber plant, a snake plant and in the bathroom a maidenhair fern in a hanging basket. They needed constant attention. Thomas watered them and sprayed the leaves. The wedding plant seemed to attract more dust than the others and every couple of weeks he would clean it, wrapping each leaf near the trunk in a damp cloth, then pulling the cloth gently towards the tip so that the whole leaf slid through. Afterwards the plant shone darkly.

With the long commute to her job in town, Mary didn't get so involved, but she seemed to know more. She gave advice. She warned Thomas when a plant needed repotting. She advised him of the existence of stick fertilisers; they had to be pushed into the earth near the trunk and left to dissolve there. Sometimes she chose attractive pots, like the painted wall pots she brought back from a business trip to Greece that he put ivy in. When the wedding plant's leaf tips turned yellow, that meant it had too much water. When they drooped, that meant it hadn't got enough. After a while Thomas began to find it all rather time consuming.

Moving down to Bristol a few years into the marriage, it seemed crazy to try to load all the plants in the car. They just took the wedding plant. At this point they had learned its real name was *Dracaena marginata*, or the Madagascar dragon tree. 'So easy to keep, it's hard to kill,' the book said. They chuckled over that. 'Not a bad plant to give at a wedding, then,' Thomas said. But when the car broke down on the M6 they forgot the Madagascar dragon was now lying on its side in direct superheated sunlight. It lay there for hours. Two days later all the leaves had fallen off.

'Cooked!' Mary laughed. 'I didn't like it that much anyway.'

Thomas, troubled, took the pot outside.

They had a garden now. Or rather, each household in the small block was allotted a patch of the ground behind. They seeded a lawn but it never really took. The thin wire fence between themselves and the open country offered no resistance to an astonishing variety of weeds. At first they worked side by side, on their knees, pulling the damn things out. Mary didn't want to use weedkiller. But it was no good. So they tried the weedkiller, but now there was hardly any grass. With a child to look after, they didn't have the energy to reseed. They would just mow whatever came up, take life as it comes. Meanwhile, the wedding plant had sprouted again.

This was an exciting surprise. Thomas had dumped the plant in the corner of the garden beside the compost. Cleaning up, in spring, he saw that the bare trunk had two sprouts on it and brought it back into the house. 'The wedding plant is not dead!' he announced, on settling it in a new pot. Now, rather than one trunk radiating leaves, there were two fresh new trunks sprouting from the withered older one and turning upwards alongside it, so that eventually two umbrellas of leaves hung down. 'We're multiplying, Goat!' Mary cried and opened a bottle of bubbly.

The leaves of the Madagascar dragon, a neighbour warned them, are poisonous to cats and dogs. Learning this, Mary worried that the plant might be toxic for the children too; they were at the toddling stage. She would gladly have got rid of it. But Thomas had allowed a vague symbolism to get a grip on him. He moved the plant to inaccessible positions. He kept it in the spare room where he sometimes worked in the evening. But though the wedding plant survived, it would not flourish as it had before. This was something to do, Thomas thought, with the way the two new shoots had come out of the trunk in diametrically opposite positions, so that whichever way you stood the plant in relation to the light, one of the two was always at a disadvantage. Thomas turned it round regularly, but this only seemed to cause confusion. The two trunks were getting a little twisted, as if chasing away from each other around the old trunk. With the second child sleeping badly, Mary had far too much on her plate to worry about such trivia.

Over the years there would be blight to deal with, and infestation. Sometimes the leaves turned brown. Once there was mealybug and on another occasion there was scale. Thomas followed instructions from gardening books and applied the appropriate treatments. The plant seemed determined to survive, but refused to thrive. Once, repotting it, he found a large black grub among the roots and dug it out with a fork. Perhaps that was the problem. He trimmed the roots and gave the plant fresh soil and fertiliser, but it made no difference. The wedding plant languished on, in the spare room, out of the reach of cats and dogs and children.

They moved north again, to just outside Manchester. The children were big enough now for Thomas and Mary not to have to worry about poisonous leaves. But the plant had grown too gnarled and wizened for them to want to show it off in the new sitting room with the new furniture. 'It makes you sad just to look at it,' Mary laughed. She didn't understand why Thomas didn't just chuck the ugly thing away. He found a corner for it in the lean-to green-house and tried to remember to water it from time to time. Why had he let the plant assume this special importance? But once you had fallen into that trap, how could you reverse the process, especially when the marriage did seem to be in much the same state as the Madagascar dragon?

When exactly did the wedding plant die? Thomas couldn't have said. Some years later a therapist asked the same question. Or rather he asked, 'When was it exactly you both realised your marriage was in rocky waters?' Some such metaphor. Neither had really known how to answer. In an email Mary told him, 'I knew I should have left you pretty soon after Sally was born. You gave me such bad feelings. But how could I do that with a newborn baby in the house?' Absurdly, reading this message, which dated the crisis far earlier than he would ever have thought possible, Thomas could not help remembering that that was when the wedding plant was out in the cold by the compost heap.

I will never give a plant as a wedding gift, Thomas vowed. Very occasionally, though, the fact that he cannot recall actually seeing their wedding plant dead and cannot remember having removed it from its pot and placed it in the composter, or simply in the bin, starts him wondering whether perhaps that Madagascar dragon isn't still alive somewhere, in a place neither he nor Mary knows how to find.

WHEREOF ONE CANNOT
SPEAK

It's fanciful, because he was gay, I know, but I always wondered whether it wasn't the female orgasm that prompted Wittgenstein to say, 'Whereof one *cannot speak*, thereof one *must be silent*'; to make a point, that is, with those bossy italics he loved, of saying that we mustn't say anything about the things we can't, technically, know anything about; we mustn't shoot our mouths off, so to speak, us men, in the dark. And in fact, so far as I'm aware, Wittgenstein never did say anything about the female orgasm.

But when did people ever accept that a can't is a mustn't? And isn't the injunction superfluous, since if we really can't, logically we won't, and hence don't need the mustn't. Or rather, we might speak of *something*, we might *suppose* we're speaking of the thing whereof we cannot speak, but, logically, it won't be that thing we're speaking of, will it, since we can't? In any event, the truth is that my friend Thomas went through a phase – our tennis days – when almost the only thing he talked about, or wanted to talk about, or imagined he was talking about, was the female orgasm, though maybe what it was all really about in the end was something entirely different.

Our tennis days lasted about eight years. Tuesday evenings. Not our salad days. More our stewing forties. Thomas had a girlfriend – a string of girlfriends, to tell the truth – and was childishly eager to talk about them. Or rather, about sex with them. It was as if, for this interval of his life – and it was a phase that had a definite beginning and a very definite end – the secret and mystery of everything, of all the things Wittgenstein ordered us we must not shoot our mouths off about, had been concealed and condensed in the experience of sex, and sex itself condensed and concealed and, as it were, *ciphered* in the female orgasm, in the absence of which Thomas was always anxious that sex hadn't really happened, that *life* wasn't really happening; and basically the old chestnut that Thomas just couldn't stop seeking to crack was: how could you ever know if she has or she hasn't . . . *come* – and if you can't know, how can you ever be sure that sex, transformative, visionary sex – the kind one no longer had with one's wife – has truly taken place?

At first I couldn't understand why confirmation of orgasm was such an issue for Thomas, since surely what mattered was my friend's – more tennis partner than friend, since we never met in other circumstances – own

experience of the embrace; I don't mean, crassly, his physical pleasure, his orgasm, which I took for granted, but,
more generously, his broader sense of a *shared* satisfaction
in the whole exchange, hence mutual gratification, mutual
gratitude.

Shouldn't that be enough?

Later, however, over beers in the tennis club bar after
bashing the ball back and forth for an hour or so, I began
to appreciate that the question of female orgasm had to
do with Thomas's sense of guilt. In bed with his wife, on
the now rare occasions they made love, it hardly crossed
Thomas's mind to worry whether this long-suffering
woman, mother of his children, had achieved orgasm; he
assumed from certain textbook signs that she did, and was
thankful for it. But when he had a girlfriend on the go, it
was important for Thomas that something beautiful, even
sacred, should occur; otherwise the transgression involved
in cheating on his wife (cheating was his word, never mine;
he hated cheating his wife, he said) was merely squalid.
So female orgasm, or rather his belief that something
extreme and beautiful had happened – because rightly or
wrongly Thomas had come to feel that female orgasm was
supremely beautiful and even *sacred* – became essential
to him.

But how could you know?

You couldn't, I told him.

Thomas found this hard. There was a woman, girl rather,
for Thomas rarely went for women more than half his age,

who almost never came. Who made it clear she hadn't come. Who expressed her frustration that she hadn't come. Who let him know that she was close to coming, but then felt all the more let down when she didn't, who wept, even – I've lost it, I've lost it! – but then occasionally *did* come and shouted loudly and covered him with grateful kisses. Thomas – we usually drank lager after our efforts on the tennis court – very much appreciated this scenario, which I have to confess I personally would have found wearisome to a degree. He appreciated, he said, the importance the girl attached to orgasm, her striving for it, her evident honesty in admitting that she hadn't got there and even in criticising him for her failure to get there, since one of the problems, Thomas freely confessed, was that the dear thing became so agitated if she got anywhere near that he just couldn't hang on and hence, inevitably, lost his umph. And again he appreciated, he said, her happiness and gratitude when it *did* happen, or when she *said* it happened – he worried that she might sometimes fake it to encourage him, as it were, to convince him she wasn't a lost cause – shouting so loud, etc.; he liked, that is, or felt *at home with*, the notion that on this occasion at least their illicit antics had been *blessed*, while on other occasions they hadn't, in which case the penitential atmosphere that her frustration created seemed the right feeling for him to take back to the family hearth, usually at one, or two, or even three o'clock in the morning.

All this was discussed back and forth at great length at a tennis club on the outskirts of Manchester. Eventually

I formulated for Thomas what I hoped was a sensible response to his perplexity: might it not be, I suggested, that precisely his anxiety that she orgasm, once transmitted to his girlfriend, made its occurrence unlikely, however great the affection and technical know-how he lavished on her? He wasn't convinced: there had been, he reminded me, the previous girlfriend, the oldest of the tribe, pretty much his own age, whom he had actually left, at least in part, because she reached orgasm so loudly and above all so *immediately* as to make him feel superfluous. This annoyed Thomas considerably. Barely was penetration achieved, or not even, and there she was yelling and thrashing and orgasming. *Apparently.* Though how could you believe it, when really he had offered nothing to make it happen? He very much preferred the travails of the younger girl.

'Thomas,' I put it to him, 'it seems to me perhaps that when betraying your wife you have to believe that the beauty you contribute to creating – your beloved's, er, ecstasy, supposed ecstasy – cancels out the transgression you can't help feeling guilty of. All this instead of just enjoying it. So why not stop the futile worrying and have a good time? Maybe it will help you get on with your wife better.'

Thomas listened carefully, but protested I was on quite the wrong track. It was more complicated than guilt, he said. Rather it was anger that life had forced him into a position where he had had to assume the baddy's role, since domestic life had become so painful he really didn't see how he could live without these adventures. And within this scenario, he had got it into his head, however irrationally – into his blood and bones, even – that only female orgasm could . . . *heal* him. Of that anger.

After making this grandiose statement, he began to talk technical, almost like a doctor exploring possible clinical treatments. He talked clitorises and G-spots and condoms and pills and jellies and sex toys, girls who came this way, if they really did, and girls who came that, if their cries and whispers were to be credited; with long and loving cunnilingus, a finger eased into the anus perhaps, or with deep and vigorous penetration, her knees maybe forced back almost to her silky hair. Thomas warmed to these descriptions, leaning excitedly across the table as if he needed to persuade me – and, together with me, himself, of course – of the transformative power of what had occurred, as if his world could be declared radically changed in all its premises thanks to the achievement of female orgasm.

Meantime it was important, I noticed, that I nod my head regularly in acknowledgement, to keep him going, as it were, to keep him believing in what he described; but in the end, invariably, he would sit back and sigh. Had she really come? He didn't know. And naturally, he said, he would feel stupid actually asking. Asking a woman if she had really come was tantamount to accusing her of faking, or alternatively to letting her know you felt insecure. Neither of which was *exactly* the case. He just wanted to know that the experience had been special, otherwise he felt somehow wrong, or perhaps *weak* was a better word. Anyway depressed, not good.

'You should stop having affairs,' I told him. 'And sort out your marriage.'

That was impossible, he said.

Then there was Sylvia.

I should say that I had reached a point where I felt our tennis days were coming to an end. Thomas was unfit, he was drinking too much, yet he could never bear losing and often contested the most obvious calls. I was wearying of this, although I always felt an affection for Thomas that even now I can't explain. He lived intensely, his unhappiness was genuine, and the person who suffered most from his misbehaviour was always himself. At the same time, with his second and youngest child now in his mid-teens, the marriage that had troubled but also formed him for so many years was clearly reaching its end.

'Sylvia is a complete mystery,' he said, some weeks after the advent of this new flame. He was radiant.

Sylvia was twenty-two years younger than Thomas. She worked in the same company as him, but not in his division. They had known each other on the most casual terms for three or four years, but only recently dated. I have no idea at all what she feels, he said. The two met on Fridays, cooked together at her place, something neither of them knew how to do, danced to stuff she pulled up on YouTube, another activity neither of them had any proficiency in, and after some resistance on her part – three Fridays, to be precise – made love.

Here was the novelty. It was not that Sylvia came or didn't come, that she struggled, or overperformed, faked, or expressed frustration, or resignation. She simply didn't seem interested in the question of orgasm *at all*. Any attempt to discuss her pleasure or his, or indeed any of the techniques and tribulations of sex, produced nothing but indulgent smiles. She couldn't care less. It was as if she wasn't properly aware that there was such a thing as female orgasm, or if she was, she made no attempt to isolate it from the embrace in general, or indeed the embrace from the dancing, or in the end the dancing from the cooking and the walking home and long drive from centre to suburbs.

Surely he could tell, though, I put it to Thomas, couldn't he, a man with his experience?

Thomas shook his head. Sylvia was responsive, he said, but not *in the ordinary way*. She hardly seemed to be seeking pleasure, or even deliberately giving it. Just doing things, instinctively.

Thomas and I looked at each over our beers. He had stumbled on an experience whereof he could not even begin to speak. He could only speak of not being able to speak of it.

Thomas began to cry off our tennis evenings now, which came as something of a relief, frankly, although, since I knew from his wife that he still told her that he was going to play tennis, and to play with me, I could not help being curious. Then, one night he didn't go home.

'I've understood,' he said, next time we played. 'I've got it.'

He seemed very pleased with himself, though on the court he had been thoroughly beaten. In fact he made so little effort I had the impression he was only playing to arrive at the beers afterwards.

It had to do with their cooking together, he said. Badly, if the truth be told. And with their dancing together in her front room, clumsily. It had to do with her laughter and her utter uninterest, not in sex, but in any talking about sex, any urgency surrounding sex.

'So does she come or not?' I asked abruptly. 'Or give that impression?'

'I don't know.'

'You don't even know if she gives the impression?'

'No.'

'But you make love. Presumably there is some kind of climax, or anticlimax, a signal that it's time to wind down. You must sense where she's up to?'

'*I* always come,' he said. 'Then it ends.'

'You haven't told me anything about her body: what she gets up to, what you get up to?'

'Actually,' Thomas confessed, 'last time I went over there it ended up we didn't make love. We talked late and fell asleep.'

'Sounds to me,' I told him, 'like she doesn't come at all and doesn't care, and you like her because she saves you the effort and doesn't worry about it.'

'Not at all,' he protested. 'When we make love, she signals something . . . But not . . . not . . .'

I watched him.

'It's as if she came from a different planet.'

'Well . . .' I waited.

'Or as if . . . as if what I'd been driving at, these past couple of years, wasn't actually sex at all but some other . . . some *thing* that, that . . . well, that was hiding, or hidden.'

I was getting bored with this. 'Something that you can't describe?'

'Right.'

'Behind sex.'

'Yes.'

'Unnameable and ineffable, I suppose.'

'Correct.'

'God.' I shook my head.

'I've decided to leave home,' he added gravely.

'About time,' I told him.

JOB MARKET

Thomas thought it was time Mary returned to the job market. She felt the children were still too young. 'You're so talented,' he told her. 'I know!' she laughed. Eventually she went for an interview. She said, 'They say it's for the export office, but in the end I'd just be a glorified PA.' 'Glorified sounds good,' Thomas suggested. 'Maybe he's an interesting guy.'

Mary was sitting at her place at the table, reading the newspapers online and eating an apple. Thomas had his back to the fireplace. 'You're an interesting guy,' she said without looking up. 'I could be your PA.' Thomas had decided not to drink tonight, but felt the pull of the fridge. 'I already have a PA,' he laughed. 'We know,' she said.

The company made designer light fittings that were sold all over the world. It seemed right up Mary's street. In the following days, Thomas had to struggle not to ask her whether they had been in touch. When he came home from work she was away doing her Pilates, or in the swimming pool, or out with the dog. The children were in their rooms, doing whatever adolescent children do. Thomas lingered by the fridge. He went into the sitting room to make up the fire. Coming downstairs, his daughter Sally had her hair in a towel. 'What happened with Mum and that job?' she asked. 'I don't know,' Thomas said. Sally sat down at the piano, banged out two chords and stood up again. 'When's dinner?' 'When your mother gets back,' he said.

The girl seemed frustrated. 'Can't *we* cook?'

'We could,' Thomas said. 'But you know how Mum is. She's probably got something planned.'

Sally went back upstairs, shaking out her hair. 'I'll be late,' she called.

On Sunday, Mary's brother came over with his wife and their two small children. Mary closed herself in the kitchen and prepared a mushroom risotto, with canapés to start and almond tart to close. Thomas chose the wines. Malcolm looked tired but pleased with himself. 'Too many hours in court,' he said. Katie talked at length of her relief at not being laid off in her newspaper's latest cull. She had a strong South African accent. 'You should be proud of yourself,' Thomas told her. 'It means you're good.' 'Yeah, soon I'll be the last man standing.' Katie shook her head. 'Woman, rather.' The upshot was that they were now working more hours than ever. 'I've figured out I'm doing three people's work, as of five years ago. Half the articles in the section, all the editing and all the layout.'

She began to talk about what had happened when the computers crashed the previous Thursday evening. Chaos. She hadn't got home till dawn. As she spoke, her young children sat on the carpet playing with their phones. Mary was silent but, passing Thomas in the kitchen with the coffee pot, she muttered, 'Proud?' And by the sink she whispered, 'I can't understand why they had children, if they're going to be brought up by Filipinos.'

'Where's Sally?' Malcolm asked. 'My favourite niece.'

Their daughter had gone to her boyfriend's.

'For the weekend!' Mark chipped in. He had chosen to sit with the adults.

'Uh-oh,' Malcolm said.

'You're not letting them spend the night together?' Katie asked. 'She's only sixteen, isn't she?' She began to say that the problem with allowing adolescents to sleep together at each other's homes was that it made it more difficult for them to split up further down the line. Everything got so tangled. She had written an article about it.

'You wait,' Mary said.

'Oh, Katie's a tough cookie,' Malcolm laughed. 'She'll keep 'em on the straight and narrow.'

'Katie's mostly out,' Mary observed.

There was a brief pause.

'What's that supposed to mean?' Katie asked.

'Exactly what it says.'

'Are you insinuating . . .'

'You bet I am,' Mary said. For the first time she seemed to be taking pleasure in having guests.

'Girls!' Malcolm pleaded.

'Mary just means that it's impossible to stop people having sex if they really want to . . .' Thomas said.

'Dead right there,' his wife agreed.

Malcolm tried to laugh.

'I can't believe this,' Katie started. 'I make one tiny criticism and—'

Mary interrupted her. 'But now we're on the subject,' she said, '*I* was offered a job, yesterday.'

There was a short silence. Mary hadn't worked since her second pregnancy.

'That's wonderful!' Thomas said.

'Doing what?' Malcolm asked.

'Running an export office.'

'High-class lighting design,' Thomas explained. 'Spiffy stuff.'

But everybody was speaking at the same time now. Mark seemed absolutely thrilled. 'Well done, Mum!' he shouted. 'Well *done*!' 'I guess now you'll see what it means, dividing home and work,' Katie remarked. 'Congratulations, Sis,' Malcolm smiled. 'Great stuff.'

'I didn't say I'd accepted,' Mary told them.

Again the silence was like a spotlight. They were all watching her.

'The fact is, I only went to the interview because Tom is endlessly bothering me about working. Aren't you, dear?'

Abruptly she stood up and began to gather the remaining plates.

'Mary! We can do that later.'

Already heading for the kitchen, she called, 'Ask him why.'

Mark ran after her. 'Mum!'

'It's crazy not to accept,' Malcolm observed. 'At least to see how it feels.'

Katie was shaking her head. 'Of course you want her to work, Tom, it would do her good.'

But now there was a tapping on the window. Sally wanted to be let in. The girl had been crying, but put on a brave face. 'Hi, Uncle; hi, Katie. You're looking well.'

The doorbell rang from the street. Twice. Sally turned to her father.

'Tell him I don't want to see him. He can just fuck off.'

She turned and hurried upstairs.

Mary had to make her decision the following Wednesday. The children were very much in favour. With them doing all the persuading, Thomas decided that any effort on his part might be counterproductive. At the same time he wondered how he and his wife had got into this state, not being able to talk together about whether she should take a job. But then why did it feel so urgent that she did? If Malcolm and Katie had asked him, he wasn't sure he could have replied.

'The truth is I'd just be a dumb PA,' Mary told the children Monday morning. 'And for a man ten years younger than me. The export-office talk is the typical bait. I've been there before.'

They were in the car taking the kids to the bus stop. Thomas concentrated on the road.

'The fact is, your father earns four times as much as they'd be giving me, so it would hardly make much difference, moneywise,' she told them over supper. 'I'd have to get someone in to clean, of course, which would cut the advantage even further. And the travel costs, naturally. Forty minutes in the car. It's hard to see the point really.'

Thomas was aware that all this was addressed to him, although apparently spoken to the children. It occurred to him he could tell her he would be in a position to work less, if she had an income. He hesitated, but let it pass. He didn't want to work less.

'You'd meet new people, Mum,' Mark said.

'I don't need new people when I have my family.'

'You're always saying we're short of money,' Sally observed.

'Well, we're not, are we, Tom?'

Her appeal caught him by surprise.

'Like when we couldn't afford the new bathroom,' Sally insisted.

'Tom?'

'Not desperate for money, no,' he said. 'After all, we did get the bathroom in the end.'

Yet he desperately wanted her to take this job. What could he do to swing it?

'Like to walk the dog to the pub?' he asked on the Tuesday evening, when the dishes were in the dishwasher.

Mary frowned. The Cross Keys was almost two miles away. There was a path over the hills. It had been an age since they had walked there. Or anywhere. In winter it would be muddy and dark.

'Who's going to take the dog out, if I'm always at work?' she asked.

'We will!' Mark and Sally cried.

'For about the first two weeks,' Mary said. 'I didn't get a beautiful dog to have him locked up in the house all day.'

'Well?' Thomas asked.

They walked up the hill and turned off into the wood. Mary had brought a torch. She stooped to let Ricky off his lead. The path was narrow here, so they had to walk single file, but when it emerged on the hilltop there was room for Thomas to walk beside her and take her arm. To their right the lights of the city flickered in the plain. Above them a sliver of moon made the evening ghostly. Through her coat he could sense her resistance.

'You got a text message,' she said eventually.

'Did I? I didn't hear it.'

He pulled out his phone and looked at the message he knew was there.

'PA working late?'

'Some dumb offer from Orange.'

'Maybe *I* could have an affair, with a younger man.'

'Excellent idea,' Thomas joked, 'though definitely unwise with the boss.'

'You're right, he probably wants to hire an older woman so as not to be tempted.'

'For Christ's sake,' Thomas tried to laugh. 'You seem to think work places are all brothels.' After a moment he added, 'Can you imagine anyone shagging Katie, for example.'

Mary chuckled and squeezed his arm.

'Malcolm should be so lucky.'

In the pub, Ricky kept running round the tables to be made a fuss of. Mary enjoyed calling him back, and telling him to sit, but as soon as they started talking he was off again, wagging his tail among the drinkers. Finally Thomas said it.

'I just think it would be the best thing for *you*. For your life.'

'Oh yeah? Driving twenty miles every morning, getting stressed out, for peanuts?'

'You'd feel more . . .' he hesitated. 'Independent.'

'I beg your pardon?'

'You know, more in control.'

'Tom, why on earth would I need to feel independent when I'm married and have two wonderful children?

Dependency is natural in a family. We all depend on each other.'

'Still, the kids really want you to take the job. They're grown-up now.'

Mary sighed and played with her wine glass. Thomas was drinking beer.

'Maybe they think it would bring some fresh air into the house.'

She waited. He was digging his own grave perhaps.

'I suppose they're excited by the idea that their mum can hold her own in the world just as well as—'

She cut him off. 'Single people are independent, Tom. Are you saying you want me to be single?'

'Mary, for God's sake.'

But somebody in the pub had begun to shout. A young woman was on her feet. 'Get that fucking dog away from me! Shoo! Get lost!'

Ricky was sniffing and wagging his tail. The woman had backed away against the wall. She was terrified. The man beside her, who seemed considerably older, tried to grab the Cocker by the scruff of the neck. As people turned to see what was going on, he asked, 'Whose dog is this?' He had a foreign accent.

'Please don't worry,' Mary said, 'he wouldn't hurt a flea.'

'He should be on a lead,' the girl screamed.

'Please get your dog,' the man said.

'He really is completely harmless,' Mary smiled.

Most of the folk in the pub were on her side. Ricky loved to be fondled. The couple were newcomers.

'That's not the point,' the man said.

Drying glasses, the publican made no attempt to intervene.

'Ricky!' Mary called. 'Come here, love.'

'It's rude,' the girl said, 'letting your dog run around sticking his nose in people's hands. Why do I have to put up with that?' She too had a slight accent, Thomas thought. Her voice was trembling with emotion. The man had taken her hand.

'Ignorant,' Mary said flatly. Ricky was already back at her side.

The girl had begun to say something else, but the man discouraged her. He got to his feet, pulled on his coat and helped her with hers. They left their drinks unfinished. But to reach the door they had to pass by Thomas and Mary's table.

'Bad manners,' the girl said sharply. Thomas was struck by her finely hooked nose and jet-black hair.

'Ignorant,' Mary repeated. As soon as the door was closed behind them, she took her dog by the jowls and stared into his eyes. 'Ignoramuses, aren't they, love? Not like wise old Mr Rick.'

'Foreigners.' The woman at the next table shook her head.

Mary drained her glass. 'That's dependency for you,' she said, still talking to the dog. 'Latching on to a man twice your age, just to be looked after.'

'No doubt his PA,' Thomas joked.

On their way home, the dog disappeared. The animal stood still for a moment, on the alert, sniffing the air, then bounded off up the hill.

'Hedgehog,' Mary sighed. 'Now he'll get filthy, or full of thorns or something.'

They walked on but the dog didn't rejoin them. There was still no sign of him when they reached the shortcut leading down through the woods. The moon had gone and it had come on to drizzle.

'We can't go back without him,' Mary said.

It was after eleven.

'What if I go over the hill,' Thomas suggested, 'the long way, and you go down through the wood. That way we'll cover both paths.'

'Okay,' she agreed, 'except you go through the wood. I'm sure he's up on the hill still. He's more likely to come to me.'

'It's further that way.'

'I like walking,' she said.

As soon as Thomas stepped into the wood, he was in the pitch dark. It really was impossible to know where to put your feet. He was still in time to turn and hurry after his wife for the torch, but for some reason he didn't. She was striding away at a great speed, yelling, 'Ricky, Ricky.' The little crisis seemed to have galvanised her.

Thomas stood still, hoping his eyes would grow accustomed to the dark. He looked up, trying to find a gap between the dark branches of the trees, then down at the ground. He couldn't see a thing. The only way to advance was by feeling your way forward, arms outstretched to touch the damp trunks on either side. Beneath his feet last year's leaves were soft and slimy. The drizzle was thickening. After a few moments he stopped again. Perhaps if he waited a little longer, he would be able to make out the path. 'Ricky!' he called. The darkness absorbed his voice. He had the impression no one would hear even if they were nearby. Looking up again, he could see a faint glow of sky through the branches, but that only made things more impenetrable when he looked down at the ground. Then all at once he experienced a strange sense of satisfaction. Of knowingness. 'This is exactly what it is like,' he said out loud. 'Being in the dark.'

He stumbled on for a few minutes, not even sure now if he was on the path. Then his toe caught a root and he was down on his hands and knees. For a moment he sat on the wet ground. How incredibly stupid this was! In the modern world, to let oneself get stuck like this. He could call Mary, of course. He had the phone. Or Anita, who had texted earlier, asking if she could call. He didn't want to. He didn't want to speak to anyone. But perhaps the phone could work as a torch. He pulled it out. The glow lighted an area of two or three steps – the path was nowhere to be seen. He had left it.

Now he tried to retrace his steps. He would go the long way, over the hill. Blundering in the dark, he remembered the girl with the dog phobia. Fear had made her very beautiful. Big round eyes. What a lucky man! And in the end she was surely right that one ought to be able to sit in a pub without having to be smelled by dogs. Yet it was pointless saying that to Mary. Mary seemed to have an appetite for these mundane confrontations. With Katie as well. But not for the world of work. Why not? Ask him why he wants me to work, she had said. But wouldn't the more pertinent question have been: ask her why she doesn't want to work? She wasn't lazy. She wasn't without ambition and curiosity. So what was she afraid of?

Suddenly Thomas was aware of the dog. A glint of eyes. Ten feet away, in the shadow, Ricky was waiting for him, on the path perhaps, sitting, panting, head cocked, watching intently. In the glow of the phone, his doggy face had the solemn puzzlement of someone making an enormous effort to understand.

'Got him!' Thomas phoned Mary. 'Only I don't have a lead, and I can't see a thing in this stupid wood.'

'Tom, you're my hero!' she cried warmly. 'Just hang on to his lovely, silky, sexy fur till I get to you.'

After midnight, in bed, she wanted to make love. Perhaps it was a kind of reward, Thomas thought. They hadn't made love in months. Neither of them had much appetite for it. Years later, lamenting with Sally about the amount of alimony he was having to pay, Thomas would sigh and say, 'If only Mum had taken that famous job they offered her. Damn and damn, why didn't she?' 'Because they never offered it to her,' Sally laughed. 'She told me the day she supposedly turned it down, and not to tell you. She just wanted to see how worked up you would get.' However, when Thomas raised this with Mark, he got quite angry: 'Dad, she didn't take the job because she knew the moment she did, the marriage was over – and the family with it. She was determined to give you one more chance.'

Even later, discussing this old mystery with Elsa in their new flat on Canning Street, Thomas's girlfriend observed that there was really no way of knowing whether Mary had told the truth, either to Sally or to Mark. Thomas agreed. He shook his head. The only thing he remembered now with any certainty was sitting next to Ricky in the dark wood, an arm round his neck, the animal's foul breath in his face, its doggy heart beating beneath thick fur, thinking of the girl in the pub, thinking of her visceral repugnance for animals, of the evident terror on her face as she backed to the wall, eyes wide, lips parted; thinking, too, of the man she was with, his tenderness as he helped her into her coat, her spunkiness when she said, 'Bad manners,' the couple's evident intimacy as they linked arms going out through the door of the Cross Keys.

'I knew I wanted that,' he told Elsa.

BIVOUAC

This flat is much larger than a bivouac, but that's how I think of it, a small, flimsy refuge exposed to every inclemency. For sure, it's not a base camp. But then, home was hardly base camp either. I must stop calling it home. The truth is I often think of my progress in terms of an extended mountaineering metaphor, although I know nothing of mountaineering and am afraid of heights. I'm not making any progress at all.

There are three main rooms. You walk into a sitting room with kitchenette opposite and one large window. Through the only other door, there is a long narrow old-fashioned bathroom to the right and a medium-sized bedroom straight ahead. That's it. I'm bivouacked, hunkered down. Not on Everest or the Eiger's cruel North Face. Nothing so grand. Possibly it's more like Dartmoor, the barren landscape beyond the prison walls. In any event, the wind is wild. Every morning it's a miracle to find myself waking safe and sound in storm-tossed sheets.

What would progress mean? A bivouac is something you pack on your back and carry onwards day by day, upwards ever upwards. I have learned how to cook in this flat. The oven is wedged in a corner with the sink on one side and a work surface on the other. Through the window come sounds of dogs and children. The custodian sweeps the paving round the front door with a nylon broom that makes sharp, rhythmic scraping sounds. It was progress when I stopped feeling that she was sweeping my exposed nerves. But I haven't yet learned to deal with the deaf couple who shout over the television in the next flat. Unless perhaps it's progress that my attention can attach itself to these minor irritations. Perhaps they are actually a source of relief. Going nowhere, I'm obsessed with the idea of progress.

For example, from cheese on toast to omelette. From omelette to lentil soup. Various soups. From various lentil soups to curries and even risottos. These are no small achievements for a man in his late fifties. It is no small achievement for a man in his late fifties bivouacked in a small suburban flat to learn to shop for a quiche Lorraine. With mushrooms and leeks. Even more, to eat whatever comes out of the oven, in peace, listening to a BBC arts programme on his laptop. Even more, to wash the dishes *before* going to bed, to drink camomile tea rather than whisky. To go to sleep sober is a very considerable achievement.

But hardly *progress*. More like the bivouac's holding up. I'm still here.

When mountaineers climb a mountain, they reach the summit, take photos of themselves, plant a pole perhaps, then return to wherever they set out from, enriched by hardships that allow them to enjoy routine again. The whole point of my being in this flat is *not* to go back to where I set out from. Nor is there any summit for me to reach and plant a pole on. The mountaineering analogy is completely inappropriate. But it was never an intellectual construct. It's a feeling. I *feel* I'm perched halfway up a mountain beyond immediate rescue in miserable weather conditions. Presumably I hoped I was heading some-where else but ended up in this bivouac on a windswept mountainside.

Actually the flat is on the first floor over the entrance of a nondescript block, built, I would imagine, in the mid-'60s, though there is no date or founding stone anywhere. This is not a building that thinks of its place in history. The thing I immediately liked about it, when the landlord showed me in, was the parquet flooring. It must have been part of a renovation job in the late '90s. They used a dark, rich reddish wood that gives the off-white room a quiet warmth. I do believe this dark wood and the warmth and comfort it gives me are what has spared my bivouac from being blown away.

I couldn't care less about loneliness. I have my work. Any number of people rely on my expertise. Sometimes in the middle of the night I get up and venture out. Perhaps I imagine I'm beginning the final ascent. Or ready to climb down, come down from my mountainside. It's not pitch-dark, but the world is indistinct, as if shadows were being blown about, imposing shapes that might be buildings or mountain slopes, except they shift and shrink and grow. Am I in the clouds? There's a crash of rushing water. I have no idea which way to turn. It's this that frightens me. Up and down are words I don't understand. Forward and back mean nothing. Everything shifts with a wild and violent purposelessness. Where am I to go? The water booms too loudly for me to imagine swimming in its flow.

Later I get up, pee, make myself another camomile tea and sit on the sofa in the dark. It's a small, formless sofa which looks nicer since I hid its grit-grey upholstery beneath a bright blue cover. Finding a shopping centre, then choosing and fitting this cover was definitely a sign of progress. I sit on the sofa in the early hours with a little street light creeping through the curtains, sip camomile and stare at the parquet. I find if I manage to focus all my attention on the slightly different shades of the parallel strips of wood, the scratches, the different levels of polish, the little stains and so on, then this calms my mind. If I can concentrate on the parquet floor, its dust and crumbs, in the low dawn light, for the whole time it takes to drink a mug of hot camomile, if I can become, as it were, and for this very brief time, one with the warm wood, with this strange touch of gentility in an otherwise humdrum flat, bivouacked on a windswept ledge, then I will be able to go to bed again and perhaps even sleep an hour until my workday begins.

I had just pulled the covers over my head when the phone trilled. I had forgotten to turn it off. It was in the sitting room of my bivouac. There is only one person who could be phoning at this hour. So there was no reason to get up to answer the phone, since the one person, who could be calling was the one person I had no intention of talking to. For the time being. I may talk to her one day, I won't say never, but I am not planning to talk to her now.

All the same I got up – it was towards five – and went into the sitting room. I should have mentioned that in the middle of the sitting room there is a rectangular glass table on which I eat, and sometimes work. The phone was lying on the table among a great deal of other clutter, trilling and vibrating harshly against the glass. The display glowed. The phone trembled a little and moved with its pathetic vibrations, like something alive. With the same old feeling of trepidation I crossed the parquet floor and came up close. Even though I was reading upside down, the letters on the display, giving the name of the caller, were clear enough. JUST DON'T, they said. The phone trilled. JUST DON'T. I'm surprised sometimes how long the phone companies allow a phone to go on trilling when it's obvious that it's not going to be answered.

Maybe it's not obvious.

The phone throbs on the table. If I pick it up, the shapeless world of swirling cloud and rushing water will rearrange itself in a familiar landscape complete with high-security gaol. The bivouac will be a businessman's urban pied-à-terre, forty-one easily travelled miles from home base. If I pick it up, every object will regain its name and meaning; up will be up and down will be down. Time and history will be themselves.

The phone pulses on the glass surface. I watch it, relishing a moment of weakness. Through the table I can see where the parquet has been scuffed by my feet when I sit eating my cheese on toast or, more recently, risotto, alone, listening to BBC arts programmes. I like eating alone.

The phone throbs and glows. JUST DON'T. I let my eyes focus beyond it on the warm parquet and wait and wait and wait until at last it is still.

That was the wildest night I spent in my bivouac. Some minutes later the phone trilled again. I hadn't turned it off. There was the clatter of two hard surfaces cursed into togetherness by gravity, fighting to be apart. Again I came to look at it. Again I saw the old command. JUST DON'T. Responding then to I don't know what impulse, I crouched and stretched myself face down in my underwear under the table on the warm parquet with the pulsing phone now amplified above my head. The way someone might choose a point of precarious safety to expose himself to the wind, to listen for hours to a wicked wind, to feel its force and bitterness, to test himself to the limit. This bivouac, I thought, does not seem to have been built of the strongest materials. I would not use it on a serious climb.

JUST DON'T.

I didn't. Not this time. Or the next, or the next. Nor will I, I thought. I didn't and didn't and didn't again. I haven't and I won't. Is this progress? Maybe. The phone is still rattling above my head. The parquet is gritty with crumbs against my bare chest. I should vacuum my bivouac more often. Above my head the phone buzzes on and on like a noisy insect at the end of a long dry season.

VESPA

Mark parked his Vespa beside three others outside Yasmin's school where it would be safe. Yasmin herself hadn't gone to school, so they had to meet elsewhere. The day was dull and drizzly and Mark had got damp riding into town. He felt a little uncomfortable, his jeans were spotted with mud, but his fingers were warm in nice new gloves. He loved his Vespa. He packed his helmet under the seat and, led by a series of text messages, took the bus three stops to Elmsley Street where Yasmin said they could make love in an empty house; there was a way in through the garden, she said. She had been there before.

They'd been making love a lot recently. Yasmin was fantastically exotic and experienced. After months of misery life was cheering up. But when he got to Elmsley Street it turned out they'd first have to climb the garden wall then go in through a broken window in full view of passers-by. Mark refused. What was the point of getting caught breaking into a house when they could make love at his parents' at the weekend? In comfort.

'Remember, my mother's going away,' he told his girlfriend.

They sat in a coffee shop on Cote Street, but Yasmin couldn't smoke inside, and even outside on the seats under the awning she wasn't sure she dared smoke her dope, which she could have done if they had gone to the empty house. She didn't mean to criticise, though, she said. Her parents had kept her home four Saturday nights in a row over poor school results, so she understood worries about getting caught.

They held hands and fiddled with each other's rings. They were in love and had been officially engaged for three months on Facebook. Yasmin wore old woollen gloves she had scissored off at the knuckles so she could roll tobacco without removing them. Her fingernails were brown and bitten. Mark loved to watch the fumes curling lazily from her parted lips. She was six months younger than him, but it somehow felt like she was much older.

When school ended, Yasmin went to her father's work to get a lift home and Mark met his mother who had come into town to shop. They nosed into three or four places on the High Street and eventually Mark's mother bought Mark a new sweater. It was a deep mauve that went well with his dark hair but he was worried it made him seem rather bulky. Mark's mother didn't get anything for herself. She seemed distracted. When they drove back to Yasmin's school the Vespa wasn't there.

The school railings were on the outside of the bend on Eastleigh Road with lots of slow traffic in both directions. It was such an exposed place it was hard to imagine how anyone could have dared steal anything. There were now five other bikes and mopeds of one kind or another lined up together, but Mark's wasn't amongst them. The rain was falling heavily.

'Are you sure you left it here?' Mark's mother asked sharply. They didn't have an umbrella. Mark was perfectly sure, but his mother was not convinced. 'Think,' she said. 'Try to remember.' Mark suddenly felt very upset, staring at the five bikes on the pavement in the splashing rain. Without the Vespa he was a prisoner in a remote house in the country. Now his mother was going away there would be no more lifts in the car. He would never get Yasmin home without the Vespa.

'For heaven's sake, don't whine,' his mother scolded. 'Think of the moment you got off the bike and locked up your helmet. Where were you?'

'I *know* I left it here!' Mark's voice quavered. 'Where else would I leave it when I come to meet Yasmin?'

'Call her,' his mother said. 'Just to check.'

Mark refused, but his mother said she wouldn't take the problem seriously until he did. It was the most ordinary thing in the world to forget where you had parked a car or locked up a bike. She had once spent an hour at the Three Lilies Centre trying to find the Fiesta.

Because you were unhappy, Mark thought. Because you were thinking about Dad.

Mark made the call and Yasmin laughed. 'The lads must have taken it,' she chuckled. There was a band at school, she said, who took bikes for joyrides and to steal parts. 'Go and look behind the school, maybe they've dumped it there.' Mark was upset; Yasmin seemed more amused than anything else. She didn't understand how important the scooter was for them. Mark's mother was making signs to say she wanted to speak to the girl, but Mark ended the call. He hadn't asked Yasmin point blank if she remembered him leaving the Vespa outside the school and the last thing he wanted was for his mother to ask her and discover she hadn't been at school. 'She knows I left it here,' he said, 'otherwise she wouldn't say to go and look round the back, would she?'

At this point his mother saw someone she knew coming out of the school, a woman who walked her dog in the park where she walked hers. They began to laugh and talk together and the woman, who turned out to be a geography teacher, said there were so many problems at the school because of the backgrounds the kids came from and how many were immigrants and it was perfectly possible Mark's Vespa had been stolen. This was probably the worst place he could have parked it, she thought. Mark's mother seemed almost too jolly and talkative. It was embarrassing. The boy started off on his own to walk round the back of the school. Turning the second corner which led him into waste ground used as a car park, the first thing he saw was his Vespa.

He felt a strong rush of joy at the sight of it. It was a sharp bright red, with white seat and wheels and a lovely streamlined shape. He felt in his pocket for his keys to get his helmet from the back. The seat would need wiping too. Then he saw the motor was gone.

It took him three or four seconds to grasp this. First he sensed the bike looked different: thinner and lighter. Odd. Then he realised the motor was missing. Between the back wheel and the seat there was an empty space. He wanted to sit down on the wet ground and cry. Now the Vespa wasn't just missing, it was dead.

'Pull yourself together,' Mark's mother said. 'For heaven's sake!' They would have to go to the police. The scooter had cost more than £2,000 only six months ago. They must report the crime, then go to the insurance people and make a claim. 'These vandals are a disgrace,' she said. But it was typical of the kind of people who lived in this part of town.

Mark texted Yasmin: 'It's there but they've taken the motor.' She texted back: 'Awesome!' Mark felt sick. Then Mark's mother said they should remove the licence plates in case they needed to be handed in some time. Both of them were getting soaked now. Mark's mother went back round the school to fetch the Fiesta which had some tools in it and Mark tore a nail trying to pull off one of the wet plates which had jammed against the mudguard. The worst thing though was the feeling in his head that life would never be the same. His pretty Vespa had been disembowelled.

It was important to go to the police station at once because Mark's mother was leaving tomorrow. She knew one, back in their part of town. On arrival, they were fourth in the queue in a room that felt like the dentist's except the posters were all about police recruitment and a bright future. Since his father left, Mark had lost any sense of having a future. Even starting at university seemed more like a kind of limbo than a path to anywhere. Meanwhile, as always, his mother struck up a conversation, this time with a stranger who was distressed about the obscene words someone kept writing on her garden wall.

'My son's had his scooter stolen,' Mark's mother told this woman, then began to explain how she was going to Zambia for six months to teach in a school for poor children who would very likely never be able to afford a bicycle, never mind a scooter. Mark did not think the other woman was listening. Yasmin had once said that her parents would never get her a scooter. She had too many brothers and sisters. He thought how nice it was when she was sitting on the pillion behind and put her arms round him, and again he felt he might cry. Almost anything made him cry these days. He was becoming a complete sissy.

'Round the back of the school, you say?' the policeman repeated, making a note. 'And why did you go round the back, if you'd parked it at the front?' 'Because his girl-friend thought it might be there,' Mark's mother said. The policeman remarked that the question had been addressed to Mark and Mark said, 'There's some waste ground, I thought it might be there.' 'She goes to that school,' Mark's mother explained. The girlfriend. The policeman said the computers were down and they would have to come back the following day to pick up the printed report, which must then be sent on to the insurance people. In the car going home Mark's mother told him he would have to do that himself. 'I'll have left already.'

The house was a semi-detached near the top of a steep hill about fifteen minutes out of town. As they arrived their dog Ricky put his paws up on the garden gate, wagging his tail furiously. After they had eaten, the animal moved anxiously back and forth from Mark's bedroom at the front of the house on the first floor, where Mark sat on the floor drawing and texting, to the kitchen at the back of the house on the ground floor, where Mark's mother spent the evening sorting out the fridge. It seemed Ricky, who was a cocker spaniel, would have liked to herd the two together, but they did not talk to each other even when they went to bed. Next day Mark's mother took the dog to friends and set off on her journey.

The following Wednesday, Mark, who was attending university in Liverpool during the week, called his father who had recently changed jobs and now also lived in Liverpool, but on the other side. Mark was in a prefab corridor in a building where he felt a fish out of water. The signal was not great. He should have taken a gap year, he thought, but hadn't known what to do. He felt limp and inadequate. His father, as always, wanted to hear good news so he wouldn't have to worry about him. He was busy. 'The fact is,' Mark told him, 'Yasmin thinks she knows who took it; she says she might be able to get them to put the motor back on.'

His father seemed to be finding it difficult to concentrate. He hadn't said where he was, exactly, but Mark had the impression he was with other people.

'You've reported it to the police, right? And the insurance too? If the Vespa turns up now, on the road, with its motor and all, they might think you were lying to get the insurance.'

Mark hadn't thought of this. His father asked where the bike was now. On the waste ground behind the school, Mark said. Mark had phoned the insurance people to give them the details and get them to check the damage to the bike, but they said he had to get it moved to a repair place before they would look at it. He couldn't see the point of doing that, though, if Yasmin could persuade the vandals to put the motor back on. He wanted his bike back.

His father didn't seem to know how to respond. Mark was between lessons and needed to hurry if he was to get a decent position in the life class. It might be better, his father thought, simpler that is, if they picked up the insurance from the old bike and got a new one. That would be the easy thing. Mark said emphatically he didn't want a new bike. He wanted his old bike back. He couldn't understand himself why he felt so strongly about that.

In life drawing they had had the same fat old model who had been posing all the first five weeks of term. Once again Mark pinned out his paper, took his pencil in his hand and looked at his subject. Why had he chosen a course where he was almost the only boy? Why hadn't he done engineering or something? The woman was sitting on the floor this time, so the twenty or so students arranged in a semicircle were looking slightly down at her. She had put a white towel on the floor, no doubt for reasons of hygiene. She had her legs out straight, slightly apart and her hands were propping her up behind her back. Her breasts and stomach sagged. Her red face was slightly tilted back, showing her nostrils.

Drawing, Mark found the woman's fat disgusting, but fascinating too, its volume and orange-peel surfaces. Every few minutes he exchanged a message with Yasmin, who had gone to school today, but there was no teacher in her lesson. Yasmin was so slim, so lithe, so living. She had had lots of boyfriends already. Mark worried what she could see in him. He felt so vague beside her, so unsure of himself. Sharpening his pencil, he decided he would try to get across the grossness of the model's fat in as few lines as possible. Fat people were gross, he thought. They were losers. His mother would never let herself go like that. She was thin and nervy and strong. She went running or swimming every day. Yasmin was naturally thin. Mark wanted to be thin too, but he had a big bum, he thought. His trousers were always tight. Most of all he did not want to be alone. It made him feel anxious when he closed the door in his tiny college room and went to sleep in a narrow bed in a space that was really a box, a sort of regulation white packaging for a no-name product: himself.

Eye moving from object to paper, Mark worked on the wrinkles at the top of the woman's big thighs where they sank down between the legs at the crotch. Now the teacher stood behind him to look at his work. 'Whoa,' he said, 'that's scary, Mike.' 'Mark,' Mark said. The teacher apologised. 'I'll get all the names before the end of term,' he promised. The model's stomach lifted and fell very slightly when she breathed. Then Yasmin sent a text to say that the motor was already back on the Vespa. 'Fantastic, I love you,' Mark texted back.

Now that his mother was away, Mark's father was happy to come home at the weekend to be with him, though Mark only went back to Manchester to be with Yasmin. He couldn't really forgive his father for leaving. Meantime he had phoned up the insurance people to say the motor had reappeared on the bike and he didn't want the insurance after all. Yasmin had assured Mark it worked fine, though he couldn't understand how she could know this since she didn't have a key to start the bike. His father, meantime, insisted that before picking it up they must go to the police again and change their report, because if by a stroke of bad luck – and his father was always expecting strokes of bad luck – the police should stop him for a routine check, or if he had an accident, God forbid, then it would come out that he was riding a bike that was supposedly stolen, or at least its motor was stolen, and they might incriminate him for having tried to defraud the insurance company. 'All these records are computerised,' he said. 'They would only have to put the licence plate in their search engine and it would seem you were a criminal.'

This time there was no wait at the police station. His father had phone calls to make and walked up and down on the pavement outside while Mark explained to a tall, alert young man that the bike he had described as being vandalised the week before was now working again. The young man dithered; he had thin, white hands that were long and alive. Mark found hands the most difficult thing of all to draw. The policeman picked up a pen and put it down, scratched a knuckle, then invited Mark to come through to a small room with a table in the middle, and left him there.

After ten minutes an older man arrived and sat down opposite. He put the previous report down on the table and laid both hands on it as if to fix it there. These hands were heavy and meaty. His forehead was puckered and his cheeks tensed in concentration and disapproval. Mark's heart sank. He wanted to phone his father and have him come and help but he knew the man wouldn't let him do this. Messages were vibrating in his pocket but he didn't dare to look at them. He felt as he used to when he was ten years old and his mother yelled at him for making a mess or losing things. His mother was writing long emails now saying how sad the squalor was in Africa but how brave the young mothers and their undernourished children were. The policeman looked up at him and their eyes met. 'So how did this happen?' he asked.

'What?'

'First a motor disappears, then it reappears. I never heard of such a thing.'

Mark hesitated. He tried to explain the circumstances, but his voice sounded defensive.

'Why did you park the bike at the school, if you were then going to take the bus into town? Why wasn't your girlfriend at school, if you say it was her school?'

Mark should have explained that he hated riding through the underpass and the two big roundabouts. He shrugged his shoulders. 'That's what I did,' he said.

The policeman's jacket was rather tight across his barrel chest. He seemed very powerful physically. 'Another thing I don't understand,' he was saying, 'is why you left the bike there after the motor was stolen.'

Mark was silent.

'The normal thing would have been to have it taken to a repair place, no? Or a demolition yard. Don't you think? As it is, it looks like you knew you could get the motor put back.'

'This never happened to me before,' Mark muttered. His hands were shaking. At this point his father knocked on the door and opened it. He asked if he could come in. Mark felt his shoulders go tight. The policeman said no, he couldn't come in and he certainly shouldn't be knocking on doors in police stations unasked. 'Wait in the waiting room. If I want you, you'll be called.' Mark felt his leg trembling. He hated himself.

'It may never have happened to you,' the policeman said, 'but it rather sounds like your girlfriend is an old hand at this, right? You leave your scooter in a prominent place and go off with her. Lo and behold, it gets stolen. She tells you where to find it. Lo and behold, there it is. With no motor. You report the theft and make an insurance claim. Your girlfriend says not to worry. Lo and behold, the motor reappears. What is this story all about? Who is this know-it-all girlfriend?'

Mark had never been so frightened. 'Her name is Yasmin,' he said. He felt he was betraying her. Her parents were Brazilian, he explained. They lived just the other side of Galaxy Shopping. She was seventeen. He had known her almost a year. They had been going out for six months.

'Does she have a criminal record?' The policeman was very blunt. 'Or a brother with a criminal record?'

Mark didn't know what to say. There ought to be someone here to protect him, he thought.

'She had some dope on her once,' he said carefully, 'when the police stopped us. On the Vespa. But she wasn't fined or anything.'

'She smokes marijuana?'

'Everybody does,' Mark said.

'Speak for yourself, young man. I certainly don't.'

Nor did Mark. He hated smoke except when watching it coil from Yasmin's lips. Somehow it was impossible to say this.

The policeman wanted the girl's full name, address and phone number. Y-A-S-M-I-N, Mark said.

'Isn't that a contraceptive pill?' the policeman asked wryly.

Mark bit his lip. Please God he wasn't betraying her, he thought. It occured to him that if anyone were a criminal in a couple it ought to be the boy, not the girl. 'Her surname is Pinho,' he said. The policeman made him spell that as well. He didn't know her exact address. But he gave the man her phone number. 'You can warn her to expect a call from us,' the policeman said. Then he dismissed the boy and called in his father; 'for a word in private,' he said. In the waiting room Mark sent a text to Yasmin telling her the police wanted to call her about the Vespa. 'I'm so sorry, but how could I say the motor reappeared without mentioning you?' His hands were shaking so much he could barely text.

Mark's father reappeared and they went outside to the car. 'The police think Yasmin is one of the vandals,' he sighed. 'Or she has a brother who is.' He swung the Audi out into traffic. 'Otherwise why would they put the motor back when presumably they removed it to sell it? You can see their point, frankly. They don't think you were involved, but they think she's leading you up the garden path; that she's not the innocent person she says she is.'

After a few moments he added, 'An ex-boyfriend, maybe.'

Mark wanted to scream.

'There's her dope-smoking too.'

'What about it?'

'Well, it suggests a lifestyle that . . .'

'Yasmin's completely honest,' Mark suddenly shouted. 'Listen, she just told everyone at school that if the motor wasn't put back she was going to talk to the headmaster, because it was her boyfriend's bike. Then it reappeared. That's not her fault, is it? It was nice of her.'

'They think at the very least she knows who they are,' his father said. 'I mean, why would they do what she wants otherwise? What do they care about her boyfriend? They stole it for a reason, didn't they? To sell it. And if she knows the perpetrators of a crime, she has a legal responsibility to report it to the police.'

'She does *not* know them!' Mark was indignant. What a pompous prick his father was, using expressions like 'perpetrators of a crime'! The fact was, he said, his father didn't like Yasmin because she was an immigrant and coloured and her dad only worked in a warehouse. 'You don't know what a nice person she is.'

'If she's telling the truth then she hasn't got anything to worry about, has she?' his father said. Somehow this sounded frightening.

From the police station, they drove over to the other side of town, to the waste ground behind Yasmin's school. They stood by the Vespa and examined it. It was looking a bit rain-stained after a week outside. Then they put the licence plates back on. 'Take it straight to the mechanic's,' Mark's father told him. 'And go really easy in case something's not working properly. The last thing we need is an accident. Check the brakes right away, and the steering.'

It was a mild October morning and, getting on to the Vespa, Mark felt good. The helmet was still there under the seat. Amazingly, the motor started first time using the battery and starter, something it didn't always do even when he'd left it in the garage. Mark rode it slowly round the muddy track on the waste ground while his father watched. 'It brakes fine,' he told him and his father said, 'Okay go for it,' and walked back to the Audi.

Mark took the bike out into the traffic. The motor was a bit louder than it had been, he realised now, and it felt a bit more powerful too. It surged and growled when he twisted the accelerator. His back responded to the sudden movement and his knees closed a little tighter. He grinned. Then he noticed that the rear-view mirror was missing. That was annoying, but he could drive without it. It felt so good when he had got through the traffic on the ring road and turned right beyond the lights, heading out towards Pendlebury. There was fresh air from the fields, which were hazy in the autumn sunshine and he felt absorbed in the movement of the bike along the strip of road between hedges and green verges with the low wooded hills in the distance. This was great. He was living again. But soon the police would phone Yasmin and accuse her of being involved with the vandals. Life was unfair. Turning in to the mechanic's, he hit a pothole, had to put his foot down and scraped his shoe.

The gangly young man had trouble following what Mark was telling him about the motor. 'I'll look it over, if that's what you want,' he said. 'The back light was missing,' he pointed out. Mark hadn't noticed. It would be ready next weekend, the mechanic said. Right at the moment he had more than a dozen bikes to look at. Now Mark had a mile and a half to walk home through the muddy countryside. He texted Yasmin to ask if there was any chance she could come out to his place and stay the night. Perhaps he could persuade his father to pick her up if she got the bus as far as Salford. Then they would find some way to get her back home tomorrow. Mark began the long climb up the hill to their house. When the phone rang he thought it must be her.

'Mr Paige?'

It was the policeman. Mark found it odd being addressed as if he were adult.

'We have been making some enquiries regarding your girlfriend's phone number, Mr Paige.' There was a pause. 'Perhaps you can explain to us why this phone is registered in your name, not your girlfriend's.'

His heart was beating fast, as if he'd been caught out. But again there was a simple explanation. When they had gone to buy her phone Yasmin didn't have any identification with her, which it turned out the phone people needed for the sort of contract she wanted, so he had given his name and address as a guarantee.

The policeman cleared his throat. Again there was a long pause. Then he said: 'So, just by chance, the very day this young, er, lady goes to get a phone she doesn't have any identification with her even though she knows which deal she wants and has presumably checked the requirements on the Internet. What's more, she just happens to go with someone who has got identity and is naive enough to lend it to her, so that now if there should be any suspect traffic on this young lady's phone it cannot be attributed to her.'

Mark was silent. He couldn't believe it.

'Could I have your father's phone number?' the policeman asked.

'Why?' he faltered.

The policeman was ironic: 'If I ask for your father's number, perhaps it's because I want to speak to him.'

'But you just spoke to him,' Mark protested.

'And now I want to speak to him again. If you don't want to give me the number, I'll find it elsewhere.'

Mark gave the policeman the number and immediately phoned his father. He explained that the police would soon be calling him, and why.

'How was the scooter?'

'Fine.'

His father asked Mark if he wanted him to come and pick him up and bring him home and Mark said he would much rather his father went and picked up Yasmin later. He didn't want to make him run about too much.

His father said, 'Okay, if I have time. I think I'd better have a word with Yasmin about all this.'

Now Mark texted Yasmin about what had happened with the phone. But it was too complicated for a text. He phoned her, but she was with friends. There was laughter, in the background. Male laughter, it sounded like. He tried to explain. Yasmin didn't seem worried at all. But for some reason this didn't cheer Mark up. 'I'm making life so difficult for you,' he texted.

Climbing the slow hill home he felt sick. Mother had put up a For Sale sign outside the house before leaving. There was an estate agent's number to call. His father thought Yasmin was a criminal. Yasmin didn't understand how upset he was. Now he would have to wait another week to have his bike back. The pleasure he'd felt riding out of town an hour before was forgotten. In the empty house he tried to follow the instructions his mother had left and prepare something proper to eat, but then couldn't be bothered. He ate cheese on toast and thought about the fat woman sitting on the white towel to protect herself from the dirty floor. The woman didn't seem worried about being fat, nor about the miserable job she had. She always had a sort of Cheshire Cat smile on her face, as if she were proud that all the students were there drawing her. Mark realised he envied her.

Her father picked up Yasmin from the bus station at four. Mark sat in the back with her while his father drove. On the radio, two presenters were taking phone calls about the World Cup in Brazil and his father made a comment to Yasmin about this being a big moment for her country but Yasmin said she didn't follow football at all. Then Mark's father asked her about the bike saga. Those were the words he used. The bike saga. Yasmin laughed and said as soon as she'd heard what happened she had just put the word around. That it was her boyfriend's bike. She'd been a bit surprised herself when the motor reappeared. 'I guess I must be popular,' she laughed. The only problem would be if the police came to talk to her parents again. Then her dad would be mad even if she hadn't done anything wrong.

'Again?' Mark's father asked.

Quickly Mark explained about Yasmin having some dope in a roll-up once. The police had gone to her house.

His father was silent. When they got back home he suggested they all have a beer together in the garden since the weather was fine, but Mark just wanted to take Yasmin to his bedroom. A couple of hours later his father called upstairs. He wanted to talk to him. Mark was grateful to him for not coming up and knocking. He pulled on his jeans and went out on to the stairs, conscious of looking tousled. 'Since I won't be seeing much of you now Yasmin's here, I'm going to head back to my place,' his dad said. Mark let him hug him, but he didn't feel the relief he normally felt when his parents went away. When he went back to the bedroom, Yasmin was in her panties at the window, smoking. Mark lay on the bed and stared at the ceiling.

'Couldn't you have told them your mother had complained to the headmaster, or something?' she asked.

'I'm sorry,' he said. He didn't seem to say anything else these days.

'They'll keep me in Saturdays again and I won't be able to come over, even when you do get the Vespa back.'

Mark stared at the ceiling.

'I wish they'd call right away,' she said.

The smoke from her cigarette drifted back into the room. It was a good job his mother was away, since she could smell the smoking even when she went out in the garden. She insisted guests went right down to the road to smoke.

'Fuck fuck fuck fuck fuck fuck fuck,' Yasmin said.

Later they went downstairs, drank his father's beers and watched TV, but both of them knew they were just waiting for that phone call from the police. Mark was supposed to read a book on the phenomenology of art for Monday afternoon's seminar, but he couldn't concentrate.

'You'll leave me because of this, won't you?' he said.

Yasmin looked puzzled. She had a small, sly mouth and stained teeth, lush frizzy hair, a puppy's body. 'Why?' she asked.

*

Since Mark had started at college and spent the week in Liverpool a sort of routine had developed whereby every Tuesday or Wednesday evening Mark's father took him out to eat, or to the pub for a pint. Mark had been drawing the fat woman again. This time the woman was lying on her side with her head propped on her elbow. She had brought three red cushions to lie on. His father took him to a Thai restaurant. 'Have the police phoned Yasmin yet?' he asked.

'No,' Mark said.

'Is she worried?'

'She's beginning to hope they won't call.'

Mark's father said he liked Yasmin. He hesitated. 'But there's no real future for you two, is there? I mean, you're from different worlds.'

Mark didn't look up from his curry.

'I wouldn't be surprised in the end if she did know the guys who took your motor,' he said.

'She doesn't.'

'In the end it wouldn't be her fault if she did, would it? She seems the kind of girl who might move in circles like that.'

'But she doesn't! Why don't you believe me?'

Mark's father asked when he would be getting the Vespa back.

'Friday afternoon.'

The waitress brought another helping of rice. Mark's father kept trying to make conversation, asking questions about the art college, about his future plans, living in the dorm, about Mum, about the restaurant, trying to be friendly, or to show he was being friendly, but Mark didn't feel like talking. The older man became impatient; he really wanted the two of them to have a nice time together, eating out in a nice Thai restaurant. Mark was very aware of this, but he couldn't have helped his father, even if he wanted to.

'Are you sure you don't want some noodles?' his father asked. 'They're so good here.'

Now he was pouring himself wine. Mark propped his chin on his elbows and watched. 'Maybe my future is turning into a flat slob,' he said. 'Covered in gross rolls of fat.'

His father looked perplexed. 'You hardly eat anything,' he said. 'You just need to do a bit of sport.'

The police called Yasmin on Tuesday to say she was invited to go to a police station near her home on the Friday morning. With both parents.

'Good luck,' Mark texted. He felt convinced it was his fault. And his parents', too. If he hadn't told Yasmin where he had parked the day the Vespa disappeared, if he had said he'd left the bike at the bus station for example, she wouldn't have tried to help by getting the motor put back on and none of this would have happened. And if his parents hadn't split up, the Vespa wouldn't have mattered so much and he wouldn't have needed Yasmin so much, and all this had made Yasmin get involved because even if she had never seemed worried about the bike, she loved him and knew he needed her, needed the Vespa so he could be with her, and so even without knowing the vandals who'd done it she had somehow made them put the motor back on and now she was paying the price for that. Maybe the police would even put her in gaol, or give her a warning so that she would be too scared to buy dope any more, which would actually be a good thing but she would blame him for it and leave him. What a bore I am, he knew. I should be like the fat woman who doesn't give a damn about her big buttocks and oceans of cellulite. His mother's Facebook page was now full of pictures of her in groups of bony black children. She said it was impossible to go running where she was staying because it didn't feel safe. On the train home on Friday morning, Mark bought a turkey and mayonnaise sandwich from the refreshment trolley and then crisps and a Coke. At this very moment Yasmin is at the police station, he thought, because of me.

Mark took the train from Liverpool, then a bus out to Pendlebury. After which it was a long walk to the mechanic's. He had texted Yasmin three times but she hadn't replied. Perhaps they had taken her phone because it wasn't in her name. Why did my parents even have me, he wondered, if they were so unhappy? His father was always saying he had been unhappy for years. How could a man who had been unhappy for years talk to anyone about their future? I wish the fat woman were my mother, he decided.

We would eat fish and chips and ice cream together on the sofa every evening. The thought made him feel oddly excited and slightly sick. The mechanic said the vandals had done a great job putting the motor back. The bike was working fine. He had put on a new mirror, a new brake light, changed the filters and checked the brakes. As he spoke, Mark was looking at a calendar above his head in which a girl crouching behind a motorbike wearing only a black jacket had propped two pointed breasts on the seat. She had the same frizzy hair as Yasmin. He would never be able to keep such a girlfriend, he thought. '£78.50,' the mechanic said.

Mark rode the Vespa home. It moaned pleasantly up the last slope. Riding it always induced a happy mood of freedom and competence that vanished the moment he shut away the helmet in the luggage compartment. As if the mood was inside the helmet. He should wear it all the time, perhaps. He went into the house which felt very empty without the dog, without his mother. His father wasn't coming back this weekend. There were so many rooms. Sometimes it seemed there must be somebody there. Once or twice Mark had even managed to scare himself by imagining intruders behind doors. There were none. Yasmin shared a room with three younger sisters and her mother, while her two brothers slept with their father. Mark thought that might be worth being poor for.

He defrosted some soup his mother had left. Why hadn't Yasmin replied to his messages? He lost patience and called her, though he knew she preferred him to text. The phone was off. Why? Didn't she realise he was worried? He was supposed to be writing his first essay for the life class: his feelings about the drawings he had done. He wriggled the drawings out of their tube and spread them on the living-room table. In the first he had concentrated mainly on the bulk of the body. There was too much detail, lots of shading and cross-hatching. More recently he had been trying to get something about the face in relation to the body. It wasn't pretty, but it was a nice face, a face happy with itself. The mouth was relaxed and soft, not like his parents'. If these things could be expressed in words, there would be no point in drawing, Mark thought. Faces are complicated things. Then he was so anxious he ran out of the house and got on his Vespa again. This time he took the spare helmet with him, strapped to the back.

He had reached the ring road when the phone rang. Mark had a strict rule that he would never answer the phone while on the bike. He broke it. In two lanes of heavy traffic he reached into his pocket. After all, if he hadn't meant to break the rule, why would he have set the ringtone on max? With his right hand off the accelerator the bike slowed and wobbled. Holding the phone he grabbed the handlebar again and gave it a little burst of speed, conscious of a bus behind. He tried to see the screen, which was glowing, but there was bright sunlight. He had to hold it right in front of his visor. The bike clipped the kerb and wobbled. The bus hit its horn and swerved. Then he was over with the bike on top and his helmet clunking on the pavement.

Mark lay still a moment trying to take it in; then a girl his own age was next to him asking if he was okay. It seemed he was. His leg hurt, he thought, but he was definitely okay. Thank God. Two men had arrived. They righted the bike and pulled it out of the traffic. The spare helmet was still attached. Mark sat on the pavement and took his helmet off. 'Thank you,' he said, 'I'd better take it easy for a few minutes.' His knee was sore. When he had got over the shock, he couldn't find his phone. It wasn't in his pockets, it wasn't on the pavement, it wasn't in the gutter or on the road. Now he really hated himself.

When Yasmin came out of school at four, Mark had been waiting almost an hour. He had thought she finished at 3.30. Sitting on his bike outside the gate, it seemed impossible he would ever find the strength to get a new phone and put all the old numbers on it. His mother would think him pathetic. His father would try to be too generous. Mark felt desperate, but bored as well. The traffic crept by on the road beside him and the clouds marched overhead in the damp sky. There was a constant windy tug to the day that he just didn't feel part of. He didn't feel part of the world at all. All he had was the Vespa. Thank God he hadn't damaged the Vespa. Then a bell drilled and almost at once kids started streaming out. He sat up. After a few minutes Yasmin appeared, but of course she was with her friends, Sandy, Mike, Ray and

Georgina. Yasmin was the shortest of the group, small and petite, her hair all over the place. But she was dressed more smartly than usual today. She even had a skirt on, a jacket, a button-up blouse. To see the police, no doubt. A mill of others hurried past. They were laughing, slouching, sharing out cigarette papers. And Mark saw at once that Yasmin was happy. She was grinning. All five of them were happy together, lighting up cigarettes, at the end of the school week.

They came through the gate and saw him.

'Hi, Marky,' Yasmin said. She was always a little cool when there were others around. They stood beside the Vespa. 'We're going to the house, wanna come?'

She meant the empty house with the broken window, beyond the canal. They were going to smoke dope.

'How was it?' Mark asked. 'This morning? I lost my phone. I don't know anything.'

Yasmin grinned. 'Fine. No worries.'

'But . . .'

'Yazzy told 'em to go fuck 'emselves,' Georgina laughed. She had a mocking smile.

'Asked 'em if they needed any spare parts for their big blue bikes,' Ray said. 'Didn't you, Yaz? Speaking of which . . .' He crouched down to look at the Vespa's motor.

'Idiot,' Mark said.

'Are you coming?' Yasmin repeated. 'How'd you lose your phone?'

'No,' Mark said. He wasn't coming.

'Oh, come on!' Sue and Jan would be there too, Georgina said. 'And maybe Lisa. You know she has the hots for you.'

Mark sat on his Vespa. 'No.'

Suddenly it was clear to him they all knew perfectly well who had taken the motor.

'What are you going to do?' Yasmin asked wryly. As if the thought that he might have something to do was funny.

Mark said nothing. He had worried so much about her.

'Let's go,' Mike said. Sandy and Ray were already moving off.

'How will I get back to your place,' Yasmin asked, 'if we don't go together? Come on. Just one smoke then back to your place.'

'Can we come too?' Georgina asked. She put on an eager little girl's voice. 'Can we come too?'

'No.'

Mark's mind was set. He wasn't going with them.

'Are you okay?' Yasmin asked. 'Is the bike going okay?'

Mark tried a smile. 'I'm really glad it was okay with the police.'

Yasmin laughed. 'Oh, they didn't know anything. Even Dad was on my side. They just wanted to scare me.'

Everybody was still for a moment. But Mike and Georgina were anxious to go.

'The bike's going great,' Mark said. 'See you later.'

'But how will we get in touch, if you've lost your phone? I told my parents I was out tonight already. When shall we meet?'

Sitting on his Vespa, Mark was slightly above the others. It was breezy and there was sunshine in his face. He didn't reply. His knee was hurting. He was fed up. Mike and Georgina started to walk after the others. Yasmin turned to follow, then turned back. Her eyes looked for his. She pursed her lips slightly, maybe forming a kiss, maybe an impatient pout. What was she going to do? Mark settled his helmet and turned the key. The bike started. He twisted a little, patted the back seat and gestured to the helmet. It was unlike him.

Yasmin still hesitated. 'Hey, dudes!' she shouted. The others were crossing the road.

Mark revved the bike and pushed it off its forks. He turned it to the road. Yasmin came to stand next to him and was shouting something again about times and phones over the noise of the motor. He shook his head. He liked this feeling the helmet gave of being separate and protected. 'Get on the back, stupid,' he yelled. He was still shaking the helmet. 'Come on, get on.' He revved the bike. Yasmin grabbed the helmet and unclipped it.

As soon as her arms were round his waist Mark surged off. The traffic was intensifying with the rush hour, but he drove faster than he usually did. He wove between the cars. He accelerated and braked hard. It was good feeling the girl thrown against him, then away. Her arms held him tighter. Once he was off the ring road and in the country Mark wound it up to max. They were pushing fifty. Yasmin was shouting something. He didn't even try to hear what. He weaved the bike from side to side a little on purpose. She was clutching him. Perhaps he was frightening her. He imagined riding with the fat model behind. The woman was naked, posing, completely relaxed while Mark forced the bike to go as fast as it could. That would be something to draw. Straining up the last hill, he was just about to move across to turn right into the drive when he saw a car close behind in the mirror. Damn. He braked to let it by, then changed his mind. Instead of stopping, he accelerated and drove straight on. He drove straight past the house, up the slope beyond the village, then on towards the wooded hills and the horizon. The sun was lower now and it was definitely colder here. Yasmin was shouting again. She couldn't understand where the hell they were going. Mark drove the bike as fast as he could between two dark hedges.

JULIE

I met Mary Paige in the dog park. She used to come late afternoon with her cocker spaniel. I had Donna, of course. She was in heat at the time, and it was keeping them apart we got together. I must have told her I sometimes looked after other people's dogs for them, because she offered me money to keep her Ricky, while she was away for a week and of course I said yes. Then she told me I must never bring Donna to the park when she was in heat. It was just common sense. She was right.

She gave me more than I'd asked to keep Ricky, and a nice present as well, a cashmere cardigan. That's the kind of person Mary is. Really generous. And full of energy. We started to take the dogs for walks together whenever I had time. Boy, did Mary take long walks! Instead of the usual half an hour with the mutts on their leads, sniffing round familiar corners, she'd drive us up the hill beyond the industrial estate and into the woods. Then we'd climb up to the ridge and set off northwards through open fields and across farmyards, through hedges, over fences, whatever. Mary was a powerhouse. Striding along with her hands linked behind her back and her shoulders pushed slightly forward, she'd just go on and on. Sometimes we'd do ten miles and more. You needed good shoes. The dogs would be exhausted. I lost quite a few pounds. It was fantastic.

And she knew so much about everything. She could tell you a million things about local history, about nutrition, health, exercise. And about dogs. She pointed out to me that Donna had a problem with her hips and told me I should get it seen to, but I really didn't have the cash to start expensive stuff with the vet. When we got back, just before lunch or just before dinner, she liked to go for a drink, maybe in the garden behind the Torrington. An aperitif, she called it. Usually sparkling wine. Sometimes a martini. She was always happy to offer. With crisps or nibbles, anything would do. In the teeth of everything she said about diet. Sometimes, laughing, she'd ask if I'd roll a cigarette for her. She used to smoke long ago, she said, though it didn't look that way when she puffed on my Golden Virginia. She looked like a kid playing with cigarettes for the first time, making elegant gestures with her hands and pouting her lips to blow the smoke here and there. Coughing. Then maybe bursting out laughing. You couldn't help but love her.

I think she wanted someone to look after. Maybe because the kids had grown up. Certainly she always showed a helpful interest in the shit I was going through at the time. I was seeing a lawyer about my ex who was refusing to give me my share of the flat we'd bought years ago, and that he was still living in. Mary talked me through the options every which way; also whether I should move in with Brad. She was very sharp about men, though it was a bit confusing how she'd swing from super-romantic to super-pessimistic: how beautiful it was being in love and having children and what shits men were when they ignored you for years and betrayed you with some young scrubber then tried to chuck you away like an old yoghurt pot. We laughed about it, but I realised she had her own troubles. She didn't talk about them. She wasn't a blab-bermouth, or after sympathy.

Sometimes she'd bring her boy along on the walks. Mark. I liked him a lot. He had a quiet, laconic sense of humour. The problem was, he really wasn't up for these giant walks. He kept complaining, saying no one had said how long we'd be out for, how far we'd have to walk. And no one had mentioned that there was no mobile signal up in the hills. He needed to send a message to someone. He felt cut off. 'For God's sake, cheer up,' Mary cried, 'the walking's good for you! Keeps you fit.' Whenever her son was pissed off, that was when Mary most fizzed with fun and energy. I felt a bit sorry for the boy. He was trying to pluck up courage to leave a girlfriend. These things aren't easy, especially the first time. When I asked him why he came along if he didn't want to, he said he found it hard to say no.

Mary was enthusiastic about me and Brad living together. She had this thing that all women should have children, though she couldn't understand what I could see in a guy twenty years older. Why not someone my age? But the fact was I got along pretty well with Brad. It was always good to be with him. I knew we would be happy. Then I didn't have much time left for changing men, if I was going to be a mother. The only headache was, I told her, that I needed all the space I had to make my dresses. I design and make dresses, super quirky dresses, with odd materials of every kind. Once a month I load them in the van and take them down to London to sell in Camden Market. If Brad moved in, there would be nowhere to work and nowhere to store all the stuff I need.

'Take a room in our house,' she said. 'Store your stuff in the garage. It's big enough.'

At first I could hardly believe she was offering me this. It seemed too generous. She wasn't asking for any rent or anything.

'Mark likes you,' she said. 'And Ricky loves Donna. It's good having someone around. Why not?'

That was the first time I realised her husband wasn't living at home. Or not always. Sometimes he was there at the weekend. The rest of the time he was in town. It was an uneasy situation. I could see everyone was on edge about it. I thought they should sort themselves out, frankly, decide where they were going and get on with it, though it was hardly up to me to say anything. Once I drove her husband – he was called Tom – to the station when he was heading back to town. At the station he asked me to roll a fag for him exactly the way Mary did. He smoked hungrily and you could see he was dying to start again. 'You're divorced, aren't you?' he asked. 'Was it hard?' 'Not as hard as giving up smoking,' I laughed. 'I never managed that.'

'I'm the other way round,' he said. 'I can keep away from cigarettes most of the time, but I find it impossible to make the final break with home.'

I told him that from the moment I walked out on Roger, nothing on earth would have induced me to go back. Not for five milliseconds. Ever. I closed the door behind me and never spoke to him again, never answered his emails, never accepted his phone calls. I did take Donna with me, though.

We were drinking a coffee at the tables outside Costa, since he had half an hour before his train. When I said this he went quiet for a while, concentrating on his cigarette. Then, stubbing it out, he said he admired my strength, but he found it very sad to have spent a long part of your life with someone and never to see them again, lose all the positive things there had been between you. 'Damn right it was sad,' I said. 'But not as sad as living with Roger had been.'

He laughed out loud and shook his head and asked me questions about Mark. He missed Mark, he said.

Brad moved in with me and I took all my work stuff over to Mary's place and set up my sewing machine and other tools in the bedroom her grown-up daughter had once used. It was full of school textbooks and sports trophies and a million old CDs. I must have listened to all of them over the months. She gave me a key to the house too. It was pretty incredible. I worked really well there. The light was great. I brought Donna and left her in the garden with Ricky, or kept both of them beside me while I worked. Dogs are good company. What Mary did meantime, I'm not quite sure. Sometimes she was out with Ricky. Most days she went swimming. Or to Pilates. She was doing some freelance stuff too, she said, with advertising companies, though I never asked what exactly. I reckoned most of the money came from the husband. The fact is you could never tell how much money Mary had. She was very generous. And there was a woman who came to clean twice a week. On the other hand she was always saving on everything. She bought the food on offer at the supermarket. The heating was always turned down low, or just plain off. I didn't complain.

I had tea and a snack with Mark most afternoons when he got back from school. It was fun talking to a teenager. He was going through a big self-esteem crisis, with not being able to fire his girlfriend. I guess the situation with his parents didn't help. I told him not to be hard on himself. It doesn't help. To be honest, I had started to feel more comfortable with Mark than with Mary, and I think Mary guessed this, because sometimes there was a sort of tension in the air if Mary got back when we were chatting.

I headed upstairs to finish my work. In the end, if Mary was nearly twenty years older than me, I was nearly twenty years older than Mark. So maybe it was natural I felt the same things for him that Mary felt for me. It was a nice kind of affection. But for some reason it confused things a bit when all three of us were together.

Then Mary asked me to drive her to France. I couldn't believe it really, couldn't believe the reasons for her going and couldn't believe she wanted me to go with her. It was like this: Mary had decided to go to Zambia for three months. She was going to do some volunteer charity work there – I never figured out exactly what or why she wanted to do this. As a result, there was the problem of what to do with Ricky. As she saw it, that is, because Mark didn't think there was a problem at all. Mark said he could look after him. He *wanted* to look after him. He loved Ricky. But Mary said he wouldn't be able to, he was out too much, he wasn't old enough or responsible enough, one day he would forget and the dog would go unfed or would be trapped in the house when he needed to get out. Mark protested, but Mary was determined. I said I was more than willing to help out. Mary said she couldn't burden me with her dog. I said it was only fair I gave a her a bit of time and help with all she was doing for me, letting me have the room and the storage space. She was making everything possible for me, I said, so I was really glad to feed the dog and take it out if need be.

Mary shook her head. Ricky was used to really long walks, she said. He was a special dog. She would feel guilty if she didn't have him properly cared for. The fact was, she had some French friends who now had a farm down in the Dordogne and a couple of dogs. She wanted to drive there and leave Ricky and the car with them. The problem was she didn't trust herself to drive such a long way on her own. She didn't get on with motorways, never mind French motorways. She would pay me for my time, she said, and the flight home. She would fly on to Zambia from Paris. I thought it would be a good opportunity to take some samples with me and show them around the markets in Paris. I had never been to Paris. So I said yes.

Weird trip. We had a place booked for the Tunnel, but Mary insisted on leaving so early that we arrived almost three hours before our slot and wasted more time hanging around the miserable little centre they have there than we would have lost using the ferry at half the price. Mary was pretty nervous, I think, but determined to be jolly, like we were girls on holiday, then worried the dog would get sick, or not have enough water to drink, or the border control people would stop us because the vaccination papers weren't in order. It was amazing how many things Mary could think of to worry about. In the end Ricky was absolutely fine, snoozing away on the back seat, but since Mary didn't like the kind of music I like, we ended up sitting in silence or listening to news stations on the radio. In French. I drove the whole way.

In Paris we shared a room in a cheap hotel that accepted dogs and she took me out to eat and the next day she took me round all the sights – the Tower, the Louvre, Notre-Dame. She knew the city amazingly well. It seemed her French was really good. She talked to everybody, button-holed people at bus stops and on the *Métro*, chattering away. I didn't understand a thing. In the evening we had to trail around to find a bistro that didn't mind dogs, but we finally found one. Ricky lay on the floor beside Mary. She had this routine of getting him to do things like sit up and touch his nose on the palm of her hand, or first his nose, then one front paw, then the other front paw, then his nose again. After which, to reward him, she popped something in his mouth. Usually she kept biscuits or some special kind of doggie treats in her coat pocket, but tonight she'd run out of them, so she started cutting tiny pieces of meat from her steak. She must have fed him half her dinner, which wasn't cheap. But the dog was so happy and cheerful, it felt like it was worth it. Ricky was one of those dogs that give you the impression they are always smiling.

Then Mary wanted to go for a second bottle of Sauvignon. She'd been getting me to eat typically French things – pâté, duck – and talking ten to the dozen about when she was a student, boyfriends she'd had, how she used to stay out all night to drink and dance then be in her lessons at nine and still get great grades.

I said I'd drunk enough.

'Come on, Julie!' she laughed. 'You're only young once, let's go for it.'

So I had to tell her I was pregnant. I'd just heard for sure the day before we travelled. 'Fantastic!' Mary cried. She thought that was fantastic and she started talking me through all the tests and stuff I'd have to do and all the preparations, and giving me stories about her own pregnancies and telling me to take gynaecologists with a pinch of salt because they often tried to scare you, just to make you do tests in their private clinics.

'But why didn't you tell me right away?' she asked.

I shrugged. I didn't really know why I hadn't told Mary.

'I suppose I still haven't got used to it myself,' I said.

She laughed and said yes this was a huge change in my life, and then she persuaded me to have one more glass anyway and said how much she was looking forward to having grandchildren herself. It would be great to have a new baby around, she said, without having to actually produce it yourself. She laughed and poured. She'd ordered a half-litre carafe. Mary really was a fantastic person to be with.

Then I asked her why she was going to Africa like this when she was so attached to her children and the dog. I couldn't understand it.

Mary frowned and sighed. She called the waiter again and ordered sweets. Something I just had to try, she said. It was called *Poire belle Hélène*. She made me pronounce it twice.

'So what does that mean?'

'Pear beautiful Helen,' she said. 'Beautiful Helen pear. Pears poached in syrup, basically. The French are good at this stuff. Trust them to put pears next to Helen of Troy.'

'Sounds sexy,' I laughed.

Then Mary said she was going on this voluntary service because she had to do something with her life. The kids had grown up. Her husband was always busy and away. She needed to prove to herself that she could still be useful and positive.

She spoke offhand, but her voice sounded brittle. She had drunk more than she usually did. I felt a bit sorry for her.

'You should leave him,' I told her. 'Kick him out. Or force him either to stay or go. One thing or the other.'

Mary smiled. She said I didn't understand. It was a long and complicated relationship, she said. 'A bit like a Gothic castle, with parts that are still liveable and parts that crumbled to ruin ages ago, and very likely parts with skeletons in every cupboard, and for sure a ghost or two in the cellars or the attic. Not to mention the secret passages! And the rats behind the tapestries!'

She tried to laugh about it. She needed to get away for a while, she said. It would be good to be doing something useful for other people. Africa was the only continent she had never visited at all. It would be fascinating.

'He's shifty,' I told her. I tried at last to be completely frank with her. 'I mean, he's a nice enough bloke, but you can see he wants out. It's written all over his face. You should go to his place in town,' I suggested, 'and challenge him. You should find out what he's doing there. A man doesn't find a place away from home unless he has another woman. That would settle it. Go there and have it out with him.'

The Beautiful Helen pear arrived and Mary did a lot of oohing and aahing over it. She didn't want to think about Tom, she said. 'What are you going to call the baby? Do you want a boy or a girl?'

Later, when we were in bed in the hotel room about to fall asleep, she told me, 'The important thing is, don't give up your career for the baby. I was too generous. Then you're left high and dry.'

The following day we drove down to this farm in the Dordogne and then Mary's friends took me to the station in Limoges and I went back to Paris to hawk my stuff round a couple of shops and markets. Mary had spent the whole drive fussing over the dog. She seemed distant, as if she really didn't like what had been said in the restaurant. She didn't want to go back there. By the time I flew home she was on her way out to Zambia.

Those three months were perfect. I took Donna over to their house every day and made my dresses. Business was going well. I'd had the smart idea of ripping out printed circuit boards from old computers and building them into the clothes I was making – on the sleeves, or the belt, or round the hems of a skirt – and people were really going for it. A shop in Manchester had agreed to take them on a regular basis. So I was finally earning enough to live, feeling almost comfortable, and the pregnancy wasn't giving me any morning sickness either. On the contrary, it was a pleasure. I kept Mark a bit of company in the afternoon. We talked about music and clothes and I made a really wacky jacket for him. He loved it and even went to college in it a few times. He was at art college now. When his scooter was out of action, or it was raining, I would give him lifts here and there, since their place was really off the beaten track. I picked up his dad a couple of times from the station too when he came to visit, though I couldn't roll him a cigarette now because with the pregnancy I'd finally stopped smoking.

'From one day to the next, I just stopped.'

'I'm all admiration,' he said.

Towards the end of the three months Mark finally managed to fire his girlfriend. We had an impromptu party that day. He was so pleased with himself. Brad came over after work with some beer and there were a couple of friends of his as well. It was quite a party, thinking back, and also maybe a party to mark the end of this little period of independence. In any event, I was really getting fond of Mark, like he was a little brother, and feeling really lucky to have met Mary in the dog park that day, when she came back from Zambia and told me I'd have to get out of the house with all my stuff as soon as possible.

Fair do's. I could hardly complain. I'd had a free ride for nearly a year. But it threw me. I wasn't expecting it. While she was away Mary had been posting a lot of stuff on Facebook. Descriptions of the school where she was working. Stacks of photos of the girls she was teaching to read and write. Pictures of her surrounded by little black kids, or by their mums wearing colourful traditional clothes. That kind of thing. I didn't really look at it very hard but it seemed to me she was having a good time and would come back positive and cheerful and maybe we could fly over to France again and bring Ricky back in the car. Instead Mary said the dog could stay with her friends. She didn't want it back. She was through with dogs. And since the car we'd driven to France was her husband's he could go over there and fetch it himself if he wanted it back. It seems Tom had taken advantage of her long absence to make up his mind at last. He had asked for a divorce.

'I have to sell the house,' she told me. 'That means I need it looking clean and empty, to show people. You'll have to move your stuff out, I'm afraid.'

Which I did. It was a nightmare, with all the orders and deadlines I had on hand, but in the end it was for the best, because it forced me to hire a commercial space and get serious and then bring in an assistant to help me. I fell on my feet. At least in practical terms. On another level, though, I couldn't understand it. I felt I'd been really welcomed into the family, I was part of it, and now suddenly I was out in the cold. Not that Mary was unkind, because she really wasn't. She was always wonderful to me. Just that with not having the dog there were no walks to go on, no reason to see Mark, no reason to go out for drinks together. I mean, we did have a drink a couple of times, but Mary was really distracted, her face was set, like she really wasn't looking at the things around us at all. So a big part of my life was suddenly blown away, and to be honest, the more I thought about it all, the more I felt the whole thing from beginning to end had been a kind of mystery, or spell. I'd got mixed up in someone else's world, thinking it was solid, when it was even more precarious than mine. I hadn't understood anything about Mary. Mark, I understood, and we did meet again a few times and he was friendly. But he had a new girlfriend and didn't have much time for anyone else. Even Tom I thought I understood, though I'd only seen him half a dozen times and never saw him again. But the more I thought about Mary, the less I understood what had happened between us. For a while I made a point of walking Donna up the hill, past their house. They hadn't sold it. Perhaps they'd stopped even trying because the For Sale sign had been taken down. Fortunately it was only a matter of months before Bradley junior was born. I thought of driving out there to show him off to Mary, but in the end decided better not.

MONEY

They met on student grants. But she had more than he did. She had won a scholarship. To him it seemed like a lot more, perhaps because she spent so generously. When first she came to visit him in his college room she brought champagne and fancy cakes. She dressed fancily too, in a gauzy blue dress wafting perfume. In fact the difference wasn't that great. It was just that his parents had taught him to feel poor.

This was Durham, 1978. To save money their first summer together he arranged a house-sit and invited her to join him. After a couple of weeks, the house owner's daughter turned up, saw them in their underwear in the living room, and reported it to her parents, who invited them to leave. So they found a little place in town on Chapel Hill Street. It wasn't expensive, being on the fourth floor without a lift. Actually, she found it. And she paid the rent, though he contributed. There never seemed to be any real difficulty with money between them. She bought good fresh food to cook. He made sure there was beer. They never ate out. It was too expensive. But they enjoyed cafés. Even now he can't remember any arguments about money. Was there some suspicion that he was being bought? Never. It was part of who she was to overwhelm a new friend with gifts. She introduced him to martinis and brandy, she made presents of nice sweaters and shirts. It seemed more impulsive than manipulative. He felt pampered.

Yet she was always practical with money. She knew how much things should cost. She knew when to complain if a bill seemed too high. She knew how to get a phone installed in a flat, what a landlord should provide and what a tenant should pay for. At twenty-three she was already an adult with money, while he was still a child eking out pocket money. Perhaps her knowledge prolonged his innocence. He began to rely on her. They argued about other things, but over money they were fine.

When he found a first job in Manchester she followed and they rented a bedsit in Moss Side. In fact the bed folded up into the wall and the toilet was shared with two other flats. Now he paid the rent, from his salary. He had a salary. Yet there was still this feeling that it was her money that made life sweet. Or the way she spent money. She bought the right quilt for the bed, the right curtains, the right fruit, the right chocolates, the right wine. All slightly outside his range. They decided to marry.

She was working now, for a magazine publisher. When her parents came to stay a week before the wedding she found a service flat for them right on Quay Street. This seemed as grand to him as their Moss Side bedsit seemed downmarket to her. At once there was a money embarrassment. He had bought a second-hand car at the cheapest possible price. The old owner had fooled him and it had worked for just three or four days before turning into a complete lemon. Driving her parents the few hundred yards from station to flat it broke down in heavy rain. She hailed a taxi. He felt pretty stupid.

Now her father insisted on a proper suit for the ceremony. He had never owned a proper suit. They went to a shop on Deansgate. Same thing with the wedding ring. He must have a good ring. 'If I want brass, I know where to get it,' her father famously said in his strong Glasgow accent when the jeweller showed them an 18-carat item. This was to be his gift, the older man said, only he didn't have the cash with him at the moment. So for both suit and ring, the bridegroom paid with a cheque. Back home, she laughed about her father, who was such an old fraud and would never pay. Thomas felt anxious at having spent so much, but proud too. As if unloading all that money had made him more mature.

To save on the wedding reception, his parents organised it for them in their vicarage home. They loved to save. His father, a clergyman, would marry them. It would cost nothing. At his wedding he felt like a boy whose life was being organised by others. During the reception it turned out that his parents had booked them into a hotel on the

North Welsh coast for the weekend, as if they had never lived together and this was their first night. It was raining and they were tired and didn't really want to go, and when they arrived the hotel was hosting a Saturday night disco and the music throbbed into the small hours. She seemed upset and wanted only to sleep. He lay awake. Was she angry, he wondered, because he would never spend what needed to be spent to be comfortable? As they were returning to Manchester on the Monday the exhaust fell off the car on the motorway and they drove the last ten miles in a deafening roar.

But how much money they made over the next twenty years! How much quiet toil and determination on both sides! How much saving and judicious spending! Moving from town to town, climbing the career ladder, discussing bonuses, company cars, pension funds. And always heading for the cheapest place to buy petrol, for the bank with the best mortgage deal. It was she who found the big house in Pendlebury. She negotiated the price. He was happy with that. The money side of their relationship worked perfectly. Everything else fell apart. Ten years after moving in, Thomas betrayed her in that house.

Now after two children and twenty-five years they are going to divide it all. Everything they have built together will be put asunder. His power is absolute now. He declares over £100,000. She less than £10,000. He is still cheap and lives on next to nothing in his bedsit in Liverpool. She still likes quality things and gives generously to the children.

Now a lawyer is trying to divide the properties they own and the money in the bank. And of course to establish who is responsible for the second child in his last year at school.

These are not happy times. The emails fly back and forth. They no longer talk on the phone. The lawyer is copied in. They use a single lawyer because Thomas refuses to be conflictual. He refuses to fight his corner. He's not man enough. Without an income, or a pension, having stayed home to bring up the children, she foresees a pauper's future. The lawyer makes fresh proposals. She has further requests, further revisions. They are detailed. He makes further concessions. When she makes still more requests, the lawyer threatens to bail out. Now it occurs to Thomas that the real relationship was always this: the different way each of them had of relating to money. And so long as the negotiation grinds on, they are still married in a way. In the end and despite all the tension, they haven't really argued yet. Not properly. They haven't really fought over money. Thomas wonders if he will ever grow up. He wonders if perhaps the day he signs the first maintenance cheque he will feel adult at last.

TOUGH CHOICES

Life always hits us with tough choices and we waste energy getting anxious over the decisions we make. If only we could know what was the right thing to do and do it, everything would be so much easier. So Thomas took ten years and more to make the decision to leave his wife and even after he made this decision he wasn't sure he'd made it, because now there was the question, should he go back to her? You would have thought ten years was enough to know you had jumped the right way, but the point his wife made was that it was precisely his leaving that had forced them both to make the changes in heart that made his coming back feasible. If he had left her earlier on, she said, without waiting so long, they would now already be back together and set to enjoy a mellow old age in each other's company. In his fifties at this point, Thomas felt guilty, thinking that by not acting sooner he had made things worse. His wife was right. On the other hand, he wasn't yet convinced that going back to her would make them better. Nor was he ready for a mellow old age. For a while he tried to go back at weekends and sleep in the marital bed again, then realised he was only doing this to correct any wrong he had done, certainly not because he wanted to. He didn't. There and then, it seemed an important distinction. But it is also important to correct the wrongs you have done. His wife talked a great deal about having understood at last what were the important things in life. Neither of them had been perfect, she admitted, but now the thing was to knuckle down and work at it, not run away. Thomas enjoyed the luxuries of his old home, in particular the fireplace, the garden, the well-stocked fridge, the comfortable sitting room. Even the dog. They made a stark contrast to his drab, poky town flat. He especially enjoyed being around his adolescent son, Mark, though the boy could be hard work sometimes and it was depressing seeing him wasted on a loser of a girl-friend and doing poorly at school; still, as his wife pointed out, this was no doubt largely to do with the boy's loss of self-esteem and confidence in life, consequent on his father's abandoning his family. The implication was, then, that by coming back Thomas would not only be righting the wrong he had done his wife by leaving it so late to leave her that their new awareness of the important things in life had come too late to bring joy to their mellow old age, but also that his return would bolster his son's self-esteem to the point that he would be able to fire his below par girlfriend and improve his exam results at college, developments which could hardly fail to cheer Thomas up. It was a lot to be heaping on the getting-back-together side of the scales and you might have expected it would be decisive, except that the enormous relief Thomas felt on returning to his flat in Liverpool on the Monday after a weekend in Pendlebury also seemed pretty damn weighty. If not massive. It would be great, Thomas thought, to act responsibly in his son's regard, and his wife's, but it would also be irresponsible not to recognise that there were powerful feelings pushing him the other way. When Thomas now made a sideways movement inviting his son to go on holiday with him for a weekend, his wife wrote an email to say that he should definitely use this time alone with him to clarify once and for all why he had abandoned them. He should explain to his son, she told him, that she (the wife/mother) was only too eager to open her arms to him again and that it was he who hadn't yet found the generosity and courage to go that extra mile. This message actually gave Thomas the rare pleasure of feeling he was probably doing the right thing, though now he wondered whether he was really duty-bound to broach the question with his son as his wife had asked. Eventually, over dinner, he mentioned it in passing – 'Your mother asked me to clear this up' – mostly because he was concerned that if he didn't his wife would quiz his son on his return and, finding he hadn't said anything, would accuse him of cowardice. His son, however, said he had no desire to talk about it; he had seen how things had gone, he said.

He wasn't blind. 'The one thing I hate about you,' he added bluntly, 'is that you won't tell me anything about your life in Liverpool. So,' he asked point-blank, 'do you have someone or not?' Thomas was eating sushi. 'I can't be entirely candid about my life,' he told his son, 'until things are settled with your mother.' The last thing he wanted, he said, was to invite him to be custodian of his secrets. 'Things will never be settled with Mum,' his son said. 'Maybe they will be *more* settled,' Thomas returned and insisted he didn't have another woman. Though there was someone he liked, he added cautiously. On returning to his flat after this weekend away he found an email from his wife mentioning that their daughter needed urgent financial help, and another including a photograph of the family as they had been three Christmases ago, which she had found while transferring files from her old PC to her Apple. Thomas phoned his girlfriend. 'I need a drink,' he told her. She said fine and they spent the night together. In the end Thomas was very happy with his life in Liverpool and his girlfriend was happy with him; all the same, over the coming months, he continued to work at worrying and making himself unhappy, occasionally going home at weekends, or taking his son away for weekends, and generally imagining he hadn't yet quite taken a decision that actually life had taken for him more than a decade before.

REVEREND

After his mother died, Thomas started thinking about his father. All too frequently, while she was dying, there had been talk of her going to meet him in paradise, returning to the arms of her husband of thirty-two years, who had died thirty years before she did. This would be bliss.

Thomas did not believe in such things, of course, though it was hard not to try to imagine them, if only to savour the impossibility of the idea: the two insubstantial souls greeting each other in the ether, the airy embrace. She had been ninety at death, he sixty. There would be some adjustment for that, presumably, in heaven. The madness of it confirmed one's scepticism.

But even assuming that she had gone to meet him, who was he? Who was he now? And if she hadn't and there are no such meetings, who had he been? Who was my father? thought Thomas. Other people spoke well of him. Quite recently, taking advantage of the Internet, a cousin had been in touch, his father's younger sister's son, Hugh. For some reason they had only ever met once before, when Hugh was just a baby. Now in his late forties, this cousin had paid a visit to Thomas's mother three months before she died. By chance, Thomas was also visiting that day. And almost the first thing the cousin did was speak warmly of the dead man. He helped me, the cousin said. He was kind to me. When and how wasn't clear. Perhaps the cousin only said this to please Thomas's mother.

Why was Thomas asking himself these questions now? he wondered. That wasn't clear. They weren't exactly urgent. On the other hand, they weren't going away. He didn't feel like doing research, putting his father's name into Google or hunting through archives. He could have looked at his father's old sermon notes. Thomas's sister had taken some papers when their mother's house was sold after the funeral. The notes would have told him something, reminded him of his father's handwriting, of the way the man thought. But he didn't want to do that. The thought of his father's sermons aroused unpleasant emotions. It was difficult to put his finger on the reason. A sense of embarrassment and irritation. What he wanted, rather, was to assemble a picture of his father as he, Thomas, remembered him. Who was he for me? A son should be able to say what his father was for him. What part of my personality do I owe him? How does this man still simmer in my life? If he does.

Occasionally Thomas would tell himself that he regretted not having asked his mother more about his

229

father. It was surely the moment to have undertaken this reappraisal, while Mother was still alive, because when a person is gone, they really are gone, and a whole world with them. All her memories of Father were dead now. He could never access them.

Yet he knew he didn't really regret not asking her. The truth was that for all this chatter of her going to meet him in the beyond, for all her occasional tears when Father was mentioned, Thomas's mother had spoken very little of his father. Very little. Perhaps the only time his name could reliably be expected to come up was when Thomas and his mother argued over something, usually something of a religious or political nature. Thomas could be provocative, stubborn, and his mother never wanted to lose an argument about things that mattered. Then, between exasperation and amusement, she would say, 'You're just like your father, Thomas. He loved to play devil's advocate, too!'

How was this possible? His father had been a clergyman. Thomas couldn't remember the man expressing a single idea that went against orthodox Christianity. How could Mother remember him playing devil's advocate? Presumably, in their own private relationship, Father had liked to get her riled, flustered, indignant. And this had been partly, though perhaps not altogether, in fun. 'He loved to split hairs, just like you,' Thomas's mother said, shaking her grey head. She did not say which hairs Father had split, and Thomas had not asked her to expand. The effect of the remark, of course, was to make it seem that

Thomas had no real investment in what he was saying, but was just arguing for the sake of it, to irritate her. While that offered an easy way out of whatever discussion it was, it did feel rather unsatisfying.

The truth was, he hadn't wanted to talk about Father with Mother. On just one occasion, after cousin Hugh's unexpected reappearance he had said: 'Well, Mum, that's the first person I've seen from Dad's side of the family since I was a little kid.' And he had asked: 'Why didn't Dad talk about his family?' And his mother, who would have been sipping a glass of sherry before dinner, which was the only alcoholic drink she ever touched, shrugged her shoulders and said, 'I suppose he didn't have anything to say.'

Thomas hadn't pressed the matter, but it was strange now to reflect on these reluctances: his mother's to speak about his father, his father's to speak about his family, his own to challenge their reticence. Why hadn't Thomas thought of these things during her lifetime? It was not that he imagined there was some secret being hidden from him. It was more as though she wanted to keep the man to herself. Perhaps she had been afraid that speaking of Father to Thomas would diminish him. Because Father was so devout and Thomas such a doubter. Speaking about him might have given her son a chance to make some disparaging remark, or simply to show once again that he didn't believe. To rock the boat. That was a favourite expression of Father's: Don't rock the boat! In any event, she had kept whatever there was between them in her heart, to the end. In her bedroom there was a photo of Thomas's father as a young man, and resting on the glass frame below his face she had placed a small square of white paper with a few lines of religious poetry:

> *Death hides –*
> *But it cannot divide*
> *Thou art but on*
> *Christ's other side.*
> *Thou with Christ*
> *And Christ with me*
> *And so together*
> *Still are we.*

Thomas respected this carefully preserved bereavement. He didn't investigate. He knew that when the cancer had gone to his father's brain he had accused his mother of all kinds of unpleasant things and that this had upset her greatly. Never for one moment did Thomas imagine that there was any truth in those accusations. It was just that the cancer had gone to Dad's head. And who does one accuse, when accusing, if not one's wife of many years? Thomas knew plenty about that. It even occurred to him that he was thinking about his father now because, in separating from his own wife, he had undone, as it were, the last thing that his father had done as a clergyman, when he'd married them, Thomas and his wife, holding their ringed hands one above the other and declaring, 'Those whom God hath joined together, let no man put asunder.'

Recently, in preparation for the divorce, Thomas had had to dig out the marriage certificate with his father's signature on it. It seemed odd to think that his father's hand had pressed on that very paper so many years ago. His handwriting was scratched and sharp, but not without a certain angular elegance. Thomas examined the certificate for a few minutes, looking at his own signature, his wife's, his father's, then put it in an envelope with the other papers, ready for his divorce.

Whore. That was it. Just once his mother had talked about it. They had been talking about her cancer, he remembered. She was lucky, she said, because hers hadn't gone to her head. Like poor Dad's. Then she burst into tears and told Thomas that, in his madness before he died, Father had said all kinds of awful things; he had called her a whore. Shocked, Thomas immediately reassured his mother that it had been the disease speaking. She knew that. In his right mind Dad would never have said such a thing. Later Thomas realised that she had told him this in order to receive his reassurance before dying herself. Once reassured, she didn't tell him anything else.

Edward Paige was born in Liverpool, on the longest day of the year, in 1920. He had two sisters, one definitely younger. Perhaps both had been younger. Thomas could have asked his own brother or sister about this – they were older than he was, they might know – but he didn't want his brother and sister to know that he was thinking about his father. Why not? He didn't want to pool their collective memories. He didn't want to have to adjust his views in the light of their knowledge. Vaguely he was aware that Mother had spoken of Father being fond of Eleanor, the youngest sister, mother of the cousin who had appeared from the blue. But so far as he could recall, Father had never spoken of her. He had never spoken of his mother, either. All Thomas remembered, from perhaps two visits when he was very small, was a tiny old woman with white wispy hair and a hooked nose.

Was his father deliberately enigmatic? Edward Paige had talked once of his father, Thomas's grandfather. They were on holiday in South Devon, and Father had wanted to visit Plymouth Sound because his father's ship had been mothballed there during the Great Depression. Thomas's grandfather had been a ship's captain and Father had spent an unemployed summer with him on that ship, waiting for world commerce to start moving again. It must have been a happy time for him, because he got quite excited as they walked along the shore, pointing out where the ship had been and the landing stage they'd rowed to when they went ashore.

Thomas knew his grandfather had been called Ernest Holden because, at some point in his teens, with no comment from Father, a sort of certificate had appeared, framed, in the hallway of the house. It was a document from His Majesty's Government declaring that Ernest Holden Paige had given his life for his country, in action, in the Atlantic, 8th June 1941. Thomas had the impression that his father had wanted to become a seaman, too, but had been held back by his poor eyesight. His sight was so poor that neither the army nor the air force had accepted him. He couldn't even get a driver's licence. So while his own hero father had fought submarines, Edward worked in Cammell Laird shipyard, doing technical drawings for marine engines. One of the happiest stories Father liked to tell was about how he was admired for his ability to hit rats with a paperweight in the shipyard workshops. It was strange to think that he couldn't join the navy or drive a car, but could see well enough to draw and to hit rats with paperweights.

Father had never spoken of his reasons for becoming a clergyman. But Thomas did know that his father and mother had initially planned to be missionaries. They had met at missionary training college. They had wanted an adventurous life. It was 1948; they had lived through a war, but only on the edge of the action. She had been bombed in London, he in Liverpool. Her father had forbidden her to join the Wrens. His father had been disappointed that his son couldn't enlist. Now they would fight the good fight another way.

Thomas's parents' marriage, he realised now – and realised that, without being aware, he had always known this – was based on a religious mission. They were partners in a task: to make the world a better place, converting people to the faith. That was the logic of their being together. If either of them were to lose this faith, their marriage would be lost with it. Wouldn't it? Their life was a life in the Church, for the Church, though, for reasons that hadn't been explained, they hadn't in the end become missionaries. Perhaps having produced children made them less eligible. The Church didn't want to be responsible for little white children in Uganda or Indonesia. Maybe we children blocked Father's career, Thomas thought. We frustrated his ambitions. First the eyesight problem, then his children. He remembered the man's impatience. His father had no time for chatter. Sometimes he barely took time to eat. He was impatient with Mother, too, impatient to be doing. But doing what? Winning souls for Christ. How strange. And how disappointing for him, then, to have failed first and foremost with two of the three souls under his nose, Thomas and his older brother.

He took our salvation for granted, Thomas thought.

Once he had decided to make the effort, it didn't take Thomas long to gather these thoughts and type them on his computer. If only because there were so few. Thomas was living in a small flat now, in Liverpool, away from his wife, in Pendlebury, away from his children, who were grown up. They no longer needed him for protection. Only for financial support. Yet he did not feel he had really got away. It was as if he had left home to climb a mountain and was now stuck halfway up, bivouacked above the treeline, free, but freezing, with no way forward and no way back. Thomas was perplexed. His wife was down in the warm pastures waiting for him. So it seemed. But he wouldn't go back. It was in this period that his mother died and he began to think about his father.

There were memories of infancy and memories of adolescence. There were two or three incidents that seemed important. Watershed moments. During Thomas's early childhood, his father had seemed busy and happy. He preached and led meetings. First in Manchester, then in Blackpool. He was charismatic and embattled. He liked a fight. His voice was vibrant. He made jokes. He was a leader. People came to him for advice. At breakfast and lunch and dinner, he said grace. In the evening, before bed, he said prayers. They were fervent, earnest prayers, the prayers of someone going to heaven, or to hell. He wasn't interested in empty, formal religion. He liked his lamb and his roast beef, his plum pie and his custard. But he was always impatient to be up and doing again. Thomas distinctly remembered his father thrusting his chair back and wiping gravy from his mouth with a white napkin. People said 'serviette' then. His father had had a rather slack mouth, poor teeth, but he was always clean shaven. He was always ready to be meeting people. To be saving their souls. Thomas could actually see the gravy stain on the crumpled napkin as his father hurried off.

But he couldn't see his father's face. Thomas tried and tried, but he couldn't quite see it. In the small flat he lived in now, he kept no photos of the past. He had no family heirlooms. What had Father looked like? A thin handsome nose, definitely; sandy hair, but receding;

grey-green eyes, very thick spectacles. Father was endlessly cleaning his spectacles, usually with a huge white handkerchief. Thomas could see the vigorous action of the hands rubbing the lenses with the cloth. But he couldn't put eyes and nose together. He couldn't remember looking into those eyes, or them looking into his. The handkerchief was in the way.

Father's body was easier. Thomas remembered an aura of vulnerability, at once wiry and hunched, tense. But not intimidated. When the family moved from Manchester to Blackpool, Father took the children swimming in the sea. He wasn't afraid of cold water. From being a tense, impatient man in study or pulpit, he had explosions of physical activity. He ran across the ribbed sand, puffing and calling. He didn't keep fit, but rode a bike to visit parishioners. At the church, they hated him because he had banned the annual crowning of the May Queen. It was paganism, he said; it had nothing to do with Our Lord Jesus Christ and his message of joy and salvation. He hadn't become a clergyman to perpetuate pagan rituals and crown pretty girls. There had been a lot of bad feeling when the May Queen was banned, but Thomas was young then and Father had seemed very confident and pleased with himself.

Once Father took Thomas to a holiday camp with some boys from a reform school. That was frightening. They were wild. They jumped off swings in motion to see who could leap the furthest. They yelled swear words and made rude gestures. Some of them had been sent to the school for robbery or violence. Father didn't seem to have any trouble talking to these boys or saving their souls. Perhaps he felt it was missionary work. He felt fulfilled. If Thomas had sworn or put up two fingers, Dad would have been furious.

It was also scary when Father talked about death and burials. There was a story about a coffin that floated in the muddy water after a storm and another that had to be forced down into the grave because it was too long. The corpse had been a giant. In the end, Dad and the sexton had had to stand on the coffin to get it underground and even then they buried it at a 45-degree angle. It seemed strange to Thomas that his father could laugh at death. It seemed strange when he changed from his ordinary clothes into his robes, the long black cassock and starched white surplice, when he raised his arms outwards and upwards at the end of the blessing, so that he was like an angel, to be gathered into heaven. 'May the Lord bless you and keep you!' His voice rang around the brown stones of the church. 'May the Lord cause his face to shine upon you!' Later, the same man would chase Thomas and his brother back to bed if they crept down the stairs to spy on guests. 'Scallywags!' he yelled. Sometimes he got seriously angry with Thomas's brother and spanked him. 'I will have the last word,' he said. 'I will thrash the stubbornness out of you.' It was frightening. But reassuring, too, in a way. Certainly it was not that memory that made Thomas sad when he thought about his father. Thomas had never been spanked, that he could recall. I was the good boy, he realised. Or the shrewd one.

When Thomas was nine or ten, his father had had a breakdown. Nervous breakdown was the expression they used then. It was Sunday and he had been due to preach. The moment had come to go up into the pulpit, but he had been unable to. He had had to go home. Perhaps the pagan people of Blackpool had finally got the better of him. Afterwards, Thomas's family had gone on the longest holiday they ever took together. A month in Devon. That was the time they went to see where Dad's father had mothballed his ship in Plymouth Sound. Thomas remembered how strange the idea had seemed: mothballing a ship in a depression. They had stayed in an abandoned zoo of all things, sleeping in old animal houses that had been converted into holiday cabins. It was the only time Thomas had met his father's other sister, Elizabeth. She came with her husband, who smoked and drank beer from cans. Thomas's parents disapproved. He had a tent made out of an army parachute from the war and he did not go to church. Thomas remembered the fabric of that tent, a very light brown and green, very soft and thin. Why had his father and mother gone on holiday with the sister he never spoke of, on that one occasion, the time Dad had been unable to go into the pulpit to preach? Why did they never go on holiday with them again?

There had been one occasion in Thomas's life when he had been unable to go into a meeting at work. Like his father, he had been in his late forties. He had had to say he was ill. It was after a girlfriend left him. That was the first time he betrayed his wife. He was in love with this girl-friend, but he could not imagine leaving his family, so after a while she left him. Then Thomas was so overcome with unhappiness that he had not gone into work one morning but had walked to her house, the house she had a room in, and stood in the street looking up at the window. It did not help. He saw no way forward.

Soon after Father's breakdown and that famous holiday with the visit to Plymouth Sound, they had left Blackpool and moved to Bristol. This was one of the watersheds and, looking back, Thomas realised that his memories of Father from this time on were different, rather sadder. The expression 'new challenge' had been used. Thomas heard the words again now without quite knowing who had said them. Dad had been given a new challenge: a big church in a thriving well-to-do Bristol suburb. People in high places believed in him. He was a man who needed to give energy where energy would be well received. An evangel-ical cannot thrive in a world of May Queens. Or not for long.

At school, Thomas had to drop his northern accent to avoid being laughed at. Did Father have to change his accent in the pulpit? To suit the good folk of Clifton? Thomas had no recollection. Thinking about this now, he found it odd. Life had slipped by unnoticed. Or perhaps he, Thomas, at ten years old, had been so focused on his new life, the need to make new friends, the new vicarage with the big garden and the bus to school, that he had barely noticed his father, who went on preaching in much the same way, it seemed to Thomas, albeit from a different pulpit.

Did he have any recollection of talking to Father, one-on-one, through his adolescence, about anything that mattered? Girls, sex, religion, smoking, drinking? He did not. He really didn't. What Thomas did remember, though, was the growing antagonism between his father and his brother, and his father's frustration with his sister's failure at school. He remembered these things because they had caused him pain. His sister was a good Christian, but not smart. One day, she had run away from school because she couldn't face her teachers. Father was angry with her. She locked herself in the bathroom, and he banged on the door with his fists. 'You shall come out!' Mother tried to mediate, but she was shocked, too: they hadn't expected this of his sister. Meantime, his brother grew his hair long, smoked, smoked dope, drank, had inappropriate girlfriends and listened to evil music. But he did well in school and could beat Father at chess, which was not easy. Thomas could not beat Father at chess. Not once.

Thomas saw clearly now how his father had failed to see things clearly then. He had failed to accept that his daughter was not going to do well at school and that his son was not going to be a staunch Christian. He had allowed these entirely ordinary developments to frustrate him beyond measure. He had castigated himself. He saw the failings as his own, because it was unthinkable that they could be God's. Still, Thomas did well enough at school and toed the line at church. He was sent to a school some miles away, to keep him from his brother's evil influence. And he kept away. His behaviour was exemplary. Thomas did not smoke or listen to psychedelic music and, when he swore, it was out of the earshot of parents and sister.

Yet even Thomas was not quite what his father wanted. He preferred literature to the sciences and Father was convinced that the truth lay in the sciences; the sciences and theology. Everything else was wishy-washy humanism. At church, Thomas was more obedient than fervent. He went to church only because he would feel guilty if he didn't. He would feel he had let his parents down. Of course, he would have preferred it himself if he had felt fervent about church. He would have liked to like his duties. It would have been such a relief. But, try as he might, he didn't.

All this was in the air, but never talked about. Father could hardly complain, because there was objectively nothing in Thomas's behaviour to complain about. Father could confront Thomas's sister when she hid in the bathroom instead of going to school. He could confront Thomas's brother when he was caught smoking at his bedroom window or when he started to paint pictures of naked women and said he wanted to go to art college. For better or for worse, there was a relationship there; there was heat. Father would bang on the bathroom door; he would shout. Sometimes he would even strike Thomas's brother, then afterwards he'd be fearfully friendly, because he had overdone it. He would embrace him, and Thomas's sister, too.

But there was nothing he could shout at Thomas about. So, in a way, Thomas didn't have a relationship with his father, as the others did. Now that he thought about it, Thomas could not remember a single conversation with his father throughout his teens. Nothing. Not a single exchange of any import or intimacy at all. When he had found that verse in the Bible, 'I know thy works, that thou art neither cold nor hot', he knew the words were meant for him. His father was a hot man. His balding dome flamed with colour when anger got the better of him. His brother was a cool customer: 'Temper temper,' he needled their sister. But Thomas was neither. 'So then because thou art lukewarm,' the Good Book said, 'I will spue thee out of my mouth.' That was how God felt about it. Mr Lukewarm, Thomas thought. I am Mr Lukewarm.

It was a Saturday evening now and Thomas was alone, sitting at his computer screen. It had been a pleasant enough day – he had gone swimming, shopping, had lunch with a friend. But now he began to feel anxious. Now he began to understand where all this was leading to, these reflections that he had avoided for thirty years. The truth was that although he had talked to a lawyer about divorce, although he had got the documents ready,

Thomas still hadn't quite done the deed. He saw that now. The thought of that final confrontation with his wife, the signing of the documents, pained him. You are marooned, Thomas told himself. Mothballed. For the depression.

He thought again of that rainy Saturday morning when, short of breath and nauseated, his father had led his youngest son in the awesome promise: With this ring . . . with this ring . . . I thee wed . . . I thee wed. First his father's voice, then his own, as they stood face to face at the bottom of the chancel steps. With my body . . . with my body . . . I thee worship . . . I thee worship. Thinking back now, it seemed to Thomas that it must have been the most intimate moment they had ever known. In the name of the Father . . . In the name of the Father . . . and of the Son . . . and of the Son. How old had Father been that day, the day before he was diagnosed with cancer, the day of the very last ceremony he would ever perform, not knowing it was the last? Fifty-nine. Dad had been fifty-nine. How old was Thomas now? Fifty-eight.

Thomas was electrified. This was what he had come back to his father for. To ask himself what the man's life had been like in his fifties, when the family melodrama was over and the decisive battle lost. But slowly does it. Put it all in order, Thomas thought, before jumping to conclusions. Go back. Back back back to adolescence.

The most memorable incident that had to do with his father, the most decisive watershed, was the Charismatic

Movement. His parents had at first resisted, then succumbed to the excitement. It must have been an evangelical version of the '68 aberration, the need for upheaval and change. Certainly, there was an American influence. Soon Mother and Father had taken to reading out 2 Corinthians 12 at every opportunity, Saint Paul's account of the Gifts of the Spirit: there were words of wisdom, gifts of healing, gifts of prophecy. Then, one Sunday morning, the curate raised his arms on the chancel steps and spoke in tongues. It sounded babbled and weird, and the man's face was ecstatic. This was the Baptism in the Spirit. Needless to say, many parishioners had been disgusted. Then Thomas had heard his father and his mother doing the same thing in their bedroom. Babbling. Then his father had declared in church that he believed in these gifts – it was the Renewal they had all been praying for – and he, too, had spoken in tongues from the chancel steps and raised his arms to heaven in ecstasy when singing a hymn. Thomas couldn't remember now which hymn. All hymns at the time had seemed painful to him, laden with sad sentiment, with some sticky emotion that held you back. To sing a hymn was to struggle through warm mud, to feel the impossibility of ever growing up and being free.

Very soon the pressure on the children began. They, too, must be baptised in the Spirit. They, too, must speak in tongues. It was never declared overtly, but it was obvious that if you weren't, if you didn't, then you couldn't be part of the inner fellowship, the core family. His sister got there in no time at all. In no time at all, she was babbling away and praising God and talking about the Latter Days. It made school exams seem rather less important. Thomas fudged it, of course. Thomas pretended he was on board, but mostly studied for his O levels. His parents wouldn't want to stop him studying. Would they? Thomas did try to see if he could speak in tongues – he might even have liked to, had it come naturally. With all the sincerity he could muster, he asked God for guidance and hazarded a few nonsense words; they were not convincing. Meantime, people noticed that he did not raise his hands during the hymns. He couldn't. All in all, it was getting harder and harder to keep your head down.

Sitting at his computer screen now, Thomas saw that Father had embraced this heady charismatic stuff to break a deadlock, to make something happen in his life. He hadn't been able to go to sea like his own father. He hadn't become a missionary in exotic lands. It was true that many souls had been won for Jesus, but then they had drifted away again. People blew hot and cold. The May Queen had been abolished, but no doubt she had returned when the reforming vicar had grown too depressed and disheartened to climb the pulpit stairs. There had been the big new challenge in Bristol and he had risen to it; he had done well, the congregation had flourished, but his daughter had failed at school, his older son was an atheist, a smoker, and a womaniser, and his youngest child a mere conformist, a sail-trimmer.

Father had written a book in those years, on the Holy Trinity, but it had not been accepted. Or, rather, it had been accepted, but only by some minor publisher, not the publisher he wanted. It had not made an impression. Exactly what was in the book, Thomas didn't know. His father hadn't talked about it, though Thomas was not so stupid, even in his mid-teens, that you couldn't talk to him about a book. So if Father hadn't talked about his book on the Holy Trinity it was because he was scared of exposing his ideas to his son's scepticism. Or maybe he didn't want to push this lukewarm lad into a position where he would have to declare himself. Either way, they hadn't spoken about it. They hadn't spoken about anything. Then suddenly this mad wave of enthusiasm was flowing through the Church; there was talk of healing and the spiritual power to transform the world. Frustrated, Thomas's father had gone for it.

To prove the worth of a weapon you must use it. For six months, a year, the tension in the family soared. They all became more and more themselves. Violently, dangerously themselves. His father prayed and prophesied. His sister was a shrill echo. His brother made fun, hissing and sniggering like a demon. His mother wept; this unkindness would bring her down with grey hairs to her grave. In response, Thomas was intensely well behaved. He hid in his good behaviour. In his room, he hung posters of football teams and tinkered with old valve radios. If he could have become invisible, he would. From downstairs came the sound of his sister banging out 'Onward, Christian Soldiers' on the piano. Very soon things would come to a head.

In his small flat, Thomas had put on the kettle for tea. Now he changed his mind and poured himself a beer. He honestly couldn't recall the details, exactly how or why it had happened, but one evening, in the lounge, around midnight, they exorcised his brother. Thomas was fifteen. His brother had come home late. Perhaps smelling of dope or drink. From his bedroom, Thomas heard shouting and started to come downstairs. The lounge door was closed. A pale-green door. From behind it came shouts and the chants of prayers, the piano, a hymn. 'Yes, Lord, yes!' And his brother was shouting, too. 'Leave me alone! Get your hands off me! You're all fucking crazy!'

Thomas stood on the stairs, looking at the pale-green paint on the door, listening. All the members of his family were in there. His father, his mother, his sister, his brother. The curate, too, by the sound of it. The loathsome curate with his ecstatic babble. They were all there, behind that door in that room, where a real drama was taking place. The drama between people who are hot and people who are cold.

Thomas was outside.

Thomas had not rushed down the last steps, burst into the room, and yelled at them to stop this nonsense.

Thomas was young. He was afraid. He was excluded. He was not really on anyone's side. He didn't want to be like his parents, but he didn't like the way his brother provoked them. 'Because thou art lukewarm, I will spue thee out of my mouth.'

Was this, Thomas wondered, why he was on his own now, forty and more years later, on a Saturday night, bivouacked on a metaphorical mountainside, with no one beside him? Because he was lukewarm? And if it was, was that really a problem? Thomas rather liked his Liverpool flat, didn't he, and his quiet cold evenings?

When the exorcism had failed, when Thomas's brother wasn't exorcised or broken but continued to be who he had always been, when the desired transformation did not take place and life returned, if not to normal, then certainly to monotony and flatness, as when a flood withdraws after the tempest, what had his father's life been like then? How had he been able to go on, to traverse day by day the grim domestic mudscape that was left? The nine sad mothballed years before the cancer choked him?

A year after the exorcism, Thomas had gone on a last holiday with his parents, to Deal on the south coast. This was where his father and mother had spent their honey-moon. They even got the same room in the same hotel, right on the seafront. But there wasn't much joy now. Thomas felt too old to holiday with his parents. His brother and sister were elsewhere. His parents seemed deflated, directionless, particularly his mother. They were going through the motions. They were trying to revive something. Father gritted his teeth. He suggested that he and Thomas rise early and take a swim before breakfast. It would be bracing. Thomas would have preferred to sleep late but didn't want to disappoint.

So they got up at seven, put on their costumes, crossed the road to the sea, laid their towels on the pebbles and waded in. The days it rained, they put the towels in plastic bags. The sea was grey. Thomas could still see his father's body, bird-like but paunchy. His skin was dead white, his old red swimming trunks baggy and slack. When the waves came up to his thighs, he would stop for a while, moving his hands back and forth in the cold water, crouching a little after a wave passed to keep his wrists covered, standing on tiptoe when the next wave rose, to keep it off his crotch. 'Wonderful air,' he shouted to Thomas. 'So fresh.' He made a theatre of puffing out his chest and breathing deeply and when finally he ducked his head into the water he would come up spluttering and protesting and flapping his arms. It was the theatre of someone trying to turn greyness into fun, trying to find a reason to rejoice. Thomas was aware now that he hadn't been much help to his father. He'd launched into the first big wave and swum steadily out to sea. When he'd stopped and turned, treading water, the Reverend Paige had been a small bald figure in a vast expanse of grey.

The years after that yielded nothing. Father started using aftershave and wearing coloured shirts, even silk cravats. He looked quite the dandy. For Christmas, one gave him bath salts or body lotion. After lunch, he snoozed in an armchair, his trousers loosened. At dinner, he was as impatient as ever. He scraped the custard off his plate and hurried off to his sermons. That was the one time when he really came alive: preaching, persuading, seducing even, in his robes, from the pulpit. To Thomas's brother, years on, Father had apologised. So his brother said. An awkward, hurried apology about the 'too much religion we drummed into you'. And once, when Thomas came home late and was in the kitchen drinking coffee, his father had come down to pick at beef bones in the fridge and, with his mouth full, muttered, 'I suppose it has been all right, in the end, this monogamous life.' Had that been an invitation to talk?

Thomas drank another beer and emptied a pack of nuts into a dish. He closed the document on his computer screen. What sort of life could his father have lived if he had openly declared that he no longer believed, no longer wanted to preach, no longer wanted his marriage? It was unthinkable. Mother would have been destroyed. His sister, and perhaps his brother, too, in a way. Thomas went back in his mind to those morning swims at Deal. Now that he thought about it, there had been a kind of melancholy father-and-son intimacy about them. He remembered the pebbles being dark with dew, their slippery hardness when he took his plastic sandals off a couple of yards from the water. Dad put his glasses in his sandals, so as to be sure where they were. 'What can you see without them?' Thomas asked. 'The sea,' Father said, laughing. 'The sky.' After a warm bed, the water was icy about your ankles. The breeze was chill. The pebbles were painful underfoot. Father began his spluttering routine, then his slow, blind breaststroke. Thomas put his head down and dived. He swam strongly, out towards the dark horizon. Stroke after stroke. A powerful freestyle. He was showing off, of course, declaring the vigour and victory of youth. Yet it had been a pleasure to have his father there, in the water behind him, between him and the shore. He had felt protected somehow. He remembered that.

Now Thomas has swum out too far and he stops and turns. He treads water, looking back at the gloomy coast, the long sweep of quaint, decaying facades, the pale clouds. The sea is all around, a slow grey swell moved from deep beneath. Dimly, he hears his father's voice. 'Tommy! Tommy!' Where is he? There. A wave rises and his father's head with it. A small white dot. I can see him, Thomas thinks, but with his poor eyesight he can't see me. 'Tommy! Hey, Tommeee!' He's worried for me, Thomas realises. He's worried that I've gone too far and may never make it back.

BLISSFUL BRUSH

SMS HSBC, 28-07-2012 11:27:44 debit card purchase £22.85 from Asda Pendlebury Supermarket, 604-612 Bolton Road, Pendlebury, M27 4ET.

SMS HSBC, 28-07-2012 20:51:08 debit card purchase £53.85 from Cross Keys, 13 Earle Street, Liverpool, Merseyside L3 9NS.

For about a year after Thomas left home he and Mary continued to draw from the same bank account. So whenever either of them used their debit card, or made an online payment, both received, as of old, a message from the bank. This was, in turns, distracting, poignant, irritating, worrying. Thomas saw the extent of Mary's veterinary expenses, and her weekend travelling. Mary wondered who Thomas could be taking to the restaurant. She was also perplexed when he made a large payment to a do-it-yourself chain in Newcastle. Thomas

figured that Mary spent far more than he had ever realised on petrol.

But of course, if he hadn't realised, it was because he
had barely glanced at these text messages when they were
together. Only since the separation had they begun to
taken on a certain interest. But it was the same for Mary.
Why, she asked herself, was she wondering who he was
seeing now, when she had always left him criminally free
when they were together?

SMS HSBC, 12-08-2012 13:15:42 your account has been
debited £315 for a direct funds transfer made on 11-08-2012.

With purchases, you could see where they were made.
With cash machine withdrawals there was the address of
the machine. But electronic funds transfers came with no
info aside from the amount transferred. Was Mary making
unwise loans to her younger sister? Thomas wondered
when £3,000 went somewhere in September. £3,000!
Mary thought she might contact Thomas over a transfer
of £5,000 just before Christmas. She imagined the money
had been sent to their daughter, who was putting down a
deposit on a house, but if you can't contact your husband
when he has just wiped five grand off your current account,
when can you contact him? Has he moved house? she was
asking herself mid-January, when the usual SMS indicating
his rent payment did not turn up. Then he paid a week
late. He was forgetful. He has forgotten me entirely, Mary

thought. She thought she might make a huge transfer somewhere, perhaps to the account she had recently opened for herself with another bank, just to see how he reacted to the mystery. Shake him up. But in the end she wouldn't give him that satisfaction. She would never give him a chance to say she had been anything less than scrupulously honest with the money.

Thomas meantime asked himself if she would figure his supermarket expenses must be for two. He felt vulnerable and stupidly guilty. When he saw she had withdrawn money in Glasgow he wondered if perhaps her mother was ill. Or could she be thinking of moving back to Scotland? But what if there were fraudulent use of the card during this period? No one would know, would they? Each of them would think it was something the other had spent.

Sometimes Thomas paid in cash to prevent her seeing how much he was spending at the Cross Keys these days, or perhaps to forestall any unwise decision on her part to drop by and see him there. Mary used the card even for the smallest expenditure, knowing that every purchase would remind him of her existence and his desertion.

At last the day came when the separation was legally settled and the account closed. Two last text messages arrived announcing transfers of equal amounts to separate accounts. This time there was no need to check why the payments were made or to whom. Afterwards, Thomas could hardly believe he could use his new debit card without Mary knowing. Or that she could go to the supermarket without his knowing. Only now did he appreciate what a strange, twilight comfort it had been to know that his wife of thirty years had just blown two hundred quid at the Blissful Brush Pet Grooming Parlour.

GRANDPARENTHOOD

This was supposed to be a trial return. They would see if it was possible, or desirable, to live together again. So, getting out of the car, Thomas was surprised to hear children's laughter coming from the garden. That took him back. Even more surprising, the children were Chinese. A boy of four perhaps, a girl of seven or eight. At the gate he stopped and looked. One of the things he had wondered in his year and more of absence was how Mary would manage the garden without him. The garden had been his territory. No one had wanted to help. Everyone protested their ignorance of plants and mowers and garden tools. All those years making the place beautiful would go to waste. But no. The Chinese children were rolling around happily on a neatly cut lawn; they had broken off a couple of irises, but there were plenty more nodding gently in the perfumed sunshine. Ricky, the cocker spaniel, lay panting in the shade. The hedges were trimmed, more or less. It was an idyllic scene.

'Hi, Tom!' Mary appeared at the French window, beaming. She clapped her hands and shouted something. Perhaps it was Chinese. The kids sat up, the little boy comically perplexed, the girl smiling. 'Lunch!' Mary announced, over-articulating, as if teaching a language class. 'Lunch,' she repeated, smiling invitingly at the girl, whose jet black hair was tied in two rose ribbons. 'Lanch,' the girl repeated. The little boy was already dashing into the house. Ricky barked. Mary turned and went in, shepherding the children one under each arm. Thomas followed.

'Can't you tell the difference between Chinese and Korean!' They were the children of Ji Won, Mary explained, who had looked after their own daughter in Seoul a couple of years before. She was on holiday with her husband and had parked them here for a while so that they would be free to visit museums and eat in nice places, all the things you can't easily do with kids.

'I couldn't say no, after what she did for Sally.'

Thomas watched his wife as she moved around the kitchen. She had rustled up spaghetti for the kids, salad for themselves. She was wearing loose jeans, an old blue T-shirt, no make-up, and seemed in excellent spirits as she sat down beside the little boy, taking his fork and showing him how to gather the spaghetti round its prongs. He was impatient, grinning and frowning, flailing his podgy arms and mucking up his mouth with spaghetti sauce. Mary laughed. Thomas didn't remember her being so indulgent with their own children.

He sat and helped himself to salad. When he smiled at the boy, who had kept his cap on, the kid pulled funny faces from under the visor. He had a fantastically round face, a gap in his front teeth, and a hilarious scowl.

'Tell Tom your name,' Mary said warmly. She repeated the phrase more slowly, pronouncing carefully.

'Tell' – she pointed at her mouth – 'Tom' – she pointed at Thomas – 'your' – she pointed at the boy – 'name. Name.'

The boy was perplexed, the spaghetti sliding off his fork.

'Your name,' Mary repeated. 'My name is Mary. His name is Tom.' Again, she pointed.

Suddenly the girl chipped in, speaking rapidly in their language. The boy frowned gloomily. 'Kwangjo,' he said, looking down at his food. Losing patience he began to bang his fork on the spaghetti to cut it up. Drops of sauce flew into the air.

'I beg your pardon?' Thomas said gently.

'Kwangjo,' the girl said.

'KWANGJO!' the boy yelled. He pulled his cap down hard on his forehead.

Everybody laughed.

'And you are?' Mary invited the girl. She pointed and repeated to help the child understand, 'His name is Kwangjo and your name is...?'

'Yuri,' she said obediently.

'Very good! My name is Yuri.'

'My name is Yuri,' she repeated.

'Hi Kwangjo, hi Yuri, I'm Tom,' Thomas said. 'Pleased to meet you both. You look a hell of a pair.'

The children grinned.

Thomas ate his salad. It was quite a mix of leaves and radishes and nuts and apples and rocket and feta cheese and fennel. Very tasty.

'I'm glad you're pleased, they really are fantastic,' Mary enthused, as the children hoovered up their spaghetti. 'Yuri is learning really fast.'

The boy banged his fist on the table. Mary hurried to the pot to get him some more spaghetti. Throughout the lunch, she was mostly on her feet.

Afterwards they went for one of their old walks in the hills. They drove up to the ruined mill and then climbed through the pine woods. Yuri held Mary's hand. The little girl was in love with her new minder and eager to please, repeating all the words that Mary gave to the things around them. Tree. Stone. Fence. Path. Sunshine. Shade. Leaves. Kwangjo refused. His frowns and pouts were gloomily melodramatic. Perhaps he was missing his family, Thomas thought.

Thomas picked up a pine cone and threw it at the boy. It caught him on the shoulder. The kid's eyes opened wide. He hadn't understood. Then he saw and yelled with delight, gathering the cones on the path to throw at Thomas. Thomas ran ahead, up the steep hill, occasionally turning and tossing a cone back at the little boy. Suddenly Yuri forgot her seriousness and dashed after them. Cones were raining back and forth, very few of them hitting anybody. Ricky came tearing out of the undergrowth and barked wildly. Mary followed, hands behind her back, smiling quietly.

In an exchange of emails the previous week it had seemed easy for the couple to discuss their many problems, to talk about a new start and what it might mean. Some of the words going back and forth were hard and firm. Both agreed that big changes were in order. But now Thomas was here, there seemed no point in saying anything. All was as it had been. At the top of the hill they sat on the steps of the disused chapel while the children ran around among the rocks with the dog.

'Don't make him mad,' Mary called. 'There are limits to his patience.'

'They won't understand,' Thomas observed.

Kwangjo was throwing cones just over Ricky's head. The dog was leaping to catch them. Giggling wildly, Yuri picked up armfuls of cones and flung them in the air any old how. Both children seemed seized by a frantic vitality.

'Reminds me of Sally and Mark,' Mary said.

This had been in the air.

'They loved throwing cones,' she observed.

'Funny,' Thomas said, 'but I can't remember our ever parking them with anyone else while we took a break.'

'Perhaps we should have.'

Thomas didn't reply. His wife would have been the last to agree to such an arrangement.

'Soon there will be the grandchildren,' she mused. 'That will be fun.'

He had picked up a twig and begun to split off the small shoots on each side. 'Not for a while, I hope.'

Sally had just married.

'Why not? You should look forward to it.'

Thomas reflected. 'I'm happy for them to have children, of course. But why hurry it on?'

'Tom!' Mary exclaimed. 'What's come over you?'

He frowned. 'Nothing that I know of.'

'You're not afraid of being called grandfather, are you?'

'Not at all. Just there are still a few other things to do in the meantime.'

'Don't be such an old sourpuss. You know you always love kids when it comes to it. You're so good with them.'

There was no point in pursuing this. Thomas watched the children. They were wrestling with the dog now, smothered in pine needles. Fortunately the animal was about as long-suffering as a dog can be. Then the boy began to shout something at his sister and she got to her feet and hurried towards them. She seemed at a loss, then came to whisper in Mary's ear.

'Kwangjo, toilet,' Thomas heard.

'Here we go!'

In a second Mary had jumped to her feet and was pulling tissues from her handbag. She picked up the little boy under the armpits and hurried him off into the trees. He was kicking his legs. She was speaking to him very clearly.

'Hold on, Kwangjo. We'll just find a nice easy place out of sight. Hold on now.'

Thomas stayed put. Smiling in a rather demure way, the girl sat beside him. Then Ricky sidled up to join them and lay at his feet. With Mary and Kwangjo away, the place seemed uncannily still. The pine needles soaked up any sound. The spring sun was pale in the clearing with the abandoned chapel. They had sat here a hundred times in the past. Often Thomas had brought the children on his own. There had been picnics, and once or twice a fire. Sometimes this place had been just the first goal in much longer rambles. Returning, the chapel was always the first sign that they were re-entering familiar territory. Nearly back. But those days were long gone, Thomas thought. It would be hard to say what was really left of them now. What is the past?

Yuri bent down to stroke the dog. Thomas would have liked to ask the girl how long she and her brother were staying, but she wouldn't have understood. The dog was lazily licking her hand now. Yuri put her face against its fur. Thomas was fascinated by her foreign eyes and hair and smile. All children are foreigners, he thought then. They come from a different country and when they've grown up they head off to another country again, leaving you where you always were.

A crashing of undergrowth announced Kwangjo's return. He came rushing into the clearing, punching his fists in the air. Still running, he picked up a cone and

264

hurled it at Thomas. 'Let's go for an ice-cream,' Mary's voice was singing behind him. 'I bet you both understand the word, ice-cream.'

In the evening they did a jigsaw puzzle. Or rather Mary pulled the thing out, cleared the big living-room table, helped get the pieces all face up, then went off to watch the news upstairs. The picture they were supposed to put together was Constable's *Hay Wain*, a horse and cart crossing a muddy stream. It would have been hard, Thomas thought, to imagine anything less appropriate for two small Korean children than this very English, very adult landscape. They sorted out the border soon enough, but the sky pieces all looked the same, and the sky was vast. The vegetation was a finely nuanced grey-green, irritatingly flecked with white, from a sun that might have been anywhere. Kwangjo was quickly frustrated. Thomas found him the pieces for the dog in the foreground. Then for a wheel of a cart. The boy put them together with a little help, then was immediately frustrated again. Eventually he ran off to join Mary at the television, but then came running back because the programme didn't interest him. He deliberately broke the border they'd made and tossed a few pieces of sky into the air. Yuri shouted at him. Thomas was relieved when the phone rang and it was Ji Won.

Now the children bounced on the sofa, grabbing the phone from each other and chatting away in Korean. Mary came down to sit with them and say a few words to Ji Won. Afterwards, Kwangjo burst into tears. Mary tried to hug him, but the boy ran away and flung himself on the floor face down.

'Put a cartoon on for him,' Thomas said. 'Didn't Mark have some manga things?' Their son was now away at college.

'Manga is Japanese,' Mary objected.

'Might be in the zone, though, for kids.'

'I was hoping they'd learn some English,' Mary said. 'What about *Batman*?'

'Put the mangas on,' Thomas said. 'He isn't going to be learning anything in the state he's in.'

The two went off and Yuri followed. Thomas sat with the jigsaw. It was strange, he thought, how Constable had fused beauty with leadenness, the dramatic movement of the sky with a gloomy stillness of the land. After a while he got up and went to the fridge. There were beers. Mary didn't approve of her husband's drinking every evening, but she had made sure there were some bottles in the fridge. At least that. For a moment, alone in the kitchen, Thomas couldn't remember where they had kept the bottle opener. Or perhaps he did remember, but in his absence Mary had made changes. He could have gone upstairs and asked her, but he didn't really want to. Opening drawers, he was struck by just how much stuff they had. Tea towels, tablecloths, napkins for ordinary meals and napkins for special meals, a brush for painting milk on pastry, moulds for making cupcakes, pie cutters and soup ladles, no end of pots and pans and plates and cutlery. The kitchen surfaces were generous and well kept, tasteful combinations of brushed steel and fine woods. It was a beautiful place to live in. But no bottle opener.

Damn! Thomas tried with a knife, slipped and cut himself. Damn and damn and damn again. Now he had to go into the ground-floor bathroom and look in the cupboard where the medical stuff used to be. His thumb tip was streaming blood. Deodorants, soaps, toothpastes, lotions, no plasters. He held the wound under the tap, dried it with toilet paper, then wrapped it in more toilet paper. At once the blood came through brightly, actually far more brightly than anything in the Constable. For some reason the thought gave him a grim satisfaction. He took the paper off and repeated the operation. Again the blood came through. But the third time the toilet paper stayed eggshell blue. Thomas went back into the kitchen and tackled the bottle top with a fork. At last it spun off. The beer foamed and he took a long swig.

Returning to the sitting room, he found Yuri bent over the puzzle. For a moment he watched her from the doorway. The child was intent, in a thoughtful, diligent way. There was something extremely attractive about her Koreanness, her Asianness, the pursed lips, furrowed forehead, sharp, narrow eyes. Beyond her, the French window was still open on the mild evening. It was too early in the season for flies and moths. From upstairs came the sound of cartoon music. Thomas went to his seat. 'Let's do the house,' he said. He pointed at the masonry to the left of the photo on the box top; one wall was whitewashed, then there were orange bricks and darker roof tiles. 'Let's do that.'

Yuri frowned, then nodded and began to look for the right colours. Her short fingers moved very fast, pulling out promising pieces and moving them round to put them on the table the right way up. Gradually they built the house outwards from the left edge of the frame. When they found a piece that fitted, she smiled and he said 'Great, well done.' 'Great, well done,' she repeated. He was rather enjoying himself, Thomas realised.

Then Mary reappeared with Kwangjo. They could hear her talking to him as they came downstairs. Did he watch a lot of manga cartoons at home? Which mangas were his favourites? 'This little boy has to go to bed,' she laughed, coming into the room. 'I just need to get him something to drink.' Clearly the boy had other ideas. He broke away from Mary's hand, ran to the table, climbed on a chair and started feverishly shifting pieces all over the puzzle, trying to force them into quite impossible homes. Yuri spoke sharply to him, grabbed the belt of his trousers. Mary came back from the kitchen bringing a small carton of fruit juice with a straw. Then she saw Thomas's hand.

'What on earth happened to you?'

'I couldn't find the bottle opener,' he grinned. 'Or the plasters.'

'And you didn't come to ask me where they were?'

Thomas laughed, 'Evidently not.'

Mary's expression, holding the boy's fruit juice so he could suck through the straw, was somewhere been perplexed and knowing.

'By the way,' Thomas asked, feeling vaguely guilty, 'how long are the kids staying?'

Mary grimaced and shook her head as if to criticise this indiscretion.

'I really don't think their language skills are a hundred per cent yet,' Thomas said evenly. 'They're not going to be upset if I ask how long they're staying.'

'Two weeks,' she said.

'Two weeks!'

'Ji Won kept Sally for a month.'

'Sally was a twenty-year-old paying for her room and board and attending college every day. Not an infant in need of constant attention. Never mind two infants.'

Mary shook her head. 'I'm trying to be generous, Thomas. Come on, little fellow,' she said, turning to Kwangjo. '*Chimdae lo idong!*'

Yuri turned with a satisfied look on her face. The boy resisted.

'I'll keep him company till he falls asleep,' Mary said. 'Come on, Ricky. Let's go to bed with the doggie,' she told the boy, 'he'll lick your hand.'

Thomas and Yuri worked on. It was past eleven now. He fed her the pieces he found; she read them with her dark eyes and tried to fit them into likely places. 'Great,' Thomas smiled. 'Great,' she repeated, smiling and waggling her pigtails. 'Fantastic,' he said, when two little clusters connected. 'Fantastic,' she nodded. They had the house almost done now, and the tree growing out of its walls and the trunks of the two trees in the centre of the picture. The leaves would be more difficult. Not to mention the clouds. Yuri yawned. She covered her mouth with a wrist. Suddenly she was tired. 'Tomorrow,' Thomas said. He put his hands together and leaned his head on them. 'Sleep now.' The little girl bowed to him and climbed the stairs. She really was a charming companion.

Alone, Thomas got his laptop from his bag and checked the day's mail. He had heard Mary talking in a low voice to Yuri as she got her to bed and had expected his wife would then come downstairs. There was a moment in particular when he thought he heard her on the landing; she must be choosing between coming down to him or going into their bedroom. Thomas wondered where he was going to sleep tonight. He wondered where he wanted to sleep.

There was nothing interesting in the mail. Another message in an ongoing discussion with his brother about the difference between knowledge and information. Something from his sister about taxes on his mother's house. An invitation to a friend's fiftieth birthday party in Hull. He knew at once he would turn it down. At least some decisions are easy.

Mary's footsteps climbed up to the loft. The children were on the first floor, in between. Down in the sitting room Thomas sat with the unfinished puzzle. He looked up *The Hay Wain* on Wikipedia and found it was painted nearly two hundred years ago. It had recently been voted the second most popular painting in any British gallery. Why? Thomas clicked on the most popular painting. Turner's *Fighting Temeraire*. He remembered it at once. An old warship being tugged to a breaker's yard in a weird mix of sunset and moonlight. Both paintings were sad, freighted with sentiment, drenched in resignation. The whitish warship had a ghostly look. Why did people like that?

Suddenly uneasy, Thomas got up and went through the French window into the garden. It was such a beautiful house. He had felt excited on the long drive home this morning. An affair that had been going on for some time was over. He thought how nice it would be to be back in these spacious rooms, to have the dewy garden outside, to be able to take his coffee and read his paper in the open air. He thought how fine it would be for the family to feel that he and Mary were together. The kids could stop worrying about them and get on with their own lives. Even Ricky had been a pleasant thought.

But did he really want to go upstairs? Did Mary really want to come downstairs for a drink and a chat? And if the house was so beautiful, and the thought of the united family so reassuring, how unhappy must he have been to have left in the first place? Then again, if Mary didn't really want, and if he also didn't really want, then why did they keep making these attempts, why did they keep wanting to want?

Thomas paced the garden for a while, then went inside. He really was at a loss now, picking things up and putting them down. An old photograph of Sally on her birthday. A few CDs, things they had bought twenty years ago. He started to climb the stairs, but stopped when he heard whimpering. Kwangjo was snivelling and his sister was whispering to him. Thomas listened. How many times had he listened outside his kids' bedrooms? Soon there would be the grandchildren, Mary had said. The voices were quietly intense, speaking in a language he didn't know. What on earth were they doing here? Thomas suddenly asked himself. Why on earth had Mary agreed to have two Korean children here, at this of all moments?

The little boy went on whimpering. His older sister went on comforting. They were sounds full of tenderness and sentiment. But nothing to do with me, Thomas thought. Turning round, he found his car keys beside *The Hay Wain*, slipped his laptop back in his bag, let himself out and headed for the car.

STORMING THE TOWER

I fell in love with Thomas because he was smart and bright and bushy-tailed, and also there was something charmingly vulnerable and yielding about him. It did not seem to me he had much experience sexually. It did not seem to me he had much experience at all. When I first saw him across the table in St Chad's it was obvious he was longing for someone to take him over. He had no idea how to achieve the ambitions he had set his heart on and very little idea how to look after himself in general. I got his phone number from Joey, who had the room next to his, and invited him to the cinema. It was a Spanish film with subtitles. Halfway through the movie I put a hand on his leg. Later we went back to my place.

He didn't know much about sex, but I felt I could trust him. He was quite moral and had old-fashioned ideas. He was shocked that I was still renting a room in my old boyfriend's flat. I liked that because it was a statement that he wanted a relationship. Thomas didn't take sex lightly.

It seems he had an on and off relationship with an old girl-friend in Bristol, but he had been trying to leave her for years, he said. She was a wonderful person, but not right for him. I liked this too. I liked the idea that I was helping him to break a relationship that was holding him back.

Almost at once we were having a lot of fun. I took a bottle of bubbly round to his miserable room in the college dorm. There was an empty vodka bottle on the floor by the unmade bed and clothes that needed washing. I felt I could help him. We were twenty-two. I liked all this. We were made for each other.

These were good times. We walked all over town. I did a lot of fancy cooking for him. He had no notion of a proper diet. After ten days we were living together and I suppose after a year we knew we were going to marry, which we did, in Bristol, about eighteen months after we met. His father, who was a C of E clergyman, married us. Not that we never argued. We had furious arguments about the most stupid things. Films we didn't agree about. Politics. I remember every time we yelled at each other Thomas thought the relationship must be over. But I taught him that argu-ments were just part of getting on. It seemed odd to me he had never realised that. I suppose his parents had been too goody-goody to argue. They kept it all bottled up.

But this is not what I want to write about. Or, I mean, at this rate I would fill the *Encyclopaedia Britannica* if I told the whole endless saga between the marriage certifi-cate and the separation papers. I just want the essence of it. To explore the ramifications would require more energy than I can muster these days. You might ask if a thing with ramifications – a sort of Gothic castle of a marriage, with cobwebby banqueting halls and secret passages, overgrown rose gardens and spinning wheels with dangerous needles in dusty disused bedrooms – can really have an essence. But I think it can. Or at least a principle that caused the ramifications, that made us start a garden then let it go to seed, or set out a banquet and then leave the wedding cake to rot. And this principle was that Thomas had grown up being a good boy for his mother and then a sinner on the side, and that is exactly what he started doing with me. He couldn't help himself. He is a pathological case.

But first things first. To start with, Thomas just needed to learn to dress better, wash better, shop better, eat better. He had no idea how to buy a second-hand car or find a flat to rent. One car he bought stopped in the rain with my parents in it on the way back from the station. Another lost its bonnet when Thomas was driving it away from the guy he'd bought it from. All of a sudden the bonnet just flew up and over the car. We were lucky there wasn't a cyclist behind, waiting to get killed.

Thomas let people walk all over him. His boss at work. His parents. One example will do for all. When he got his first job in Manchester we had rented a place from an old Hungarian and his wife in Moss Side. They were gloomily religious with little Madonnas and photos of the Pope all over the place, but about as miserly as folks can be. Basically, we just had the upstairs of the house, they the downstairs, with no real separation between us. This meant they had total control of our heating, the cost of which was to be included in the very steep rent. Of course they scrimped. Even when the heating was on, you shivered. When it was off your only chance was to keep a hotwater bottle on your lap under a mountain of blankets. Then in early May these two old skinflints announced they were off to Majorca for their annual holiday, and since all controls to the boiler were in their kitchen and since their kitchen and sitting room would be locked, for privacy, the heating would be off for two weeks.

I remember it snowed in Manchester that year on May the first. 'You've got to go down and tell them we won't accept it,' I told Thomas. He hated any kind of confrontation. He just didn't have the stomach for it. Still, he went. I suppose I shamed him into going. Needless to say, he didn't get anywhere. 'They won't budge,' he said. 'But you've only been at it five minutes,' I protested. 'You can't give up when you've barely started.'

Our landlords were leaving at seven the following morning. They had a taxi booked for the airport. 'Set the alarm for six and go down and simply demand that they give us access to the boiler. It will be freezing at six. They can't say no.'

Actually it was freezing all night. We slept under at least four blankets. This was before everyone had quilts. The crazy thing was that the person who would suffer most without the heating was Thomas. He always had frozen feet. But he was more worried about confronting these old Eastern-bloc bigots than dying of cold.

We woke at six. Down he went, shivering, and in just two minutes he was back. 'They absolutely won't leave us the keys for the heating,' he explained. 'They say it would ruin them. Can you believe they're filling their suitcases with tins of luncheon meat. To take to Majorca!'

I threw off the blankets, rushed downstairs in my night-dress and told those old crones I was going to lie in the street in front of their taxi and make a scene they would never live down. How could they surround themselves with Jesuses and Marys and treat us like this?

They looked terrified; they were two bent and stooped old scrooges who spent the days in their kitchen sitting by their Aga, as if we were in one of those Tolstoy stories where peasants sleep on the stove. 'And don't imagine I won't, because I will!' I yelled. 'I'm even looking forward to shaming you. I'm going to scream my head off.' It was ten to seven and raining heavily. They gave us the keys to the house. For two weeks, while they had miserable weather in Majorca, we roasted.

Thomas loved to tell this story. And others like it. At dinner parties with his friends. He was proud of me. Yet the more the story got told, the more I sounded slightly eccentric, bizarre, even a loose cannon, and what he never realised was that I had to be like this to make up for his being such a wimp, such a good boy, and such a sneak too. It would be the same throughout the whole marriage. I decided when we moved and where we went. I found the house we rented, then the houses we bought. I haggled over the prices. I decided when it was time to have a child. *Not* because I was bossy. The picture he would paint to his friends of a henpecked man having affairs because he was pushed around at home was absolutely false. Simply, he couldn't decide; couldn't even decide who he was, I think. He didn't know what he wanted. Twenty years into this marriage, one of his friends said to me, 'You do realise Thomas is having an affair, don't you, Mary?' I denied it out of loyalty. When I told Thomas, he said, 'With friends like that, who needs enemies?' 'But is it true?' 'Of course it isn't,' he said. 'For Christ's sake!'

I knew he was lying. At the same time, I think I wanted him to lie. I wanted to believe he was the good boy, the innocent boy he had been when we met, the boy I could rely on. All the same, an idiot could see that something had changed. He wasn't frank any more. So maybe here we are getting close to the principle behind the Gothic castle of our marriage with its endless bits added on to make it liveable when really it should have been pulled down years before. I confronted the world for Thomas, who was incapable of confronting it. But I couldn't confront him, and meantime he presented the world with a completely false picture of me.

Of course the main addition to our life were the children. Two wonderful children. I loved Thomas as a father.

His good-boy character was positive in that department and perhaps all the stronger for not knowing who he was in others. Yes, I reckon it was a relief for Thomas to be a father and to know what a father's responsibilities are, and it was a relief for me to love him as a father and see him doing what a father ought to do. I think he loved me as a mother, too. So two splendid new wings were added to our castle. And who is going to bring down a stately home they have just added to, who is going to confront a husband when they have just had a child, are completely vulnerable emotionally and, above all, economically?

To sum up, then: he was proud of my spirit, but found marriage inhibiting. I loved the father he was, but he humiliated me. We still loved each other, I think, maybe, but he wanted to be shot of love; his only problem was that if he left me it would look like he had behaved badly. Thomas was obsessed with whether people thought of him as good or bad, whereas I really couldn't care less. I couldn't give a damn. It doesn't matter to me what people think. I just want to understand what happened, or understand a little better.

So, to have done, I'll go straight to the moment that keeps coming back and back in my mind, the moment that decided it all, that pulled away the foundation stone, I reckon, which is also the moment I least understand: when he insisted we go to see a therapist.

I was suspicious from the start. It seemed to me this was a card he was playing with the kids. The kids knew now that he had had an affair. Let's leave aside the details.

It certainly wasn't me who told them. Now, proposing therapy, he could present himself as good again, as the guy who was trying to solve things. In fact, when I resisted, the kids pressed me to go. He had scored a point.

I went but I was angry. If he wanted to get the marriage back together he could take me on holiday or just be nicer in general. Not to mention the money. Here was a guy who was generally tight with money, paying a fortune for this therapist who worked in tandem with another therapist who was going to 'observe' us from behind some kind of two-way mirror. I was only going because if I didn't the kids would say I was in the wrong. In the car on the way he said, 'You're wearing muddy shoes.' I said, 'So what? I just took the dog out.' He said, 'You might as well just announce out loud that you don't want to be there. You'll dirty their floor.' 'Good,' I said. 'They're being paid enough to employ a cleaner, aren't they?'

The therapist tried to be a mix of uncle, priest and friend. He had a strong Liverpool accent. I found him creepy. He refused to condemn Thomas for having affairs. Needless to say, Thomas did some crying to give the impression he cared. Thomas has this thing that if he presents himself as overwhelmed by his problems, above all overwhelmed by the impossibility of making up his mind about things, then people will take pity and forgive him. He always breaks down in tears. It's not very helpful.

The therapist went out to consult the woman observing from the other side of the mirror in the wall. He was a long time coming back and I thought probably they wanted to watch us on our own to see how we reacted to the first part of the session. I said how dingy the furniture was, what a miserable decor in general. How were you supposed to cheer up a relationship in a sad place like this?

When he came back I told the therapist I had given Thomas all the freedom any man could possibly ask for; perhaps he had had a dozen mistresses, I don't know, there was no lack of opportunity. So I couldn't see what more he was asking of me. Then the therapist said maybe freedom wasn't what Thomas wanted and of course Thomas immediately nodded and said no, it wasn't, and I realised then that the two of them had ganged up against me and it wasn't worth going on.

After that first session Thomas seemed pleased with himself. He had his virtuous cap back on. Maybe he saw the £250 as some kind of penitence. It irritated me to think of that cash going to waste when there were so many other things to spend it on. What can I say? I didn't see any improvement in our relationship over the following weeks. Essentially, Thomas kept out of my way and I returned the compliment.

At the second session, the therapist asked how we had reacted when our love started to stall and we lost direction. I said I had frequently invited Thomas to come away on holiday with me up to the Highlands. The therapist asked Thomas why he hadn't agreed to these holidays, and Thomas said because I was always inviting him to places I knew well and he didn't. Places where I had family. Instead he had invited me to India, which would be new to both of us. I began to explain that I had no desire to spend my holidays sweltering in impossible heat and confronted with abject poverty. Then I stopped. There was no point in going on. I wasn't saying what I really felt and I wasn't talking about what really happened between us. 'I'm going,' I said. 'I don't need this.'

I stood up. It was good to see the therapist taken by surprise and Thomas with the wind falling out of his virtuous sails. 'If he wants me,' I said, 'he can storm this tower to win me back.' And I walked out. Back home, in the kitchen, Thomas came from behind while I was cooking and said, okay, he'd be happy to come on a holiday with me to the Highlands. He put a hand on my shoulder and tried to turn me to face him, but I said it was far too late for that stuff now.

There it is, then. That was the therapy. And what I don't understand about it is what really happened then, when I stood up in the therapist's gloomy office and said that stuff about storming the tower. The fact is I didn't know whether Thomas really wanted to get things going between us again, or whether he was just waiting to be told that the marriage couldn't be saved and he wouldn't be criticised for leaving. If that was the case, why did I play into his hands as I did? Did I do it on purpose? And what does it mean to say you did something on purpose if you don't know if you did? What kind of purpose is that?

I also don't understand why, when I walked out on the therapy, giving him the moral high ground and the signal he wanted, he didn't walk out on me right away. Why wait two miserable years more? Then why did I say those words about storming a tower? Could I really imagine him on his knees with his arms round my legs? Or buying flowers for me every day? Did I even want that? And why was I a tower he had to storm? Why didn't I offer a garden he could discover?

I couldn't. I acted how I had to act. He always wanted me to be someone else, but I am who I am. I did what I did. I couldn't change who I was.

So why do I regret it? Or do I? Does it ever make sense to regret the things you feel you have to do?

Does it make sense to want things to make sense, when all that really matters is to set your mind at rest?

Perhaps the truth is that when you live with someone who doesn't know who he is you pretty soon lose your own identity too. You have to retreat into a tower to feel you're anyone at all. You have to say: if you want me you'll have to become the kind of hero who can storm a tower, instead of a wimp who doesn't . . .

Thomas stopped. After a long pause he put his pen down. He was getting nowhere. Mary remained a complete enigma.

Perhaps you had better stick to your own side of the story, he decided.

WINNER

People are successful or they are failures. There are no two
ways about that. If you apply for a job, for example, you
either get it or you don't. And if you get it, you either
do well at the job, or you don't, you make a career of
it, always on the rise, or you get stuck in some paper-
pushing backwater. These distinctions are very clear.
Who would dispute them? In Thomas's family it is good
to be successful. He and Mary are agreed on that. They
met at a good university where they were considered high
achievers. They were high achievers. Now their children
are expected to do well at school. Not that Thomas and
Mary are obsessed. They don't want to make monsters of
their offspring with cramming courses and trying to get
them into top schools. They want them to be normal. It
is simply expected that whenever they do something, they
will do it well. Play the piano well, do their exams well,
write good essays, play smart football, tennis, hockey, etc.
Not that they are punished or ever would be if they didn't

do well, having given of their best. Thomas and Mary are not slave drivers. They are not unkind. But inevitably there would be a certain disappointment, if only in sympathy, as it were, with the child's disappointment. Who doesn't want to be successful? The truth is, Thomas and Mary find it hard to think of themselves and their children, individually or as a group, as failures.

But of the four of them, who is the most successful?

It's a question neither Thomas nor Mary wants to ask. Success should unite the family, not divide it. Yet children these days seem to approach life in a more anxiously competitive and comparative spirit than in the past. There's no stopping them. From a very young age Sally is calling Mark a klutz, he's useless at this, useless at that. 'How thick can you be?' the firstborn asks. Mark suffers but has learned not to do the same things as his sister. Not to choose the same subjects at school. When their end-of-year exam results come in, it's easy to say that this school is known to be easier than that, or that school tougher than this. Actually, Mark is doing pretty well at school these days. It's Sally now who has to say her school is tougher. Mark has no idea, she says, how tough her school is.

Mark fights his father on the ping-pong table. Thomas doesn't want to lose on purpose. That would be false. 'When you beat me, you'll really have beaten me,' he tells his son. 'You can really feel proud.' And eventually his son does beat him. Thomas feels disorientated, even though this has been on the cards for a while, even though he wants his son to do well. Sally cheats at Battleships. Thomas is sure she does, but he lets it go. He doesn't mind losing at Battleships; it's mainly a game of luck. In general, he doesn't mind losing if the other person cheats, just as he doesn't mind other people in his profession being more successful than himself if they obviously had a head start or preferential treatment. It's losing on an even playing field that's unnerving for Thomas. Sally insists she doesn't cheat. Perhaps she's just really lucky. Or really good!

Mary doesn't play games with the children. She doesn't like playing cards or board games or ping-pong. And since she left work to concentrate on bringing up the children, she's given up the idea of a career. So she's not in competition with Thomas there. Or with anyone else, for that matter. She is a successful mother, bringing up healthy and generally successful children. She's a great cook. Hard to beat her in that department.

Sally is good at the piano but wants to give it up. Thomas and Mary are disappointed, but not slave drivers. 'If you still don't like it when you're fourteen, you can give it up then,' they tell her. Sally gives up lessons on her fourteenth birthday. On that same day Mark starts taking the piano more seriously, more happily. In a few months he has become a pretty good pianist. Thomas thinks that if he had let Sally give up when she was twelve, Mark would have had a chance of becoming a virtuoso. But how could he have known this?

Sally is also good at skating, at karate, at basketball. Her instructors take Thomas and Mary aside and tell them to encourage the girl to invest more time in this sport, she could be a major success. Each time this happens, Sally drops the sport like a hot potato. She concentrates on making small pieces of jewellery. This was not something Thomas or Mary had foreseen. Mark's piano teacher encourages him to go to the conservatory to study piano, but Mark decides against this. He starts to draw and make zany posters. Rather surprisingly, Sally compliments Mark on his posters and Mark compliments Sally on her jewellery creations. They are successful adolescents.

Thomas is a high-flying advertising executive. Sally opts to study pharmacology. She gets good grades and is happy. Her father can't understand a thing when she starts to explain about dose–response complexities. Mark gets into computer graphics and design. Years later, both children will change direction. It turns out they don't really like pharmacology or computer graphics. Separated from Mary now, it occurs to Thomas that perhaps they chose those fields because that way they could dream of career success without competing with other family members. Did we do things wrong? he wonders. Obviously, he wishes his children well in their new ventures. He hopes they will find paths they enjoy and jobs they can be happy in. He no longer feels the need to be proud of their achievements or to tell friends how well they are doing. His life is going better now, though never without an undertow of regret.

Some hours after signing the separation papers, Mary texted:

The winner takes it all. Remember the song? Her destiny. Standing small. A loser.

Thomas cancelled the message quickly.

MISSING

'I'm supposed to record your responses, is that okay?'

'If they remain anonymous, sure.'

'There should have been something about it in the email.'

'Maybe there was. I just said yes when I saw it was a request from inside the group.'

'Very generous of you. Anyway, the research is quantitative. There are no names or anything. They take people's opinions on an issue, then they're sorted into categories, statistics, and so on.'

'Go ahead.'

'Just some basic data to start with.'

'Okay.'

'Age?'

'Fifty-nine.'

'Occupation – Accounts Director, right?'

'More or less.'

'Nationality?'

'Brit. What else?'

'Sorry, it's routine. Marital status?'

'Do you really need all this?'

'I guess they're just categories they divide people up into.'

'People could lie.'

'They could.'

'Married, then.'

'Okay. Those are the formalities. Now the question under examination: Is it possible to miss someone, yet not want to see them?'

'What?'

'It's a bit of a conundrum, isn't it? Is it possible to miss someone, and still not want to see them? Meaning this someone.'

'Why on earth would anyone want to ask a question like that?'

'Don't ask me. It's not my brief to explain the point of the research, I just put the issue to people and record their responses.'

'Quite, but . . .'

'It's cognitive psychology. Some research your group is sponsoring.'

'Which makes you a psychology student, I suppose?'

'Well, I'm an undergraduate, yes. But this is just a way of paying the bills. I'm not actually involved in the research in any serious way.'

'But why was I selected for interview?'

'I don't think anyone was *selected*. As I understand it, they were starting with people in the group in the hope they would be more amenable, given that the group is sponsoring it all. Then because they have your company emails to fix appointments. It's quite difficult getting people to stop on the street. Everyone's busy. Then for this project we're supposed to encourage in-depth responses.'

'I haven't got oceans of time myself. Talking about depth . . .'

'Of course. Let's say five minutes. Just a couple of quick reflections. Is it possible to miss someone, yet not want to see them?'

'Hmm. Okay. I think so, yes.'

'In what circumstances?'

'God. Hang on. Well, you could take the case of someone who is dead.'

'I don't understand.'

'Take my mother. She died last year.'

'I'm sorry.'

'For heaven's sake. She was in her nineties. But the fact is, I'm still not used to it. I still think, Oh, I'll call Mum about that. Automatically. Then realise she isn't there. Or I think, Mum would have given me good advice about that, knowing of course that she'll never give anyone any advice again. In particular, when I go to London – she lived on the outskirts, near Twickenham – it seems strange not to touch base with her first thing on arrival, not to spend one of my London days with her.'

'So, you would say you miss her.'

'The term seems to have been invented, yes, to describe these emotions.'

'How much?'

'Sorry?'

'How much would you say you missed her? On a scale of one to ten, say.'

'Oh, I really can't do the one-to-ten thing. I mean, you can't put feelings in relation to each other with numbers. It's not like volume on the radio.'

'I know what you mean. I said that myself when they asked me to put that question. What about something more subjective: intensely, occasionally, mildly?'

'Intensely occasionally. Mildly more often.'

'I'll leave them to figure that out.'

'Give the shrinks some work to do.'

'Right. So. Where were we? You miss your mother. With occasional intensity. But you don't want to see her. Right? Why not?'

'Well, what would it mean to see her?'

'Sorry? It would mean seeing her, surely.'

'Precisely. But seeing what, exactly? Where is Mum now? If I want to see my son, I know where he is. He's at college. He's nineteen. Four or five years younger than you, I guess.'

'Six, actually. I was a slow starter.'

'I find that hard to believe.'

'It's true.'

'Anyway, I can imagine meeting my son. I can visualise his smile, or perhaps frown, when he finds me on the doorstep. We would grab a coffee together, no doubt. Or a beer, perhaps. Depending on the time of day. He would tell me what he's up to. It would be fun. Or maybe he would tell me about some problem with an exam and I would sympathise and give advice. Or he might even be upset over a girlfriend and I would have to offer the proverbial shoulder, perhaps worry for him, but in the end that is fine too. It is always lovely to see one's children.'

'Yes, I like to see my father too. But how does that fit in?'

'You're not playing dumb now, are you? Do they ask you to do this?'

'No, not at all. Did I miss something? You miss your mother, with varying degrees of intensity, but you don't want to see her. That's the particular combination that's being researched. I just didn't quite get the connection with your son, who you miss but do want to see.'

'My mother's dead. She's a corpse, isn't she? Or rather, not even. She's ashes. How could I want to see her? She won't be smiling when I show up on her doorstep.'

'You could see her ghost.'

'It's a charming idea, but I don't want to see her ghost. Seeing ghosts would upset my entire belief structure. I'd wonder if I wasn't going crazy. I prefer missing Mum and leaving it at that.'

'You could see her in a dream.'

'I could. I *have*. I have seen her in many dreams. But I don't actively *want* to. I mean, seeing her in dreams isn't seeing her in reality. I just wake up reminded she's dead. It's sad.'

'I'm sorry.'

'Please don't be. As I said, it came in the fullness of time.'

'You wouldn't like to put the not wanting on a scale of one to ten?'

'No. Actually, I don't see how an absent emotion – not wanting something – can be put on a scale.'

'Well, people do say: I *really* don't want that to happen. Using an intensifier.'

'I don't want to see her, and that's that. No intensity.'

'Okay.'

'So, case closed; it *is* possible to miss someone and *not* want to see them. Are we done?'

'Well, someone might object that those are rather special circumstances; the person's being dead.'

'Nothing special about being dead. It happens to all of us.'

'Of course, but in this case it is a particular category, isn't it? We don't spend all day missing the dead.'

'I try not to.'

'So what if the person you miss isn't dead? Is it still possible not to want to see them?'

'You said five minutes.'

'I did. I'm sorry. You're free to end the interview whenever you want, of course.'

'Hmm. Is it still possible . . .? Yes, yes it is.'

'You don't seem quite so sure of yourself now. I'm supposed to ask you about levels of certainty. You seemed very clear before.'

'No, I am sure of myself. But the point is, now it gets more personal, doesn't it?'

'I don't understand.'

'Well, the fact of my mother's being dead is hardly anyone's fault. It doesn't require a particular narrative.'

'No.'

'Everyone loses a mother. Unless you die first yourself, of course.'

'Right.'

'Well.'

'Well?'

'I'm surprised you can't see what I'm driving at. You said that the dead were a special category. But in regard to the question you're asking, is it possible to miss someone and not want to see them? – which means, I suppose, to live in a conflicted state, to feel the impulse that normally makes you want something, and yet not want it – well, in regard to this question, the dead person is a special category only in so far as the conflicted state – missing, not wanting – seems natural, forgivable, no blame or disappointment need be attached.'

'I'm afraid you've lost me.'

'I don't believe that.'

'This is my fourth interview this afternoon. Could you maybe explain in a different way?'

'Damn. Can I invent, rather than giving a personal example?'

'By all means. Nothing was said about personal or impersonal. My brief is just to get as many in-depth responses as possible.'

'Okay, imagine a father happy with a son, enjoying his childhood and adolescence. Then the son turns nasty. Who knows why? Perhaps he gets into drugs and bad company. He despises his father's way of life. He becomes offensive. He leaves home. Now you might miss him. But you don't want to see him. You just know that any meeting would be unpleasant. In fact, you're almost afraid to see him because the meeting would confirm your worst suspicions.'

'Intensities? The missing, the not wanting.'

'No, sorry, I refuse to get into that. Though I can imagine that in this case both feelings would be quite intense. You miss the boy, you really don't want to see the man.'

'Okay. So, the dead mother, the prodigal son. Actually, you've created another situation where someone misses a person as they were in the past and then doesn't want to see them because they are either dead or otherwise changed. Really, it's the same thing.'

'That's it. That's how I think the situation you describe becomes possible. Are we done?'

'Would you mind if I pushed it just one question further? What if I ask: is it possible to miss someone, yet not want

296

to see them, even when that person has not changed in this dramatic way? Death, drugs, downfall, whatever. I mean when it's the same person you always knew.'

'I must say the nature of this study is pretty perplexing. I mean, how can they do a quantitative analysis with these kinds of questions and answers?'

'That's not my job, unfortunately. I'd love to know that myself.'

'I've heard that psycho researchers often have goals quite different from those the interviewee imagines. I mean, for all I know, this might actually be about how an older man reacts to a younger woman interviewer.'

'Oh, I don't think so, because in that case I would be a kind of bait, wouldn't I? Anyway, you've behaved like a perfect gentleman.'

'I left the door open!'

'I noticed.'

'One feels obliged to these days. But do they really not tell you what the exact object of the research is?'

'Honestly, no. My official brief is to explore the question they've given me, put it in as many ways as possible, ask about intensity and circumstances and take back the recordings. They give us a few hours' training, a long list of follow-up questions, and send us out.'

'And how do most people respond?'

'People contacted by email through the group usually give us a few minutes. But not everyone.'

'I meant, what kind of answers do they give?'

'All kinds, really. Some people are pretty inventive. Others are surprisingly sentimental. Somebody was talking to me about a pet rabbit. But if you're in a hurry, maybe we could clear up this last category: missing someone, who hasn't changed, but still not wanting to see them. Is that possible, as you see it?'

'It is possible, yes.'

'Ah. You sound very sure this time. And the circumstances?'

'I suppose if the person hasn't changed, other things will have changed. I mean, in order for the missing/not-wanting-to-see combination to hold there has to be a narrative, otherwise you'd be happy to see someone you missed, all things being as they were at the time when it was a pleasure to be with this person, and presumably at some point it *was* a pleasure, otherwise you wouldn't miss them.'

'So what are the other things that have changed?'

'The purpose of this research is to collect people's stories, isn't it? It's not quantitative research at all. They want to see how willing people are to confide their personal life.'

'What can I say? My brief is just to collect in-depth answers to this question for further analysis. If you'd just like to finish that reflection we could call it a day. You've been very generous with your time, Mr Paige.'

'But why would I want to go on, now I feel fairly certain I'm being misled? I wonder how ethical this is.'

'It's your call. Actually you seem to me a person who rather enjoys sorting things out. Maybe they're testing how willing people are to take on complex emotional conundrums.'

'But I don't like to be manipulated. I think they should tell us what the goal of the research is.'

. . .

'You're not going to tell me?'

'I'm as much in the dark as you are, honestly.'

'What if I don't believe that?'

'I can't make you believe me.'

'You seem too astute an interviewer not to be in on what the nature of the research is. I mean, you're not just ticking boxes.'

'I'm just holding a voice recorder. But for your information, no one else has asked me these questions so far. I mean, most interviews were over in about five to ten minutes. No one else seemed worried about the reasoning behind it.'

'Maybe the research is to find out how *you* respond when someone asks these questions.'

'That's fine by me. I'm paid by the hour.'

'How come? I would have thought by the number of interviews.'

'They seemed eager for long interviews, so they're not going to encourage us to keep them short.'

'But how would they know how many hours you really worked?'

'They have the recordings.'

'Right. You're recording.'

'It's anonymous.'

'A voice isn't anonymous, though, is it? If someone wanted to identify me.'

'You've hardly said anything that could be awkward for you.'

'That's not the point.'

'I'm sorry you feel this way. Do you want to close, then, with the case of missing someone who hasn't changed, or shall I turn it off?'

'This is a bit crazy, but, okay, my wife if you want to know. My ex-wife.'

'Didn't you say you were married?'

'I'm separated.'

'Ah. I'm sorry.'

'No need to be. I'm not.'

'Ah, that's good. You did say you were married, though, earlier on, didn't you? Yes.'

'Perhaps that's part of the missing. It's an easy answer to give. As if nothing had changed. And a separated person is theoretically still married. Legally.'

'But something has changed.'

'Right. And not my wife – that is, the person missed – in this case. In fact that was the problem, probably. I changed, or life's circumstances changed. Not her. Maybe even a simple question of age. Which actually is not that simple.'

'I wouldn't know.'

'Evidently not.'

'You don't want to say a word more about the nature of the change? In this case?'

'They didn't choose the interviewees on the basis of who was divorced?'

'I have no idea how they were chosen. Anyway you said you were separated, not divorced. I just know that you were sent an email and agreed to give a few minutes.'

'Almost fifteen, if I'm not mistaken.'

'Okay. I'll turn off. Unless you'd just like to say a word more about the circumstances.'

'One lives with someone for many years, through good times and bad. Decades. One changes town and job together, brings up children. One appreciates that the marriage has fallen apart, that there is a whole area of the relationship you simply can't deal with, and yet there's also a functioning routine: in the end you're constantly obliged to be close to that person, and there are still rare moments of fun. Finally it's all too much and you leave. You feel if you don't break out of this stalemate it will kill you. But having left, you inevitably miss this person. Leaving doesn't solve everything in a flash. Simply, they are so intensely connected with your life. You miss them, and you miss them as they are now. They haven't changed. At all. But you don't want to see them, because it would only be painful to them and confusing to you. In fact you feel it would be extremely unwise to see them. Intensity? Considerable. I mean you really don't want to see them.

Feelings of guilt and so on. Revival of an impossible dilemma.'

'Thank you. That's a very full reply.'

'God. I need a drink. You've turned off the recorder?'

'Yes.'

'Want to come along?'

'Sorry?'

'Would you like a drink? I feel a little upset. Thinking about that stuff.'

'Ah. I'm sorry. Thanks. I'm afraid I have a few more interviews, though. I mean, I have to make my quota.'

'You're a good interviewer. I can't imagine many people who would have coaxed that out of me.'

'Why, thank you.'

'On a scale of one to ten I'd give you . . . nine.'

'Not ten?'

'Maybe after a drink.'

'Sorry, I really can't.'

'What's your name?'

'Deborah.'

'Pleased to meet you, Deborah. I'm Thomas.'

'I know.'

'Some other time, then.'

'You're really asking me out for a drink?'

'Is it illegal?'

'Maybe dangerous.'

'On a scale of one to ten?'

'I suppose I'll only know that if I accept.'

CONCRETE

Maturity. The contentment of older couples. He puts the cat out while she stirs the camomile tea. Each knows which part of the paper the other wants, whose feet will be cold when. The ripened fruit in the familiar basket, the leaves to be gathered from the lawn. Winter trips to warmer climes, brightly wrapped presents for grandchildren. Accumulation, sedimentation. Her dying mother, his sister's motor neuron. The real more real every day. The sofa shaped to their two backs. The gentle scratching of her nails on his nape. He takes her calloused feet in mottled hands. Smiles through cataracts and a healthier diet. A yearly pact to rearrange the photographs. Why wasn't that our destiny? Thomas wonders. Thomas wonders how to deal with a past of erosion and unravelling. How to tell a story that is quicksand? He goes over the facts with his analyst. He goes over them again. She is paid not to be weary of it, he thinks. He goes over them again. She nods, she interprets, she interjects, objects, suggests, shakes her head. He goes over them again. They won't stay still. His wife won't stay still. His ex-wife, XYZ wife. I'm obliged to learn a new language, Thomas thinks, to speak in a different tongue. Thomas thinks his analyst is too sympathetic, too patient. In the end it was he who undid it all, he insists. 'It was my fault.' He explains his attraction to stone hearths, to the business of lighting fires, the pleasure of arranging the logs, watching the flames catch. He explains how much he loved gardening. He loved putting the bulbs in, pulling the weeds out. I'm getting nowhere. Fullness, repletion, plenitude, satiety, roundness, sagacity, serenity. These words plague him. The unquiet ghost. Me now. Exact opposite of the imperturbable patriarch. The haunting, obsessive return, without repose, neither here nor there, without burial.

'You want to be buried?' his analyst enquires. 'Alive?'

Thomas goes back to his rented bedsit and cooks vegetable biryani with his girlfriend. Afterwards, she feels they rather overdid it with the black pepper.

MARTHA AND EDWARD

'Is that you? Edward?'

'Martha!'

'So it's true! Praise the Lord! All true. Even the streets of gold!'

'Purest gold.'

' "As it were transparent glass . . ." Revelation 21:21.'

'My Bible girl! I've got you back.'

'Hallelujah! It really is all true!'

'Martha dear! Did you doubt it?'

'Oh, Edward, I did. Yes, at the end I'm afraid I did, a bit. It was so horrible, I was so sick. Everything was so heavy and dark, the room spinning. I feel I'm waking up from a nightmare.'

'Poor Martha. But how marvellous to see you again.'

'Edward?'

'Yes?'

'I wish I could *see* you.'

'Ah.'

'I mean, how did you know it was me? I . . . There must be so many . . .'

'You just sense it, dear. Then it was time for you to come. Who knows how these things work? You knew it was me, didn't you?'

'At once, yes. But without . . . without really seeing anything. I mean, much.'

'We left our bodies on earth, dear. And mine's been burned to bits, of course.'

'I sprinkled you in the river.'

'I beg your pardon?'

'I sprinkled your ashes in the river, Edward.'

'Did you? Did you really? How . . . Indian. I thought we'd agreed on a rose tree. In the North London Crem memorial garden.'

'I changed my mind. I mean, it seemed more beautiful in the river, where we used to walk and you loved to row. Oh, Edward. It's all *true*! It's like Christmas. And I feel no pain. I was in such pain. It was killing me. Silly, it *did* kill me. Can we hug?'

'Martha, love!'

'Can't we?'

'You'll have to get used to how it is here. See, people just drift through each other. We have no substance now.'

'*Through* each other?'

'By the gateway, look – there, with the sapphires. That group coming out.'

'How peculiar. Just coloured air. A sort of brightness.'

'If you like, we can occupy the same space. Let me. There! We're one inside the other now. Superimposed. We're absolutely together. Like we never were before.'

'I can't feel anything, though.'

'We don't have feeling, Martha. You think it. It's a thought. We're one inside the other. Enjoy that thought, in your mind.'

'You were the thinker, Edward dear. Not me. It does seem a shame, though, after thirty years, not to hug.'

'Everybody says that, at first. Then you get used to being all spirit.'

'We can talk, though. Thank heavens for that.'

'Actually, we intuit each other's thoughts.'

'Ah. You're right. I knew something was odd. I'm not actually hearing you. Oh, Edward. What a huge relief to find you here and to know it's true. There were moments . . . Oh dear. I haven't quite got over it yet. Thomas was squeezing my hand, the last day, you know, while I was dying, and every squeeze told me he thought I'd soon just be dead. I'd be nothing. A lump of senseless flesh. That was what was upsetting him, bless him. But it didn't help me with my faith.'

'Thomas has done quite well for himself, hasn't he?'

'Oh, all right. I suppose. He has a good job. Seems he's quite a whizz. But his marriage failed, you know, poor thing.'

'Ah. And that was the very last wedding I celebrated. What a shame!'

'And he won't be coming to heaven either, will he, love, if it's all true? We won't ever see him again.'

'No, dear, I'm afraid not. Nor Jim.'

'But doesn't it grieve you, Edward? Two sons. Both lost. Oh, it takes all the shine off it.'

'I've got used to the thought now, Martha. What can you do? Jim was always such a cussed boy. He always had to have the last word.'

'He didn't come to see me at the end. I suppose it was a terribly long trip to make at short notice. Oh, Edward.'

'What is it? Martha, what is it? What's the matter?'

'I want to cry and I can't. The tears won't come.'

'No, dear.'

'Don't tell me we can't cry.'

'You need a body to cry, love.'

'How silly. I spent half my life trying not to cry and now I can't. Poor Jim. Poor Thomas. If only we could have proved to them all this existed.'

'It is extraordinary, isn't it? The walls of jasper. The gates of pearl. And it goes on for ever, you know. You can just keep breezing along for ever. And the light is always astonishing. Always the same. It's the glory of the Lord. It never stops.'

'"And the foundations of the wall of the city were garnished with all manner of precious stones." Revelation 21:19.'

'Martha! How funny having you with me again. Nobody quotes the Bible here, though, you know. No one reads it.'

308

'Oh, really? I thought we'd be reading Scripture all day long.'

'There are no days! Or nights. No sleep and no waking. The fact is we just don't need it now – do we? – once we've got here. There wouldn't be any point. Actually, I'm not sure there are any bibles. Or any doctrine. I mean, I always thought when I got here I'd finally understand the Trinity and so on, except it just doesn't seem to matter any more. Nobody discusses it. No one writes. No one reads at all. Martha! Please. Don't be upset. You could hardly imagine what it would be like when you were back on earth, could you? Nobody could. Come on, now. Tell me which part of the river you sprinkled my ashes in.'

'Kew Bridge.'

'Ah. Kew. Looking towards Strand-on-the-Green? Or Brentford?'

'Strand-on-the-Green, of course. The Steam Packet. Though there was a silly breeze blowing the wrong way. You kept coming back in my face in gritty bits.'

'To think I've been telling people I was in North London Crem. I wonder what they'll do with yours?'

'My ashes are going in the vicarage garden. At Whitton. It's a lovely place.'

'You think! I thought I knew where mine were going. But no doubt Elaine will tell us in due course. Elaine will definitely join us. At least one child. Nothing could shake her faith. Then we'll be a family again.'

'It just won't feel right without the boys, Edward.'

'We did our best. What else could we have done?'

'It's true. We prayed and preached and wrestled with their hearts. The truth is, Satan had them in his grip.'

'Satan.'

'What is it, dear?'

'I haven't heard anyone mention him for ages. I suppose the struggle is far behind us here. One forgets.'

'Edward! From the sound of your voice, if you had a face, you'd be smiling. Oh, I remember your dear face so clearly. What is it?'

'I was thinking I almost missed him, Martha.'

'Who? James?'

'No, Satan. It was so exciting, wasn't it? When we did the exorcisms. When the devils squealed and ran.'

'Do be careful, love. Isn't that sacrilege?'

'It's the truth. It was exciting.'

'Yes. I suppose it was. I never thought of it like that. Oh, I can hear singing, Edward. "Great and marvellous are thy works, Lord God Almighty; just and true are thy ways, thou King of saints." Where are they? Let's join in. Let's give thanks for being reunited. I want to see the Lamb of God.'

'Those are angel voices, Martha.'

'Oh, but they're so beautiful. So perfect. I could listen to them for ever.'

'You will. You will.'

'Let's go and join in. Edward? Come on.'

'I'm afraid *we* can't sing, love.'

'Because we don't have bodies.'

'Right.'

'But what do we do, then? Oh, I'm sorry, it's just I'm feeling a bit lost.'

'It's hard to explain. We just, sort of, *are*, Martha. We go into a trance, of adoration of the Lord. We are one with Him, with this brilliant light and the glory all around us. It really is very beautiful, once you've settled in.'

'"Then shall the righteous shine forth as the sun in the kingdom of their Father." Matthew 13:43.'

'Right. Sort of. It's like an endless beatitude. Time just flies. If it is time. Absorbed in the light. It's only when someone from the past arrives that you're disturbed a bit. For a little while.'

'Disturbed?'

'You start remembering things. Details. Then you colour the air, just a little bit. Stain it, I suppose. Otherwise we're quite transparent. Oh, Martha! Don't worry! The Lord has everything under control. Promise.'

'You sound like Elaine now. She kept saying that while I was dying. Except it didn't feel as if He had.'

'Dear Elaine.'

'Well, no doubt I shall get used to it. I suppose I'm just a bit miffed we can't have a hug.'

'Martha.'

'Remember our Saturday morning lie-ins?'

'I do, dear. I do.'

'And the hot baths on winter afternoons? With tea and scones afterwards. They had quite nice scones in the

311

hospice, come to think of it. Just I was too ill to enjoy more than a crumb or two. I presume we don't eat here, then, Edward? There are no set times for anything. Or sleep?'

'No. Martha, we don't. But remember, we will get our bodies back one day.'

'Of course. On Judgement Day.'

'When the world ends and the dead rise from their graves.'

'Or out of the river.'

'Right. All those bits of ash from Hammersmith and Chelsea and Greenwich, and miles out to sea.'

'Remember when we visited the Isle of Dogs?'

'And Gravesend!'

'Edward! You never could resist a pun, could you?'

'So, you see, Martha, we do have something to look forward to.'

THE SECOND MRS P

'I wonder if the second Mrs P will have such big breasts,' Mary said.

Or she said: 'That definitely looks more like the third Mrs P than the second.'

A tall slim adolescent was walking by. Thomas hadn't noticed till his wife spoke. These were the early days of their marriage. It was a joke.

Now, with hindsight, he wondered if she hadn't always foreseen the end. Or if by mentioning the possibility, light-heartedly, she meant to prevent him from going where she imagined all men wanted to go, even though at the time no such notion had occurred to him. He was too busy being married and starting a family and pushing forward his career.

'I wonder if the second Mrs P will have dreadlocks,' Mary laughed. 'Or a tongue-piercing.'

'Oh, I doubt if she is born yet,' he said, joining in the fun.

And in the end, of course, this had turned out to be the case. What will Mary think when she finally finds out? Thomas wondered, boarding the train that will take him to a home that is home no more.

Looking out of the window at the familiar landscape, Thomas reflected that he had commuted too long between the old life and the new. Was that cruel of him, or just inept? And on her part? Was it cruel of her to tease him with second Mrs Ps, to let him have such a long leash, but nevertheless insist it was a leash? Had that been smart? Perhaps the truth was they had both somehow come to have a double narrative of their marriage: they would continue man and wife into ripe old age; they would sink and split. Both stories had felt true. Logically, they were mutually exclusive, but that didn't stop them believing in both. Like knowing you will die but living as though you are immortal.

The occasion of his visit today was the sale of the flat that had once served as his office. Both signatures were required. They had decided to meet beforehand at the house to discuss the division of the furniture. In the past Thomas would have had his car waiting at the station, or Mary would have come to pick him up, or one of the children when they were old enough. Or at a push he would have taken a bus. But now the weather was sweltering and he felt impatient. On impulse he went to the taxi stand, which would cost him £45. 'I can barely afford *one* Mrs P,' he remembered joking years ago, 'never mind two.'

'I guess it will have to wait till you're chairman of the board,' she laughed.

'Just after the bend, on the right,' Thomas told the driver and was overwhelmed by the thought that what he should have said was that he loved her and that all this talk of a second Mrs P was nonsense and she should never mention the idea again. You should have forbidden her from ever bringing up the idea at all, Thomas thought, climbing out of the cab. That would have reassured her. Instead you fooled around, and so confirmed her suspicion. What could she do in response but start to disinvest in the relationship? Which in turn would prompt him to feel that something was badly wrong and that he had better prepare for the worst. You made a terrible mistake, Thomas thought. Despite the heat he was in a cold sweat. Worse than a mistake, a crime. Destroying a family. Thomas gave the taxi driver a large tip.

Beyond the wicket gate the familiar garden was in full bloom. Roses flamed over the front windows. The lawn was the brilliant green that betrays a chemical fertiliser. But Thomas was surprised to see the French window closed. Why? Both Mary and their daughter Sally loved to sit in the breeze by the open window. It was such a fine spring day.

Thomas put his nose against the glass, but the room was empty. And had changed, he thought. Perhaps some piece of furniture had been moved. Or a picture. He couldn't quite see what.

Going round the side of the house he reflected that Mary had not had any trouble replacing his gardening skills. Both jasmine and wisteria were very neatly tied up. Suddenly he was struck by a strange silence hanging about the place. Everything was perfect, but very still, as in a photograph, or a film set before the actors arrive. Or after they have gone, perhaps. He pushed the doorbell. Even through the heavy door the ring was loud.

Immediately there was a response. But it came from the garden behind him, behind the jasmine. A dog whined. Thomas had always hated this dog, a Dobermann, which was left out all night in the next yard and often barked. What was its name? He couldn't remember. Meanwhile there was no sign of movement in the house. This was irritating. He rang the bell again. Again the dog whined. It scratched at the fence. The sounds only made the stillness heavier. She will be in the bathroom, Thomas thought. Mark must be out. Though actually he was a little late for lunch and Mary had assured him Mark would be there, otherwise he wouldn't have accepted the invitation. He would never have agreed to have lunch with Mary on her own.

Waiting, he turned to look over the fence at the dog he hated. Why, he wondered, had Mary got rid of her dog, Ricky, shortly after they had separated? It was strange. Just when you thought she would have been grateful for the company of the animal she got rid of him. Life was mysterious. Thomas looked over the fence at the Dobermann and remembered its name was Rocky. Rocky and Ricky. He'd never noticed that the names were so similar. Such close neighbours. Seeing the face appear over the jasmine, Rocky barked loudly and ran around his stump of a tail in excitement. The bark echoed painfully between the two houses. Thomas hated it, but nevertheless felt a certain affection for the dog, seeing it after so long. For its doggie nervousness, its disquiet.

But why was no one answering the door? It wasn't like her. He was nervous too. Listening to the bell respond to his finger for the third time, Thomas suddenly realised what had happened. She had killed herself.

The film set – for the whole thing has taken on an eerie theatricality now – comes complete with a glass-paned lean-to against the wall by the front door. This narrow shed is a clutter of garden tools. Tracked by a camera overhead, Thomas moves swiftly towards it. He untwists a wire that keeps the latch on its hook and steps inside among spades and garden forks and crusty old work boots. Now there is a close-up of his staring eyes as he rummages through old flowerpots on the shelves. Where have they left it? Cobwebs stick to his fingers. Then he has the spare key.

She has hanged herself. She knew he was coming. She knew he would be the one to find her. Aware of the camera focusing on his trembling hand as he tries to push the key into the lock, he knows these are moments he will remember for ever. The lock turns. Inside, the silent perfection of the place convinces him that an awful revelation is at hand. Rocky has stopped barking. The stillness is uncanny. Mark too? he thinks, as the camera tracks round the empty room. Please God, no. The piano is where he left it four years ago. The chairs, the shelves, are all where he left them. There is no blood on the floor. 'Mary?' he calls. His voice in the overhead mike is courageously firm. 'Mark?' He turns left to the kitchen. It is neat and clean. There is no sign of cooking. They never meant to eat.

Thomas raises his voice. 'Mary!' Later he will recall how extraordinarily aware of his body and posture he was as he started to climb the stairs, tensed for nightmare. Each turn of the staircase – and there are three floors – takes a year off his life as a new part of the old house falls into his field of vision. Nothing. Nothing at the first turn, nothing at the second. But then, how could they have hanged themselves here, when there is no place in the ceiling to attach a rope? No banister to dangle from.

The bathtub scarlet with blood. He pushes the toilet door, ready to vomit. A bright beam of sunlight glistens on the white enamel. Mark's room, then. Another door to push. It's a shocking mess, but that in itself is hardly a shock. On the contrary. The camera behind his left shoulder now, Thomas gazes at piles of clothes overflowing from an open cupboard, papers everywhere, the computer on the floor where he always puts it when he sits with his back to the bed. Seventeen years ago Thomas had sat in that very spot singing a tiny child to sleep. Now he is in a cold sweat.

To the right the small guest room waits with dusty patience for guests. This is where Thomas slept when he could no longer bear the conjugal bed. A guest in his own house. But why is he wasting time here? He slams the door shut, very aware that he has merely been putting off the only two rooms that matter, the only rooms with rafters.

The camera holds his anxious face as he pauses on the landing. Thomas looks into the lens. Eyes and camera seem to be questioning one another. What is all this about? Decisively he moves to his daughter's old room, long empty at the back of the house where the roof comes down low and the ceiling is wooden slats with one large beam near the outer wall. Thomas pushes the door determinedly. Nothing. The room is breathlessly still. Except, moving into the middle, Thomas catches the movement of his own body in the floor-to-ceiling mirror his daughter once asked for so she could watch herself dancing. The very emptiness of the place seems to demand her ghost.

So it must be in their own bedroom, under the roof up the last flight of stairs, that she has done it. But you *knew* that, Thomas realises. Where else? In the sanctum of their withered intimacy. The camera knows it too, turning before he does to track along the passageway.

'Mary!'

The house is drawing him upwards. Everything else has been a diversion, or a preparation. The scene is set. In confirmation, the camera fuses with his eyes, his point of view. They will discover the slaughter together. Her feet, swinging from the big central beam on which the roof rested, dangling over the bed where love had been made countless times, where Mark himself was conceived.

Tom!' a voice called. 'Is that you, To-om?'

Thomas closed his eyes and sighed deeply. The call came from behind and below him.

'Really not smart,' Mary was shaking her head as he reached the bottom stair. 'Leaving the front door wide open. With all the stray cats around here. Not to mention the cat burglars!'

Mark went to his father and they hugged.

'What were you doing in my bedroom? I'd prefer it if you didn't go up there without asking.'

'You're sweating, Dad,' Mark stepped back. 'God, you're soaked. Let me give you some deodorant.' Laughing, the boy pulled his father into the downstairs toilet and began to spray something icy cold into his damp armpits.

As he came out, Mary unleashed a wry smile.

'Alone still? I half thought we might have to provide luncheon for the second Mrs P.'

Turning to the kitchen, she began to open a big pack of sushi. She hadn't felt like cooking.

'I've decided to skip the second Mrs P,' Thomas found himself on automatic pilot, 'and go straight for number three, or even four.'

Mary laughed good-heartedly.

For a moment then it was hard to tell which of those two old stories of their marriage they were presently in.

SHRINK

Thomas was furious with his shrink and finally found the courage to tell her as much. Perhaps three weeks without analysis over the long Christmas break had given him the chance to get his head together and reassert his independence.

'The fact is,' he began, 'if it hadn't been for you, I wouldn't have left my wife. I would still have a home and family and an identity that made sense to me. Not to mention the financial side of it all.'

Made worse, of course, he might have added, by these £90-an-hour sessions.

His shrink is a small squat woman in her mid-seventies who shuffles around a stone floor in slippers, smoking ultra-thin menthol cigarettes. She has never asked Thomas's leave to smoke during his visits, which, given that this is theoretically a place of work, is quite possibly illegal, he reflects, and certainly disrespectful. On the other hand he hasn't asked her not to smoke. She exercises a strange power over him that Thomas is beginning to find rather irksome.

The shrink got up to look for a shawl. She must be cold. Now she sits again and taps away a little ash. Looking up, her raised eyebrows seem to say, Go on, then.

'I came to you in a dilemma over my marriage; you took the decision for me after only two or three meetings. From everything that's emerged in our conversations since, and that's nearly eighteen months' worth, it's become clear that you are viscerally opposed to marriage in general, above all long marriages. No doubt you tell all your clients to leave their husbands or wives. Basically my whole life has been radically and negatively transformed just because in a moment of weakness I took a friend's advice and came to the wrong shrink.'

The shrink draws on her cigarette and pulls the brown shawl tight round her shoulders.

'How was your Christmas, Mr Paige?' she asks. 'And New Year. Did you go away?'

'No. I was here in town. My girlfriend went back to her family. In Dublin.'

The shrink waited.

'In the end I took advantage of the situation to get a lot of work squared away so there'll be more free time when she gets back.'

Again the shrink did not speak. When Thomas did not continue she simply settled back in her chair as if to make herself comfortable. She appeared, Thomas thought, to be observing him carefully, even sympathetically; on the other hand he had long since realised this must be any shrink's default setting. Well, he wasn't going to oblige, he decided. He could stay silent as long as she could. Already he was thinking that at the end of this hour he would very likely discontinue their relationship. But as soon as his posture began to assume a hint of defiance, she enquired:

'Was this the first Christmas you've spent away from your family?'

Thomas reflected: 'The second.'

Again she made her encouraging face; again he hesitated; again as soon as it seemed he might stay defiantly mute she had a question ready.

'What stopped you from getting in the car and driving over there?'

Thomas too was in an armchair, still in his overcoat. It wasn't clear to him whether the question came from genuine interest or a desire to provoke; he decided to take it for the latter.

'That would have been a big decision,' he said, 'precisely thanks to all the drastic steps I've taken this year.'

He didn't say, *under your influence*, but felt he could trust her to read the accusation in his voice.

The shrink grinned and sucked the last wisdom from her cigarette. She leaned forward and stubbed it out carefully. The ashtray was clean because, as Thomas had noted some time ago, she always emptied it before the next client and opened the window for a few minutes, which was perhaps why she had felt cold. Outside it was raining on slushy snow.

She waited.

'It would hardly have been fair on Elsa,' Thomas added, almost involuntarily. It annoyed him that he tended to throw more into the conversation than was perhaps necessary. Sometimes the whole hour was pretty much his own monologue. Which was rather letting her off the hook, he thought. My motormouth making her money. On the other hand, he was there to be analysed, not to keep things hidden. In the end, the whole quandary boiled down to the question: was she friend or foe? And if foe, why on earth was he paying her to fight him? Suddenly he felt he must solve this question today.

'Sometimes,' he announced, 'I feel that if my wife were ever to find out the kind of advice you've been giving me, she'd take you to court for destroying our marriage.'

The shrink did at least seem very attentive now, which was gratifying.

Thomas waited. He would decide this very day if it made any sense at all going on with this farce.

'Tell me about Christmas in the family,' the shrink said.

Thomas sighed.

'I always wanted a traditional English Christmas,' he told her.

She made her encouraging face.

'I mean, having a tree. As big as possible. With fairy lights. A turkey lunch. Plum pudding. Exchanging presents on Christmas Day itself. Seeing them under the tree on the days beforehand. We used to have lunch, which was pretty heavy, with quite a lot of wine, something special and expensive, open our presents together sitting round a fire, then collapse into bed or go for a walk.'

'Sounds idyllic,' the shrink laughed. 'I can't see why you didn't drive home, then.'

Thomas felt angry.

'Obviously it wasn't quite like that. Or, it was like that, but it didn't feel as it should have felt. Or as I always hoped it would feel.'

The shrink proffered her questioning, knitted-brow look. Sometimes it seemed she worked more with facial expressions than with words.

Thomas tried to focus on Christmas. For some reason he found himself saying, 'The ghost of Christmases past.'

The shrink ignored the allusion.

'Actually it was all very tense. First Mary didn't want the tree because it dirtied the floor with its needles. She didn't want the turkey because she didn't feel like cooking it. She didn't want to wait for Christmas Day to exchange presents because why not use things once they'd been bought? Very likely she was right and it was stupid of me to insist. I think she thought we were doing things too much the way my family had always done them, while her family had never really had a Christmas tradition. It didn't seem they really did anything at all at Christmas. It was all Hogmanay with them. Being Scottish. Glaswegians, even. The children loved it, though. When I said, Okay, I give in, not this year then, they'd start clamouring for the tree and the turkey and so on, and then Mary changed her mind and we did it anyway, but with a feeling that it had all been quite an effort to get to that decision.'

The shrink nodded.

'Probably it was my fault. Probably I shouldn't have suggested anything at all.'

The shrink pulled out a face that seemed to mean: how depressing, but there you go.

'Then it would have been up to her to suggest what to do and she would have felt more in control and positive about it all.'

The shrink frowned. 'Your wife wasn't working at this time?'

'Freelance jobs. Now and then.'

The shrink waited.

'I remember one time she called in the decorators between Christmas and New Year.'

Here the shrink raised her eyebrows, as one both surprised and amused. It was the most spontaneous of her expressions so far.

'Tell me,' she said, feeling down the side of her armchair for her cigarettes. Thomas was aware of a sudden recip- rocal warmth between them. He was rather good at telling stories and she was an attentive listener. He tried to remember.

'I had invited my mother up that year. Or rather, we had invited her. I would never have invited my mother for Christmas, or anyone else for that matter, if Mary hadn't agreed. Maybe it was even Mary who suggested it. I can't remember. Actually, they got on pretty well. Mary was generous with guests, she put on a big show for them, but then she'd get impatient, especially if the stay was extended. It was also the first year of the dog. He was still a puppy.'

'Ricky,' the shrink said.

Thomas smiled. If there was one aspect of the shrink's performance you couldn't fault her on it was her memory. Gradually she was becoming a repository of his entire life. Often he wondered how she could do that for all her clients, the same way he wondered how pianists could recall all the pieces they played. No doubt it was this that gave her her hold over him. She did not forget. She possessed his life.

'That's right. Ricky.'

'The trophy dog,' the shrink added. She was rubbing it in, but he could hardly deny these had been his words.

'That wasn't a problem,' he said quickly, 'since my mother always loved dogs. We always had one when I was a kid.'

The shrink waited.

'Anyway, the house needed redecorating. Or rather the walls needed repapering. My wife liked them to be smart and fresh. I wasn't too concerned myself. Probably I'm a bit lax that way. I think men and women differ over stuff like that. She had waited till the children were pretty much grown-up and had stopped putting fingerprints on the wall. Anyway, she managed to get a cheap price from a couple of guys who worked for a decorating firm. They would do it over Christmas with the firm's equipment, but moonlighting and paid under the table.'

Thomas cast about for the actual sums of money but couldn't remember. 'Anyway, it was pretty cheap. I mean, it was a serious saving. Mary was always smart that way.'

'Except it was Christmas.'

'Right. And my mother was staying. She wasn't well, either. I think she'd had her first operation that year.'

The shrink nodded. 'Presumably you objected to bringing the decorators in.'

'I wasn't enthusiastic. I felt we should do it in summer when it wouldn't matter having the windows open for everything to dry and the hell with the money since we didn't really have a money problem at the time. I think Mary was naturally a little anxious over money at this point. Not sure why. She didn't use to be when we were younger. Then it was the other way round. Me worried, her not. Anyway, she called them in. I think it was the day after Boxing Day. If not Boxing Day itself.'

'So,' the shrink observed. 'You were insisting on a traditional Christmas show for your mother, and your wife got the decorators in.'

'Actually, Mary *liked* cooking turkey. I mean, once she'd decided to do it. Having my mother there gave her a chance to show how good she was. And she really was. Really *is*. Certainly much more elaborate than Mum ever could be. Mary is a great cook. In fact, from the moment we agreed it would be right to have Mum over, because it might well be the last year she would be well enough to make the trip, I can't recall any of the usual argument about whether we should have a traditional Christmas lunch or not.'

The shrink waited.

Thomas sighed. How weird, suddenly to be going over all this old stuff again. He felt torn.

'Basically, it was a disaster. My wife was still in the phase when she thought the dog needed a two-hour walk every day. I mean, she had got herself an outdoor kind of dog and she felt guilty if she didn't walk him enough.'

'Guilty?'

'She said he needed to be walked. She had a responsibility. Obviously my mum couldn't go with her because she was pretty much reduced to a few steps around the garden. That meant I had to stay at home. So Mary would take Mark for company. Of course he would rather have slept in. Mary would bribe him by taking them to the coffee bar for a cake or something, but then they had to walk for two hours and they came back irritated and annoyed. Even the dog was exhausted.'

'And your daughter? Presumably she was home at Christmas.'

Thomas laughed more heartily. 'Sally? She wouldn't have dreamed of going. She just says no. Refuses point-blank.'

The shrink smiled. 'There's always someone who does that.'

Thomas stopped and breathed deeply. What was that supposed to mean?

'I was on her side,' he said, as if this altered anything. 'She was studying pretty hard for her finals then. To make matters worse, if I remember rightly, Mark's girlfriend had left him on Christmas Eve, the same day Mum arrived, which rather put a damper on the Christmas lunch. He was really upset. That was his first serious girlfriend. Of course we were being as sympathetic as possible, but no doubt he could see that we were all pleased as well, because it was pretty obvious to everyone that they weren't really suited to each other. We were glad it was over.'

'Ah,' the shrink nodded, sagely.

'In fact, as I recall it, I was thinking this was a major piece of good news, them splitting up – you know one's always terrified of one's children choosing the wrong partner, right? Mary and I were a hundred per cent agreed about that. All the same, the break-up put a very big damper on the party; Mark is usually a lot of fun and seeing him take it so hard and then texting all the time wasn't encouraging. Plus of course there was the worry they would get back together. And then things would have been worse than before.'

The shrink raised a very wry eyebrow here, which again seemed to be trying to tell Thomas something. His mood had definitely shifted. It felt good to be telling the story of this awful Christmas, though dangerous as well, exhilaratingly dangerous. Like walking along the edge of a cliff. Suddenly there was a rush of memory.

'The fact is, over the next few days I felt so angry I wanted to die. I really wanted to lie down and die.'

In response to this the shrink sat up with a face of intense concern. It was almost comical. Sometimes Thomas thought of her as Yoda in *The Empire Strikes Back*. There was the same mix of exaggerated facial expression and supposed wisdom. 'Imagine Yoda smoking ultra-thin menthol cigarettes and you have it,' he had once told Elsa, but then it turned out she hadn't seen *Star Wars*. She hadn't been born then.

'People who feel angry often want to hit back,' the shrink pointed out, 'but not to die.'

Thomas hesitated. Was he really going to go there?

'Normally,' he stalled, 'I would have joined in the walks, even with my mum being there – I like walking – but somebody needed to stay home and be around while these guys did the decorating. There was lots of heavy furniture to move and cover up. That's it, I remember now. It was part of the cheap deal she'd negotiated that they would find each room ready to paint or paper when they arrived in the mornings, without having to do all the preliminaries. And I knew if I didn't cover things up properly, masking tape round the skirting board and so on, and they got paint drippings on them, or if the rooms weren't ready, there would be trouble. I was tired that year and not feeling too well at the time. Bad back and the rest. I don't want to go into that. It was an old problem I'd been having. But what drove me mad was these two guys – and we're talking your classic working-class decorators, one middle aged, one young, a real double act – they could see perfectly well what the situation was between myself and Mary and they were faking respect for me but actually smirking and my mother could see this as well and the children too and the guys would ask me questions, what to do about this corner or that mirror, and when I answered they said maybe you should phone the missus in case she sees it differently and they were right of course, so I did, and she asked me to pass the phone to them so she could speak to them directly and I realised they had only asked me first to save themselves the cost of the phone call because they could perfectly well have phoned her directly and left me to get on with what-ever I was doing, and then right in the middle of it all, the day they were going to do the big bedroom, our bedroom, I made a mistake and put everything but the bed out on the terrace – the bedroom was on the top floor and had a kind of roof terrace – the bedside tables, an armchair, the carpets, the lamps, a chest of drawers, a low table, etc., etc. and then a little later when I was downstairs making a coffee for Mum – one problem was we couldn't put the heating on because of the need to keep the windows open, so it was freezing, except in the kitchen where I'd fixed a space heater – the day suddenly clouds over and this huge, but really huge gust of wind comes along and blows everything about, including a nice lampstand with a madly expensive glass shade that shattered into about ten million pieces over the chairs and rugs, and the decorators pretended to be sympathetic but were really sniggering. So then for the rest of the morning I was dreading my wife coming back, which she eventually did, with the dog looking more knackered than ever and Mark in a state of angry misery, and Mary sighed as if to say what could one expect, and she said maybe this was a good moment to get rid of the big painting above the stairs that was a favourite of mine but that she had never liked. My mother, needless to say, was looking like all she wanted to do was to be allowed to get on the next train home and die in peace, she wasn't used to people arguing, and . . .'

Thomas stopped. The shrink had been chuckling, but now used a drag on her cigarette to change the expression to a frown. Thomas knew then that she knew he wasn't telling her the half of it. He felt cautious.

'I remember having a dream,' he began. 'One of those nights.' Again he stopped.

The shrink watched. For the first time she seemed sceptical.

'I'm not sure if it was really one of those nights. But it comes back to me now.'

The shrink sighed. 'Tell me.'

'I had a girlfriend at the time,' Thomas said, a little sheepishly. 'A mistress, maybe you'd have to say.'

The shrink was hardly surprised. They had been through this.

'Let's say girlfriend,' she said.

'I'd been with her maybe a year at this point. We got on pretty well. Anyway, I dreamed we were in a mountain valley. It was green and very beautiful and we seemed happy and relaxed and she was dressed very beautifully and rather chastely in a long flowery skirt down to bare feet. I think my feet were bare too. I almost always have bare feet in dreams. Go figure.'

The shrink nodded.

She's being paid for this, Thomas thought. I'm paying her to nod like this.

'It was beautiful, I mean the whole scene just said: beauty, serenity, happiness. A caricature. Except there was the problem that we needed to go somewhere to eat and sleep. There was nothing in the valley but beauty. You can't eat beauty. So we were following a path downwards that seemed to be taking us somewhere, except that it led into a tunnel. It seemed to be an old railway tunnel, disused now, and we started walking into it, thinking we would soon be out. It was pitch dark, which was worrying with us being barefoot, but there was something faintly white in the distance and we thought it must be daylight, even if it didn't look like daylight; in fact when we got there it was ice, or maybe frozen snow, blocking the tunnel from top to bottom, there was no way through, it was packed tight, and I remember waking and thinking how strange it was that there could be snow inside a tunnel when there was none outside and wondering how it had got there.'

Thomas stopped.

The shrink stubbed out her second cigarette and smoothed out her dress, which had rumpled when she leaned forward.

'You were telling me about that Christmas.'

'I drove my mother into town to the station, probably New Year's Eve, both pretending it had been a great stay and that everything was fine, even though we each knew perfectly well that the other knew perfectly well that on the contrary nothing was fine, everything was wrong. And driving back home I thought for the thousandth time that my wife was behaving the way she was because of my mistress, not that she knew about her, but I suppose these things are sort of in the air, so I called her, my girlfriend – I stopped in a service station, I remember – and told her we would have to stop, it was over. She was terribly upset, couldn't believe it even, because we had been getting on so well, and naturally I felt a complete shit, not to mention spectacularly unhappy, but also like I had no right to complain, since it was hardly fair of me to have this mistress, fair on either of them I mean, Mary or her, and when I got back the dog had wagged his muddy tail all over the new wallpaper to one side of the front door and Mary was just laughing and I couldn't understand why she wasn't angry. I suggested we go out to a celebratory dinner for Hogmanay but she said the dog couldn't be left alone because the fireworks would drive him mad and the children couldn't dog-sit because they both had parties of their own, at one of which needless to say Mark got back with his inappropriate girlfriend. So all those tears had been for nothing and on the day . . .'

'Mr Paige.'

Thomas stopped.

'I'm afraid our time is up and I have another appointment.'

The shrink smiled kindly, but somehow sadly too.

'Let me just ask you, though, was this Christmas you've just spent on your own better or worse than that?'

Thomas had already moved forward on his chair to get up. He felt foolish.

'Well,' he grinned, 'friends kept commiserating because I was alone, like, how awful, Christmas on your own, you know, but actually, well, actually, it was fine. I felt fine.'

'And your girlfriend is coming back soon?'

'This evening. I'm going straight to the airport right now to meet her.'

Saying this, it was embarrassing how unable he was to hide his pleasure.

The shrink stood up, smoothed her crumpled dress, picked up the ashtray with her left hand and offered her right to Thomas to be shaken.

'Next Thursday, then. Same time. Do feel free to call me if you need to.'

In the hallway, Thomas passed a man who was struggling to pull off a motorcycle helmet. During the bus ride to the station, watching sprays of slush from the filthy gutters, he reflected on the shrink's method. Was it a method? He felt ashamed of himself and rather happy.

MUSIC

In the concert hall Thomas tries to concentrate on the music. He is sitting beside his girlfriend. The programme is Verdi, symphonies and arias. As a result, the concert hall, usually half empty, is full. Verdi is popular, it seems, though his symphonies are rarely played. Thomas and his girlfriend are near the front but way over to the left, so that they have to look right to see the faces of the first violinists.

What does it mean to concentrate on music? Thomas remembers sitting in the same position, though in a different concert hall, many years ago to listen to Bach's organ music. An entirely different cup of tea. He had been beside his wife then. He had always sat to the left of his wife, as he now always sits to the left of his girlfriend. Is it he or they who make this decision? Has there ever been a woman he sat to the right of? On that occasion too there had been the problem of concentrating. He had been tormented by the dilemma: should he leave his wife? His unhappiness made it impossible for him to follow the music. In one fugue he had forced himself to imagine that the notes of the dominant voice, at once so random and so perfect, were moving around the concert hall, probing at hidden places in the walls and roof. Trying to find a way out, perhaps. This game had allowed Thomas to hold on to the notes for a while, his eyes shifting in the high corners of the hall, above the organ pipes, imagining the music moving there, feeling, pushing, looking for space and light. Doing that, he had remembered that at school there had been a poem by Robert Browning where an organist thinks of the notes of a toccata as a kind of search, or quest for something hidden. He hadn't been able to recall the name of the poem at the time, and still can't recall it now, thinking back from Verdi to Bach, from his girlfriend to his wife, who then sat tensely by his side as he tried so hard to concentrate on the music rather than their problems by following its imagined movements around the concert hall, all too aware that this could hardly be what was really meant by concentrating on music; truly to concentrate on music would surely mean having your head full of the sound, its qualities and harmonies, without these words and this constant effort, this forced and fanciful analogy of notes probing for a way out of the concert building, which of course, he realises now, had been just him hoping for a way out of his dilemma – his marriage, rather – not to mention the gnawing, pathetic, mean concern that since he was incapable of concentrating on the music he was actually wasting an evening that had cost a lot of money.

The orchestra winds up one piece, pauses for applause, then begins another so similar to the first that Thomas would be hard put to prove that the musicians are not just repeating the same thing. You cannot follow Verdi's symphonies round the room, he reflects. The notes don't go anywhere. Rather they turn in on themselves, like a maypole dance, girls and boys in circles, ducking under each other's arms, hands meeting in the air holding ribbons and handkerchiefs. Or like patterns in old lace tablecloths, predictably frilly, charming enough in their way, but not something anyone really has much use for these days. Perhaps it's not his fault he can't concentrate. It's Verdi's. No wonder no one ever plays these symphonies. At least Bach was challenging.

Beside Thomas his girlfriend, who once studied music at the conservatory, seems happily focused. No doubt she is hearing all the nuances that escape him. Marvelling at her absorption, Thomas feels envious. His wife too had given the impression of being absorbed on the few occasions they went to concerts, though with his wife he had felt – and this was true of himself too – it was more a desire to be absorbed, a craving to concentrate, consequent, in reality, on an uneasy feeling of exclusion – this cathedral of sound excludes me, this beauty excludes me, I want to get into it, I want to be part of it, but I can't – and this had given his wife that disquieting tension she had, something visible, palpable even, in her slightly forward leaning posture and set facial muscles. There had definitely been an aura of

anxiety around his wife and indeed himself, in these situations, at concerts and the like; they both tried too hard
to experience the thing, whatever it is, that people should
experience at concerts, hence both felt unable to relax.

Alas, we were very much alike in that, Thomas thinks.
So that now Thomas wonders why he and his wife hadn't
been able to make common cause of that feeling of exclusion, their being locked out of things, locked into their
own worlds, their own uneasiness. Why had they turned
against each other? Why had the marriage become a battle,
rather than a friendship? Whatever music he had listened
to at home, his wife tended to make fun of it. 'Such a
bore!' she wailed. 'Turn it off!' 'Another whiny woman's
voice,' she complained, 'you're giving me a headache!' For
his part, he had observed that the music his wife liked was
not really music at all. Tom Paxton. Frank Sinatra. Ironic
words, romantic words. All text and no tune. Yes, if you
were looking for the reasons why it really was necessary to
leave your wife, Thomas now tells himself, and the truth
is he is always looking for such reasons, you need go no
further than the way you both react to music, always criticising each other's taste, making it impossible for either
to listen to anything when the other is in the house.
'A Toccata of Galuppi's', he suddenly recalls, and simultaneously the people around him burst into wild applause;
a tall dark woman in her fifties has appeared on the stage.

Thomas seems to have missed the moment she came
in. He wasn't aware the second symphony was over.

They've switched to the arias. His girlfriend squeezes his hand. Incredible, though, to have remembered the title of Browning's poem forty years on. 'A Toccata of Galuppi's'. That is a kind of success. The orchestra strikes up and the singer opens her arms, throws back her head and lets out a note of extraordinary shrillness. This promises to be a different ride, Thomas thinks. Perhaps now at last he can focus on the performance, forget marriage, forget Browning.

Chin lowered, arms by her sides but slowly lifting, the singer pushes out her chest. It's all very physical; her voice bobs up and down like a boat on stormy waves. It's true this is another cerebral analogy, but there must be some kind of contact with the music if you can change the image you have of it. Then, on a large white screen above the musicians' heads, these words appear:

> *Non san quant'io nel petto*
> *Soffra mortal dolor!*
> *Vieni, Edoardo amato,*
> *O morirò d'amor.*

Thomas reads the words and immediately feels differently about the singing. Not that he understands very much, just that it takes on a wordy content. He has no idea what '*quant'io nel petto*' is all about, but the second line must mean 'suffers mortal pain'. Or perhaps 'grief', or 'sorrow'. And the last line has to do with dying. Dying of love, no less. Funny that pain rhymes with love in Italian, Thomas reflects, while the singer sings on with a great show of passion, her face glowing. Then a translation fades in to replace the Italian:

> *No one knows my heart*
> *What mortal pain you suffer!*
> *Come, Edward, beloved,*
> *Or I will die of love.*

Of course the rhyme is gone in the English, Thomas notices. But it's the same with advertising copy. You can't keep the puns in translation. His wife, he remembers, was always rather brilliant at rhyming and punning; it's something Thomas misses sometimes, or rather, one of the things that he remembers fondly. Mary would certainly have passed some mocking remark on these words now. She had no time for romantic guff. His girlfriend is listening with a faint smile on her face. Or I'll die of love, Thomas shakes his head. That's quite a threat. Not something anyone tried on him, fortunately, though Mary had certainly wept. Well, they both had.

The singer's voice is reaching a crescendo; her head is thrown right back, her shoulders are shaking. *Morirò d'amor*, she repeats for the nth time. Or so he supposes, reading the text. The '*or*' shoots up into the rafters, or rather the acoustic panelling. His wife had wept with her face bowed forward, buried in her hands. A very different sound. A sobbing in the guts. At the core. *Dear dead women*, Thomas suddenly remembers, *With such hair, too.*

The public explodes in applause. They are ecstatic. Thomas too begins to applaud. He is weeping. It's Browning's fault. *What's become of all the gold used to hang and brush their bosoms?* His girlfriend's face turns towards him, a wry twist on her lips. She moves her mouth to his ear. Her breath is moist. 'You'd have thought at least,' she says, 'they might have managed to put the right aria on the screen. What a cock-up!' For a moment Thomas is convinced the voice shrieking ENCORE two or three rows behind is Mary's.

EVEN TENDERNESS

Being an avid reader in his spare time, Thomas loves to look for his own personal story in novels, and more generally in the lives of literary folk he studied at university. But it's hard to find a precedent. He didn't lock his mad wife in the loft like Mr Rochester, or in a mental hospital like T S Eliot. Nor did he auction her off at a Wessex fair like the Mayor of Casterbridge, or have her imprisoned and beheaded like Mantel's Henry. His story is not Angel Clare's, repudiating a beautiful girl because she was not what he supposed. But nor was he betrayed by her, as Monsieur Bovary, or Count Karenin, or Gerald in *Women in Love*. He didn't chuck the mother of his children out of the house as Dickens did, or Mr Harmon's father in *Our Mutual Friend*; he never tried to get between her and the children, never wrote to the press to deem her unworthy. He didn't let the whole thing just go for ever sourer, only to turn sentimental when she was gone, which was Thomas Hardy's trick. He isn't Jude or Jules or Jim. He never slapped her about as Lawrence did Frieda, nor was slapped about as Lawrence was by Frieda. He hadn't Philip Rothed her, or done a Gilbert Osmond. He didn't drag her into poverty with his drinking and gambling, as Dostoevsky's characters might, or propose partner-swapping as Updike's must. He hadn't had sex with a maid, like Sam Pepys, or a slave as Old Colonel Sutpen did. He didn't humiliate her as Shelley did Fanny. Nor did she do any of these things to him. She hadn't become a nympho like Elsa Morante's Aracoeli. She hadn't tried to seduce a son-in-law like Giovanni Verga's Lupa. He hadn't asked her to have sex with someone else as Joyce asked Nora. Nor was he ferociously jealous, like Maurice Bendrix, or Othello. No, the more Thomas cast about for comparisons, the more he was bound to reflect that his and his wife's relationship had followed no literary pattern. It really was their story, and it really had happened. Year after wonderful, difficult year. When this truth finally came home to Thomas in a sharp rush of rude reality it brought with it a new affection for his wife, ex-wife, and a new respect – they really did go through all that together – even tenderness. For a moment or two he thought of phoning, but in the end decided against.

CIRCUMAMBULATION

Every day Thomas walked round his new home in down-town Liverpool, but he could never go into it or take posses-sion. Sometimes he thought back to his old home where Mary now lived with Mark. What a beautiful house that was, with its generous spaces, its garden front and back, its stone fireplace, its views over the valley. He didn't miss it. Thomas found this not-missing strange. But he really didn't miss it. Rather he yearned for the home he couldn't enter. So every morning, after grabbing a coffee in Starbucks, instead of going directly into the office, he took a small detour and walked around the building.

Apparently it had once been a factory, or warehouse, in the days when such buildings could be noble. The facade was brick, with generous windows high above the street and elegant white-stone surrounds. Built about a central courtyard, it occupied almost a whole block – eventually there would be more than a hundred flats – so that to walk around it meant to turn down Hope Street off Canning

Street, left on to Rice Street and left again on to Pilgrim Street, thence back to Canning. Thomas's flat was at the corner of Hope and Rice on the second of four floors. And it was all finished and good to go, complete with the beech parquet he had chosen in sitting room and bedrooms and grey-pink tiles in the two bathrooms. It was shortly after putting in those tiles that the builder in charge of the project failed. The site was closed.

Thomas felt let-down. Worse, this state of affairs seemed to confirm the emotional paralysis his life had sunk into. He saw no way forward. On leaving home three years ago he had rented a modest one-bedroom flat above the main door of a decaying '60s block inhabited for the most part by pensioners and recently arrived immigrants. I won't be here long, he thought. For some time then he had been torn between going back to Mary and inviting a girlfriend to move in with him. Weary of his indecision, the girl-friend had withdrawn. Only then did Thomas appreciate that he really could not go home. He felt he would die. So he must make something of his life in Liverpool where his new job was. But what? To make something happen, he had set out to buy a house.

A year passed in that process, a year in which Thomas realised how little his lifetime's savings were worth in the town centre. He saw flats that were too small, flats that were old and decaying, flats that were too expensive, flats that were too far away from his work. What was the point of coming to live in town if he were in some squalid suburb? There must be somewhere, he thought. Sometimes, in desperation, he emailed Mary and asked for her advice. He sent her links to photos of flats on offer. And very generously she gave her advice, which on these subjects was always astute. 'No,' she wrote, 'this is not the place for you, Tom. It's too poky for your taste.' But however good Mary's advice, Thomas felt it had been a weakness to ask. He was getting nowhere. He had left home, but he did not have a new home. He was still in a bivouac. He was temporary. He might be forced to return to base at any moment.

Finally, not half a mile from the office, in an area that was, as it were, on the edge of the centre, rundown but maybe on the up, Thomas saw a handsome gentrification project. The following day a Polish girl showed him a roomy flat with high ceilings and gracious windows. This was it. He knew at once. And he had arrived at exactly the right point in the renovation process to choose the flooring and the bathroom tiles. Putting down a large deposit, and signing the papers that would wipe out his savings, Thomas was delighted. He had done something on his own at last, something really adult. The flat would be the hub of a new life. Handover in six months, the developer said. Only days later the banks began to collapse, and in the months that followed the whole economy was sucked down with them. The builder failed, but the developer would not pay back the deposit. This was a brief delay, he had said. Two years ago.

Thomas walked round the building. On the ground floor the huge windows had yet to get their glass. The rain blew in. There was still scaffolding on two sides of the building. His own flat, twenty feet up, was locked and finished and snug, but unattainable. This was the future that was denied him. He had seen a way forward and it had been closed off. Thomas saw a lawyer, the lawyer wrote a letter, the developer did not reply to the letter. But one day the developer phoned Thomas and assured him it was only a matter of time. 'Even if you sued,' he said, 'we couldn't repay the deposit right now. We don't have the money. But things will be moving again before the year is out. Hang on.' Thomas wanted to believe the man was telling the truth, but he felt rather stupid.

Meantime, the situation in the bivouac deteriorated. In itself the flat was not unpleasant; a little gloomy perhaps, the kitchen area poky, the furniture shaky and sad. But the space was sufficient. The heating worked. There was a window over the courtyard, which had a patch of grass and a tree. The problem was noise. Thomas felt hemmed in from all sides. On the floor below, the electric lock on the block's main door clunked with surprising force. Some malfunction caused it to fire home its bolt four times at intervals of about five seconds whenever someone went in and out. And people went in and out every few minutes. In the middle of the night those clunks were loud enough to wake him. In the basement of the block there was a music rehearsal room. In bed Thomas could hear drums thumping till midnight. Not every evening, but almost. He read late in bed.

Then there were neighbours on three sides. Beyond the sitting room an old couple kept their television on day and night at surprising volumes. They must be deaf. In the flat whose front door opened beside his own, a young couple threatened each other and their children with serious violence on a daily basis. 'You little liar, I wish I'd never had you!' 'Evil bitch! Fuck off!' Thomas's own married difficulties began to seem a rather tame affair. What on earth had he been complaining about? But the couple looked cheerful enough when he ran into them on the stairs. On the bedroom side of the flat another elderly tenant was interminably on the phone explaining her ailments and cooking projects to whoever would listen. Her voice boomed.

And still this wasn't all. In the flat above Thomas's, a fifty-year-old fellow, who wore cowboy hats and rolled dead cigars between his lips, kept two large Labradors that spent much of their time padding backwards and forwards above his head. Thomas could hear their claws clattering on the floor. True, they did not bark, but there was a Border collie in one of the flats across the courtyard that did. The animal yipped and howled with its paws on a windowsill, frantic that the lazy Labradors wouldn't reply. In summer, going down the stairs for their walks, the dogs left a carpet of hairs on the steps and in the hallway. Very soon Thomas had a runny nose and rheumy eyes that would not go away and he began to sneeze once, twice, three times in succession. Day in, day out.

Thomas languished. Every morning the porter swept the courtyard with a witch's brush made of stiff green nylon fibres. Thomas had the impression she was sweeping them directly over his exposed nerves. The woman hailed everyone entering and leaving in a shrill voice. She engaged the postman in interminable conversations right under Thomas's window. Every month or so a small truck arrived with strimmer and leaf blower and spent an inordinate amount of time sprucing up the handkerchief of lawn. On one of the higher floors above the courtyard a retarded woman shrieked like a peacock at her open window. She shrieked at all hours, or laughed hysterically. Thomas sneezed. Then, irony of ironies, renovation work began on the building immediately beyond the open courtyard. There were piledrivers and pneumatic hammers. Meantime, any work on his own block was a distant memory.

It was not that Thomas risked going insane. He had his earplugs. He had his antihistamines and nasal sprays. He did not think of himself as a victim or an object of compassion. It just seemed incredible that a reasonably successful advertising executive in healthy middle age should be trapped in this sterile, uncomfortable life. He really should make an effort to get his deposit back from the developer and buy elsewhere, or maybe just rent a different place. But the fact that the flat he had bought really was absolutely the right flat for Thomas stymied him. What if he made a move and immediately afterwards building work resumed? How dumb would he feel then?

352

'Not long now,' the developer promised again. He called about every three months. 'We're negotiating with the banks, we're nearly there.' Thomas enjoyed his morning coffee at Starbucks and walked round the building, before walking on to work. The developer was a liar, he thought. The banks were shot. He remembered reading somewhere that circumambulation was a common feature of magic spells and ancient rituals. You walked round a bride-to-be three times. Or round an icon. You carried a coffin three times round a cemetery. You walked three times around an altar before slaying a firstborn lamb. Soon I will have walked three hundred times round this building, he thought, and still the windows gaped, still the crane was idle, nothing moved.

Then he kissed Elsa. To tell the truth, Thomas had been meaning to kiss Elsa for quite a while now. Unfortunately, it was painfully evident that Elsa had not been meaning to kiss Thomas. One could well understand, given the age difference. Unusually, Thomas had no fantasies about the girl. It was pointless yearning for her in the way he used to yearn for girls, in the way he yearned now for his new flat. Yet he sensed, observing her at work – discussing a conference agenda, for example – that Elsa was a good woman, possibly the right woman – why not use that expression? – should it ever cross her mind to kiss him. Meantime, it was promising that she enjoyed the occasional drink with him on leaving the office in the evening. Less so that afterwards she always had somewhere to hurry off to. Needless to say, there was a boyfriend. 'We are very stable,' Elsa said. A strange choice of words. At least I'm not tormenting myself, Thomas had thought.

But one evening it came over him to kiss her *anyway* and she returned the kiss, and before Thomas knew it the boyfriend had been fired and only weeks later Elsa had moved into his little bivouac and was getting to know the old couple and their booming television and the young couple and their ferocious battles and the old lady and her ailments and recipes, and the retarded woman and her peacock shrieks. Very soon Elsa was wincing in the early morning at the sound of nylon fibres on cement and very soon she too had a runny nose just like Thomas and from time to time her big black eyes ran with tears. She sneezed. And the wonder was they laughed about it and loved each other and loved the bivouac that kept them warm that winter.

At New Year the developer rang and said building work would soon resume. In spring, he said. Now Elsa was beside Thomas as they circumambulated the building after morning coffee. 'One day it will be ours,' he said. 'Yours,' she corrected him. 'Ours,' he insisted. Elsa looked up circumambulation on Wikipedia. 'Odd,' she said, 'that all religious circumambulation around a sacred object is anticlockwise. And so is ours round the new flat.' 'Only because our Starbucks is at the corner of Canning Street and Hope Street,' Thomas laughed. 'It wouldn't make sense to go clockwise if we're then going on to the office.' 'We can call it our Kaaba,' Elsa suggested. 'That's the most circumambulated building in the world, in Mecca.' 'Careful you're not accused of blasphemy,' Thomas warned her. When he sneezed, she laughed.

In June, the crane began to move. The building would be finished in October, the developer said. But only in November did workers begin to fix the windows on the ground floor. Thomas calculated that he had now walked round the building more than five hundred times. It was a kind of penance, he thought, a purification ritual. 'Ready in December,' the developer said. Walking round the building was more exciting now, watching materials arrive and scaffolding come down. Thomas and Elsa went to a furniture warehouse and ordered a kitchen. Thomas was surprised what a pleasure it was to contemplate furniture with Elsa. They took their time, assessing all the choices, bargaining over the price. I am glad the building was delayed, he thought.

Mid-February, the developer said they could move in at Easter. For real, this time. As if he had obviously been joking on previous occasions. On their morning circumambulation Thomas and Elsa were now able to walk in and inspect the courtyard of the renovated building. It really was almost finished. The windows and doors were in place. The crane had been dismantled. Men were laying out the garden. But Thomas shivered. 'I feel like Moses looking into the Promised Land,' he said. 'I'll be sixty soon.' 'Sixty is the new fifty-eight,' Elsa laughed. 'And Moses didn't get to walk round the Promised Land five hundred times.'

In the dark when they made love it was slow and happy. Down in the basement a bass guitar thumped a heavy pattern. 'If this happens again I'll kill you,' a voice yelled. When the bass fell silent, the front door clunked, three times, four. Coming back from the bathroom, Thomas sneezed, and sneezed again, and, climbing into bed, sneezed a third time. 'Imagine,' Elsa whispered, 'that all our neighbours move when we do and they all reappear on each side of us in the new building, with the two Labradors above and the peacock woman across the courtyard and the porter sweeping outside.' 'Cruel girl,' Thomas told her. 'And a building site across the way,' she murmured. 'And the television and the ailments and the recipes.' 'The insulation will be better,' Thomas told her.

They lay in the dark holding hands for quite a while, listening. 'From tomorrow no more circumambulation,' he eventually said. She propped herself up on an elbow. 'Why not, Tom? Right when we're nearly there. We can't stop now.'

'No more circumambulation.'

'Tom!'

Thomas took Elsa in his arms. 'I just feel like I've already arrived,' he said. 'The flat is a detail.'

I was on a roll and decided to go all in.

"Thank you," I said. "Your Honor, now might also be a good time for the prosecutor to reacquaint his witness with the penalties for perjury."

It was a dramatic move made for the benefit of the jury. I was expecting I would have to continue with Torrance and eviscerate him with the blade of his own lie. But Vincent stood and asked the judge to recess the trial while he conferred with opposing counsel.

This told me I had just saved Barnett Woodson's life.

"The defense has no objection," I told the judge.

penguin.co.uk/vintage